STEADYING
THE ARK

About the Author

A proud graduate of Choate Rosemary Hall, Middlebury College, and the University of Arizona James E. Rogers College of Law, Rebecca K. Jones now lives in the Phoenix, Arizona area, where she has been fighting crime since 2012. This is her first novel.

STEADYING THE ARK

REBECCA K. JONES

BELLA
BOOKS
2022

Bella Books, Inc.
P.O. Box 10543
Tallahassee, FL 32302

Printed in the United States of America on acid-free paper.

First Edition - 2022

Editor: Cath Walker
Cover Designer: Kayla Mancuso

ISBN: 978-1-64247-346-9

PUBLISHER'S NOTE

Dedication

To the women and men who work tirelessly on the side of truth and light in the service of society's voiceless and most vulnerable victims. Thank you for all that you do.

PROLOGUE

It was dark for ages before she had the courage to leave. She didn't know what time it was, but she waited until the lights went off and the ice maker stopped churning. She didn't have a clock, a radio, a cell phone—nothing showing the time was allowed. Her head hurt so much that she couldn't keep track. She was hungry. She shivered. She wished she had some clothes. A blanket. A towel, even. She had undressed when she went into the room, folded her dress and left it on top of her shoes like she always did. He had come and taken everything.

Her legs were cramped and numb but at least they didn't hurt. She sat there, crisscross applesauce, for hours, waiting. She was good at waiting. She could leave her body and watch herself, waiting until it was time to go back inside. She played games while she waited. Sometimes she played Count The Holes In The Ceiling Tiles. Sometimes she played Count The Hairs On His Head. She was good at counting. There were fourteen thousand three hundred and twelve holes in the ceiling tiles. Sometimes she played possum. When she learned that phrase, years earlier, she realized that she already knew what it meant.

She did it all the time. She stayed very still to see how long she could go without breathing or moving. Sometimes she played pretend. She pretended that she was a princess and he was a dragon. She pretended that he could breathe fire. She pretended that she could slay dragons. Sometimes it felt like he could breathe fire—his breath scorched her pale skin. She could wait out the pain, though. She was good at waiting.

She thought back to the first time. She didn't remember when it started, couldn't be sure how old she was. She wasn't good at waiting then—didn't know how to play the waiting games. The first time, she stayed inside herself and felt every burning breath. She learned to leave quickly, and soon she could wait outside herself instead of feeling anything at all. Now, sometimes she waited outside during school or piano lessons or family dinners. Sometimes she waited outside for no reason at all. She was so good at waiting, she couldn't help it.

She waited for him to come back. He always came back. After several hours, though, she thought maybe he had fallen asleep. She picked at a scab on one bony knee and hissed when it started to bleed. Maybe he had forgotten to come back. He had never forgotten before, but maybe she had finally waited long enough. Sometimes she played How Will I Ever Get Out Of This? so she knew just what to do. She could find the window, even in the dark, and she knew exactly how far to open it so it didn't creak and wake anyone. He had very good hearing, but he never heard the games she played. He didn't know how good at waiting she was.

It was time to go. She wished she had something to eat. Something to wear. Shoes. She knew she couldn't wait any longer, though. Last time, she had screamed, and he had breathed fire with his hands and his belt. She wouldn't make that mistake again. Couldn't wait for next time. She had to go.

She eased the window open and slipped outside, shivering anew in the cold night air. She glanced back to make sure the lights were still off. Good. She had waited long enough this time. She turned left and tried to run. Her bare feet hurt too much when they hit the pavement. He was good at breathing fire on places no one looked. She tried walking, and that came easier. She didn't look back again.

CHAPTER ONE

When Mackenzie Wilson's work phone rang at 2:00 a.m. that Tuesday, the lithe blonde was fitfully awake. She was stretched out on the couch, making her way through a three-week buildup of reality programs on the TiVo and sipping an Angry Orchard hard cider. She had finished a big trial the previous Thursday, and the Tucson jury was still deliberating. After seven years, the assistant district attorney still couldn't get a full night's sleep while waiting for a verdict. That night was no different.

While watching TV, Mack had been idly flipping through a police report on a pair of home invasions in a neighborhood less than a mile from her condo. The police suspected the burglaries were sexually motivated, but as far as Mack could tell, they had no hard evidence to support that theory. They certainly didn't have a suspect, and she wasn't even sure why they'd bothered to send her the report this early in the investigation.

The phone rang again.

She sighed, hit the pause button on the TiVo, pulled the

phone out of her gray Arizona State sweatpants pocket and tossed the reports onto her table. "No Caller ID" showed on the screen, which meant it was probably a cop. Unfortunately, she had drawn the short straw and was the on-call sex-crimes attorney that week. In addition to waiting out her deliberating jury, she could get called at any moment on a breaking case.

"This is Sex Crimes. ADA Wilson."

"Hey, Mack," a familiar baritone voice said. "This is David Barton."

She had known and worked with Dave, a sergeant with Tucson Police Department's special victim squads, since she had started working sex crimes five years ago. Mack liked and respected him and his detectives. If Dave was calling at 2:00 a.m., it was serious.

"Hey, Dave. What's up?"

"I'm sorry to bother you," he said, sounding tired, "but I need you to come out to a scene I've got going."

Mack was surprised. One of the few advantages to working sex crimes, as opposed to homicides or gang cases, was that there were almost never active scenes. It was extremely rare for police to ask for a prosecutor's presence during a new investigation—especially so late at night. This was the first time she'd gotten such a request. The fact that it came from a trusted colleague, a big and gruff long timer who hated these calls himself, caused her to shiver involuntarily.

"About two hours ago," he continued in a monotone, "we got a call that a naked kid had wandered into this Circle K." Mack heard someone asking the officer something. "Sorry, hang on a second, Mack."

It was hard to hear Dave clearly, but there was excited conversation in the background. Within seconds, she heard a car door slam and the noise died down.

"That's better," he said. He coughed. "The clerk thought the girl looked to be about eleven or twelve. She tried asking for her name, phone number, anything, but the kid wouldn't say jack."

Mack had a hundred questions already but tried to be patient.

After another pause, she heard Dave sigh. When he spoke again, he sounded sad. "She's dirty and bloody, so we're going to take her in for an exam and try to interview her."

"Try?" she asked. Tucson's forensic interviewers were known as some of the best in the country, and Mack had never seen a kid they couldn't get talking.

"Mack," he said, a tremor in his voice, "she hasn't said one word since we got here. Not to anyone. This is totally beyond anything I've ever seen. That's why I want you in on the ground floor on this one. I didn't just call the on-call phone—I called *you*."

She sighed. Her couch was warm and her sweats were comfortable, but Dave was appealing to her professional instincts. She promised to meet him in twenty minutes, as she shuffled toward her bedroom. The convenience store wasn't far from her condo in the foothills north of the city, and there was unlikely to be traffic at that hour.

Mack traded her sweats for jeans, an Oxford shirt, a sweater, and a fleece jacket. In the first week in January, Mack shivered every time she left the house. After years in Tucson, her blood had warmed, and Mack didn't know how she'd ever survived living in New Hampshire during her undergrad years at Dartmouth. She swept her blond hair into a messy ponytail and grabbed a Burberry scarf from the hook near the door. She shoved on a pair of battered black Converse All Stars. She didn't bother with makeup or checking the mirror—even barefaced she would be the freshest-looking person on the scene.

When she eased her beat-up old Saab 93 into the parking lot of the Circle K and saw the flashing red and blue lights, she knew she had the right place. There were three marked and two unmarked police cars and an ambulance. Before she could get the door open, Dave appeared at her window. He wore a standard-issue bulletproof vest over a hooded sweatshirt and black cargo pants, and a Tucson Police baseball cap covered his shaved head.

"There's something else, too, Mack," he said, bouncing

lightly on the balls of his feet, as she hauled herself out of the bucket seat.

Mack groaned. She took her glasses off and rubbed her eyes. There was always something else with cops, and it was never good.

Dave led her across the lot to the ambulance, its open doors revealing a female EMT sitting next to a stretcher on which a little girl sat, pale face streaked with dirt and lined with tear tracks. Her short blond hair was in disarray, matted with twigs. She looked like she couldn't have been older than nine or ten. Certainly not twelve, as Dave had said. She was draped in a sterile blanket, so Mack couldn't tell if she was still naked, but at least she knew that any evidence on the kid's body would be preserved for collection during the medical exam. Dave hung back as Mack walked closer, and the girl looked at her inquisitively with large hazel eyes. Mack smiled at her.

"Hi," she said softly. "My name's Mack. What's your name?"

The kid continued to stare without speaking.

"Where are your mommy and daddy?" Mack asked.

No response.

Gently, Mack tried a couple more times, asking how she got there, where she went to school, and when was her birthday. Each attempt was met with the same silent stare, and finally she gave up and walked back to Dave.

"So what's the deal?" Mack asked. "She's mute? Deaf?"

"We don't know yet," he said, taking his cap off and rubbing his head, "but watch this."

He walked toward the ambulance. As he approached, it was like he'd flipped an invisible switch. As soon as he got within five feet, the kid started screaming. When he backed up, she stopped. He walked back to Mack.

"She does that whenever a man gets close. Women can get right up next to her, can touch her, even, no problem. But a man so much as comes near her and she wails like a banshee."

Between the silence and the shriek, Mack fully understood Dave's earlier comment about how hard it would be to interview the girl. Whatever had happened to this kid, she was badly traumatized.

CHAPTER TWO

Mack followed Dave and the ambulance to the closest child advocacy center, a central location that police, child protective services, interviewers, and nurses all share, so that already-traumatized kids don't have to be shuttled from one office to another. She was glad Dave was in the lead. Even though she had been to the center over a hundred times, the surrounding row of nondescript ranch-style buildings blurred together and she could never find the right one.

It turned out that there was *one* perk to being out at 4:00 a.m. Mack found an empty meter right in front of the center and headed toward the building, the kid on her stretcher in the front of the line. A pair of matching petite brunettes, forensic nurse Lindsay Evans and forensic interviewer Nicole Rose, were waiting outside the door, both clutching large cups of gas-station coffee and shivering in the cold morning air. Mack grinned when she saw them. She had worked with both Lindsay and Nicole during several tough cases and knew their work stood up to even the harshest defense attacks. A bad interview or a shoddy medical exam could sink a case at trial.

"Hey, Lindsay," she said as Dave unlocked the door, "Nicole."

"Hi, Mackenzie," they said in unison. Lindsay yawned.

"Thanks for coming out," Dave said, motioning the EMT and the stretcher to go ahead. "This is a weird one. I'm glad we got you two."

"You know us," Nicole said, "the weirder the better!"

"Who's up first?" Lindsay asked. "Do we have parents coming?"

"No parents," Mack said. "We don't know who they are. Let's get the medical done first."

She looked at Dave, wondering if she had overstepped her role as observer. He smiled, though, like he could read her mind, and shook his head.

"Whatever you say, Counselor."

As Lindsay set up the exam room, Nicole prepared to introduce herself to the kid. Interviewers are supposed to meet a kid three times before they do an interview, and Nicole followed that protocol as closely as possible. They approached the waiting room together, where the girl had been transferred from stretcher to armchair. Mack crouched down, so she didn't tower above them, and made the introductions.

"Hi," Mack said. "Do you remember me?"

No response from the kid.

"Well, I'm Mack, and this is my friend Nicole."

"Hi," Nicole said, sitting on the edge of the coffee table and smiling widely. "My name is Nicole. What's your name?"

Nothing.

Nicole stood and whispered in Mack's ear.

"Do we know for sure she's hearing?"

Mack shook her head.

"We don't know for sure that she's *anything*," she said.

Nicole nodded and sighed.

"Okay, then," she said. "I guess I will see you later, okay?"

She smiled at the kid, who stared blankly back.

By then, the paramedics had left and Dave had caught Lindsay up on the very little that they knew. Lindsay knew that no one had gotten the kid to speak, but she did her best as she began her exam. She went through the whole routine, asking all the normal questions and giving the kid a chance to respond before moving on to the next step.

Forensic medical exams evolved out of a recognition in the child-abuse community that most doctors, including most pediatricians, don't know what to look for in diagnosing cases of childhood physical and sexual abuse. Emergency room doctors and nurses often misdiagnose routine skin conditions or accidental injuries as the result of abuse, and—more importantly—clear indicators of abuse as accidental injuries. This recognition spurred the education and training of a generation of physicians and nurses specializing in childhood abuse. They conduct head-to-toe exams of suspected victims, documenting everything with copious notes and photographs. Mack had seen a number of cases where the medical exam and the documented signs of abuse were the only corroboration for a child's disclosures. It wasn't just that she had seen those cases. She had won several at trial. Medical evidence, when it existed, was among the strongest evidence Mack had in her arsenal.

Because no one knew what had happened here, Lindsay did a more thorough investigation than she might have under other circumstances. She did a full physical, a genital exam, took swabs of every body part she could think to swab, took blood samples, and requested that the kid be radiographed at Pima Juvenile Medical Center the next day.

The kid's behavior during the exam was bizarre. She didn't seem to be in any pain, and, although she looked at Lindsay when she asked questions, she didn't respond. The weirdest thing, though, was that whenever Lindsay moved some part of her body—lifted her arm, had her get into position for the genital exam, whatever—the kid stayed perfectly posed. She didn't move a millimeter.

When Lindsay finally finished, she left the kid on the table under a blanket and came out to the break room where the other three were drinking coffee and chatting.

"Well," she said, pouring herself a cup, "you were right, Dave. This *is* a weird one."

"Did she say anything?" Mack asked.

"Not a word," she said, dropping heavily into the empty chair at the table.

"She been abused?" Dave asked.

"Yes," Lindsay said. "Sexually and physically."

Mack grimaced. Even the most brutal sex assaults couldn't phase her, but having to see physical injuries on a kid made her nauseous.

"She's got evidence of old injuries, lots of scars," Lindsay said, "as well as penetrative trauma. She's malnourished, and I think she's closer to fourteen or fifteen than eleven."

"Really?" Dave asked. "She's so small."

Lindsay nodded and pulled her curly hair into a ponytail. "I think that's the malnourishment," she said. "Based on physical development, she's older."

They all shook their heads and sighed. They knew that any case with multiple forms of abuse was likely to be more challenging because the victim was more likely to have ongoing issues. Mack had found that those abusers who inflicted multiple types of abuse were more likely to be sick sadists, rather than the more typical perverted, narcissistic losers.

"Great," Mack said, "our weird, hard case just got weirder."

"And harder," Dave said.

Nicole drained the dregs of her coffee and stood.

"Let's get on with it," she said.

Lindsay headed home. If she was lucky, she told them, she'd have time for a nap before her daughter got up for school. Mack and Dave looked down at their watches and groaned. It was already 5:45 a.m. Dave could wear his slacks and polo shirt to the office, but Mack couldn't appear for court in jeans. Worse yet, she had taken the suit she normally kept in her office to the dry cleaners the previous evening. She would have to go home—at least twenty minutes in the opposite direction from the office—before she began the day. That meant she would miss her early morning hearing in front of Judge Spears, a notorious stickler about unpunctual attorneys. Someone would have to cover for her, but it was too early to start calling to ask for help.

Mack went into the exam room and saw the small girl was

still naked. She rummaged through the cupboards but could only find a pair of adult medium-sized scrubs. The kid pulled them on and Mack shook her head. They dwarfed the petite child.

"Better than nothing," Mack said, guiding her back to the waiting room.

Nicole came out for her second chance to "meet" the kid.

"Hi," she said, again sitting on the low table. "In a couple minutes I'm going to have you come back in a different room with me, okay?"

The kid just stared at her.

"Would you like something to drink before you go in?" Nicole asked. "Are you hungry?"

Nothing. Nicole got up and smiled at her again before going back into the interview room. Dave went to turn on the recording equipment in the monitoring room, and Mack was stuck keeping the kid company.

Great, she thought. Mack had realized early in her career that, despite working with children so often, she did not particularly enjoy spending time with them. She felt the awkward need to impress children, which she never felt around adults, and she began to fidget as the kid stared at her.

"Do you drink coffee, kid?" she asked, simply to break the silence. "Lemonade? Coke? Vodka martinis? Anything?" Mack picked up a kid's magazine off the table and flipped through it. "Do you like to read? Play soccer? Dance?" She sighed and gave up, too tired to keep trying. She flicked through the magazine until Dave and Nicole returned, ready to start the interview. She followed Dave down the hall to the monitoring room where the interview would be recorded and kept for the trial.

Forensic interviews emerged out of the same basic realization that produced forensic medical exams: when people who are not specifically trained to deal with child-abuse victims *do* deal with child-abuse victims, things get screwed up rapidly. With physical exams, the problem is medical personnel, while with interviews, the problem is cops and prosecutors. In the wake of the day-care sex-abuse hysteria of the late 1980s and early

1990s, the child-abuse community took a hard look at how kids were interviewed. Recognizing that children were questioned by police in much the same way as adult perpetrators, there was a national push to implement more child-friendly interview methods. In Arizona, detectives, child protective service workers, and prosecutors alike are subject to many hours of training on the state-sanctioned interview method before they're let loose with victims. There are also people like Nicole—dedicated forensic interviewers. Mack appreciated that Dave had called Nicole in to this interview, especially since they weren't sure what they were dealing with.

Mack and Dave watched as Nicole and the kid settled into matching plush armchairs in the interview room. A teddy bear sat on an end table, and a coffee table between the two chairs had a variety of art materials in a basket on a lower shelf. Nicole started the interview like any other, with rapport building. She introduced herself to the kid a third time and asked the standard questions about birthdays and school. Unfortunately, where a normal kid would answer with narratives from which the interviewer could get a good language sample, this kid sat stonily, hands clasped in her lap. She wouldn't even look at Nicole. Instead, she stared at the art supplies on the shelf. After several unsuccessful attempts, Nicole tried another tactic.

"Would you like to draw a picture for me?" she asked.

Surprisingly, the kid gave a single abrupt nod.

"Great!" Nicole said, thrilled at this first real indication that the kid could hear and understood English. Nicole left her chair and knelt in front of the table, grabbing the basket and unloading paper, colored pencils, and crayons. "Come on down here with me."

The kid knelt next to Nicole and crossed her hands on the table, waiting until Nicole arranged everything on the tabletop and told her to "Go ahead!" before she dug into the crayons, selecting a deep emerald green.

Mack and Dave watched the child's undeniable talent from the video room. They were amazed as she drew a detailed fantasy landscape. An imposing gray tower rose from a green hillside. Inside a high window, a brunette princess looked out over an imposing purple and black dragon that breathed fire at the base of the tower. The girl drew for almost ten minutes before setting the purple crayon down and clasping her hands again on the tabletop.

"Wow," Nicole said. "That's really good! Can you tell me about it?"

The kid stared at the paper before her.

"Who's this?" Nicole asked, pointing at the princess. "Is this you?"

The kid unclasped her hands and tapped twice on the princess with her right index finger. She folded her hands in her lap.

"And who's this?" Nicole asked, pointing at the dragon. "Is this someone?"

The kid looked away and a long moment passed before Nicole tried again.

"Would you like to draw another one?" she asked, reaching for a fresh piece of paper.

As soon as the blank sheet was before her, the kid started to draw, this time in colored pencils.

Again, she drew a tower with a brunette princess and a dragon. This time, though, there was a man riding on the dragon's back, carrying a flaming sword. The man's eyes were red and his teeth were bared in a wide red smile. The man had wings, black and purple, like the dragon. After coloring a final steel-gray cloud in the sky, the kid set down her pencil and once more folded her hands in her lap.

"So, this is you," Nicole said, pointing at the princess.

The kid tapped the princess twice with her right index finger before returning her hand to her lap.

"Who's this?" Nicole asked, pointing to the man riding the dragon.

The kid stood abruptly and returned to the armchair, crossing her legs as she sat, appearing even smaller in the over-stuffed chair. The "interview" was over.

CHAPTER THREE

Mack sighed. They were no closer to knowing the girl's identity, where she had come from, or what had happened to her. She knew what they had to do next, even though neither she nor Dave relished the idea of getting the media involved.

"We have to," she said.

"Yeah, I know."

"We should do it now," she said, "so we can get it on the morning news."

"Yeah," he said again.

They agreed that, since the girl was apparently scared of men, Mack and Nicole would do the honors. They asked her to stand against the wall of the interview room and Nicole tried to pat down her hair, but it was still pretty wild when Mack took the photo. She texted it to Dave, confident that, by 6:45 a.m., the picture would be all over the state.

Mack pulled her ponytail out of its elastic band and ran her hands through her disheveled hair. She desperately wanted to go home to shower and change. She even had hopes of being able to sneak in a nap before driving back downtown to work. But there was more to do. She commandeered an office and looked at her watch. Anna Lapin would just be finishing her morning run.

As the phone rang, Mack idly noted, as she always did, that Anna was the only person she knew who still paid for a ringback tone. Unlike the woman herself, it was nothing classy—the early-nineties classic "Cherry Pie," by Warrant. Finally, Anna picked up, sounding composed as always, a hint of Long Island in her voice even after a decade in the Southwest.

"Mack!" she said. "To what do I owe this pleasure? It's much too early for you to need a favor."

Mack laughed. "You nailed it, Doc." Anna hated being called Dr. Lapin by her patients or her colleagues, and she *really* hated being called Doc. Knowing this, Mack tried to work it in as often as possible.

Anna groaned.

Mack and Anna had dated early in Mack's time in the sex-crimes unit. They had met on Mack's very first trial. A man on probation for masturbating in public, in treatment with Anna, had reoffended. Mack was instantly attracted to the petite psychologist. Anna was five years older than Mack, her trim body obviously the result of careful attention, and short dark hair effortlessly falling over olive skin and one of her piercing green eyes. When Mack learned that Anna's stunning looks were outpaced by her brains and a dark gallows humor that matched Mack's own, her attraction solidified into a deep crush.

Mack was content to leave it at that, sure that Anna must be straight, until the case finished and Anna proposed drinks to celebrate Mack's first sex-crimes trial victory. That night was the start of a one-year relationship, which, when they realized that they talked more about work than about anything else, had simply faded into a firm friendship. In the intervening four years, the two worked together on over fifty cases, did six trials as a team, and only revisited the idea of dating when one or the other had a few too many drinks. Anna was one of Mack's very best friends and was usually the first person she turned to with difficult situations either at work or in life.

Mack quickly described the silent kid and asked if Anna had any ideas to get her to talk.

Anna thought it over. "Nothing ethical, I'm afraid," she said, and they both laughed. "Give her time, Mack. When she's ready—if she's *ever* ready—she'll talk."

"Some good you are," Mack said. "Even I could have come up with that."

Mack promised to call Anna when she got a verdict from her deliberating jury so they could schedule drinks—either celebratory or conciliatory. A Child Protection Service worker was on the way to pick up the kid and set her up with an emergency foster placement. They turned on the television to catch the news, eager to see if the press release got out in time. It had. Mack composed a quick email to James Harris, her unit chief. She also gave him a heads up about the media coverage the case was already receiving, in case he started getting calls. James wrote back immediately, copying his boss, Michael Brown, the executive assistant to the district attorney, as well as Charlie Waters, the public information officer for the office, letting everyone know he had seen the coverage and expected Mack to keep them all in the loop as things developed.

Mack's next call, made from the car as she sped home against early rush-hour traffic, was to Jess Lafayette, Mack's coworker in the sex-crimes unit and best friend. She hoped that Jess was at work already and was at least partially caffeinated. Otherwise, she was likely to refuse, or to require more extensive bribes than Mack's modest government salary would support.

"Sex crimes, this is Jess," she said, sounding alert and surprisingly cheerful for 7:30 a.m.

"Hey, dude, it's Mack."

The sound of typing in the background stopped. "What's up, friend?" she asked.

"Look, I had a call-out, and—"

"An actual call-out?" she interrupted. Her voice made her sound much younger than her thirty-seven years. "That's crazy!"

"I know," Mack said, "and it only gets crazier. I'll tell you all about it. But, look, I stupidly forgot—at 2:00 a.m. when I left my house, totally flustered—to bring a suit with me, so I'm on my way home to change, and I have an eight o'clock in front of Spears. Can you—"

"Can I cover for you?" she interrupted again. "Of course. But you will bring me coffee. And it will be large. And it will be black. And it will be accompanied by a bagel. With cream cheese. And you will still owe me one. You know Spears can't stand me."

Mack laughed, grateful, and agreed to her terms. After explaining the hearing, Mack promised to take Jess' next grand jury presentation—a task Mack didn't mind and knew Jess hated.

"Sold, to the lady with the bagel," Jess said. "The cinnamon bagel."

CHAPTER FOUR

Mack found time for a twenty-minute nap before racing through a shower and throwing on her navy-blue Tuesday trial suit. Early in her career, Mack realized that she was too lazy to get dressed every morning if it required any thought or effort. To compensate, she bought a series of suits, shirts, and shoes in basically matching colors, and designated an outfit for each day of the week. Anyone who knew the pattern could tell what day it was and whether she was in trial based solely on her suit and shoes.

She fixed her hair and sighed as she looked in the mirror. A splash of dark freckles stood out against her pale skin. In the two years since turning thirty she had begun to notice bags under her eyes, and she tried to conceal them on trial days. She had never been much for makeup, and even though she sat through several department-store tutorials, she still found it challenging to apply enough to look put together without veering into homicidal clown territory. She ran a brush through her hair a final time, put in her verdict earrings, and steeled her shoulders.

She was worried about the kid. A text from Dave said that, after some initial drama, CPS had picked her up. The on-call caseworker, a nice guy who Mack had actually worked with on a few cases, had shown up unaccompanied. When he walked into the waiting room the girl screamed bloody murder. Dave had forgotten to tell the supervisor that the kid had issues with men. He got a female coworker while Nicole got the kid calmed down again.

The kid drew three more pictures while waiting for the other caseworker. Dave described the first two as basically more of what they had seen earlier that morning—a scary dude on a dragon attacking a princess in a tower. The last, set inside the princess's tower, introduced a new character. The dragon was still visible outside the window, but the princess was not alone. A second princess with long blond hair lay on a bed against the wall, apparently sleeping. She wore a purple dress, while the brunette princess near the window wore pink. Nicole had tried asking who the second princess was, and Dave said it looked like the kid almost answered before tapping the sleeping princess and retreating from the art supplies to sit on the waiting-room couch.

Mack grabbed her bag and the files she brought home the night before and double-checked that she had her wallet and keys. The bagel shop was less than a mile from her condo. One of Mack's favorite things about Tucson was that it was laid out on a grid. The major streets are a mile apart and run north-south and east-west across the valley. In the suburban parts of town it meant Mack was never more than a mile from groceries, coffee, or a taco. In her neighborhood, she could add a bagel place, a Chinese restaurant, and a dry cleaner to the list of walking-distance amenities.

As she pulled up to the drive-through window, waiting for her two cinnamon bagels with blueberry cream cheese and two extra-large coffees, Mack thought about last night's incident. Anna had emailed her an article on post-traumatic mutism while she was in the shower. Although she only skimmed it while brushing her teeth, she learned that mutism was apparently a not-unheard-of trauma response in children. She pulled out her phone and tried finding more on the topic, lost in thought until the clerk shoved her order through the window and Mack grabbed it just in time to avoid coffee-colored upholstery.

By the time she got to the office, Mack's jury had resumed their deliberations. The clerk emailed that she thought they would return a verdict that morning and she should be ready to head over at any time. Mack winced as she looked at her desk and considered this mixed blessing. On one hand, she wouldn't get any real work done until she got a verdict. On the other hand, the fifty-eight cases she had neglected over the previous three weeks *all* needed real work, and the longer she stayed "in trial," the longer she could avoid facing them. Plus, she reasoned, if the verdict wasn't in her favor she would rather just keep waiting.

Three more charging submittals had found their way to her already overflowing in-box. Those three little packets, no more than fifty pages each, represented the possibility of untold hours of work as they made their way through the system with Mack as their shepherd. She picked up the top one and glanced at the cover sheet before deciding she was not ready to face it and dumped it back in her in-box.

Mack went looking for Jess and was relieved to find her in her office. That she had made it back from Judge Spears' courtroom meant it was unlikely Mack had missed anything important. Jess confirmed it, gave Mack the new court dates, and dug into her bagel without a thank you.

Jess had been a prosecutor five years longer than Mack and had long since dispensed with many of the social niceties Mack still upheld. She was known around the office as a brilliant— if abrasive and eccentric—trial attorney and had taken Mack under her wing. They had done several trials together, and often spent weekend evenings taking in a movie or enjoying a dive bar halfway between their homes. Jess was perpetually and unhappily single, and Mack enjoyed hearing about her remarkable series of horrible first dates. Her favorite was the accountant who, upon hearing that Jess was a sex-crimes prosecutor, told her about the time when he was ten and gave his sister fifty cents to let him touch her private parts. He did not get a second date.

"Why, yes," Mack said, "you're absolutely welcome for breakfast. It was absolutely no trouble at all." She made herself comfortable in one of the chairs in front of Jess' desk.

Jess pushed her dark-brown hair behind her ears. "Thaaak oooo," she said through a mouthful.

"Have you decided on the rest of my debt?"

Jess nodded vigorously and pushed up the sleeves of her gray cardigan, then rummaged through the pile of files and papers covering her desk. She was set to begin a six-victim rape case the following week with an unpleasant defense attorney, so Mack forgave the mess. Finally, she pulled out a slim file and waved it across the desk. The stack of bracelets on her wrist clinked gently.

"This fine young cannibal," she said, looking at the label, "Benjamin Allen, is set for grand jury on Monday. Can you take it?"

Mack reached for the file and smiled.

"Yes, as long as it's still AFT Lafayette." In sex crimes the attorneys kept whatever cases they charged, and Mack wanted to avoid getting stuck with another trial if it wasn't absolutely necessary. If Mack presented this case at grand jury and they found probable cause and issued an indictment, James would assign it to her for trial—AFT—unless Jess agreed to keep it.

"Oh, totally," she said. "It's a stupid voyeurism, anyway. I was just the only person around when it came in."

Mack skimmed the short police report. Allen had been caught in a grocery store taking a photo up a woman's skirt with his cell phone. The police hadn't found any similar photos on his phone, and he had told the officer that this was the first time he'd ever done anything like this. He was twenty-four and had had no other arrests, as far as the police could tell. His three days in jail before posting bond were probably enough to scare him straight. It would be an easy case to resolve.

"You know what?" Mack asked, "I'll even keep it. AFT Wilson. You'll owe me one."

"You, sir," Jess said, "are a gentleman and a scholar."

Mack laughed and unwrapped her bagel. She always had a hard time eating—and keeping food down—while in trial, and the blueberry cream cheese, which had sounded so appealing an hour before, turned her stomach. That helped to explain why she had lost ten pounds over the previous year, in which she did seven trials.

"Now, tell me about the weird case that kept you out of Spears' division." Jess sat back in her chair, arms folded across her chest, and cocked her head.

Mack was recounting the morning's events when her phone buzzed. Both anticipating and dreading a verdict, she warily opened her email. It was Dave. His detectives had fielded calls all morning in response to the news item. They thought they might have located the kid's parents. The couple was coming down to the advocacy center at noon. Was there any chance Mack could be there? Her heart beat faster. She had expected the press release to be productive, but not that quickly. Mack shot Dave a message telling him that she would be there.

"What did we even do before social media and the twenty-four-hour news cycle?" Jess asked, taking a long swig of her coffee.

"Amen, sister."

Jess looked at Mack and smiled innocently. "What does Anna think about it?"

"Why do you assume Anna knows about it?"

Jess gave her a withering look. She adjusted the oversized silver watch on her left wrist before answering.

"Mack," she said, somehow stretching her name into a three-syllable word dripping with condescension, "I know you. You called Anna before you called me. Anna has sent you at least two articles she thinks might be helpful. *Anna* cited some obscure psychiatric condition you've never heard of but are now convinced is afflicting this poor girl."

By her final use of Anna's name, Jess' tone was full of disdain, but Mack had to admit that she was right.

"Post-traumatic mutism."

Jess laughed. "See?"

Mack left without responding, shutting her door to block out the sound of Jess' continued laughter. As soon as she walked back into her own office, her computer had signaled new mail. There were three new messages: one from Jess, saying only, "Hahahahahahahahaha," one from the clerk informing her that the verdict would be read at 11:00 a.m., and the third from Dave, giving a heads-up that the kid's suspected father was Steve Andersen, a respected local politician and golf buddy of District Attorney Peter Campbell.

Mack sighed.

It was a good thing she had only eaten a few bites of her bagel. Any more and she would have puked.

CHAPTER FIVE

"We the jury, duly impaneled, as to Count Twenty-two: Molestation of a Child, do hereby find the defendant, Javier Martinez, guilty," read the clerk.

Mack finally relaxed. Guilty on all twenty-two counts. The judge thanked the jury for their service as Mack watched the defendant realize that he would die in prison. A single tear ran down his lined face and into his foot-long beard. He seemed to shrink in his seat. His collared shirt, borrowed from the public defender's office, looked three sizes too big. Behind her, Mack heard his daughter Evelyn, the mother of his three victims, begin to cry. The assigned detective, who had sat through every day of the trial taking meticulous notes, clapped Mack on the shoulder and squeezed gently.

"You did it, Counselor," he said softly, leaning close. She could smell the coffee he'd been drinking before the jury came into the courtroom for the verdict.

She nodded and exhaled shakily, not trusting herself to speak yet. It was a hard case, and she had been worried right up until the end. Aside from his three young granddaughters, Javier had molested Evelyn and her sister Estella. This was justice for them, too, as well as for any of his potential future victims. The backbreaking work, all the hours spent, the blood, sweat, and (often literal) tears invested—they were always worth it for these sweet moments of justice.

Mack stood, numb, as the jury was excused, and turned toward Evelyn. It was 11:45, and Mack had to leave immediately to meet Dave, but she wanted to make sure Javier's daughter understood what the verdict meant for her and her daughters.

"Ms. Wilson," Evelyn said through tears, clutching Mack's hand in both of hers, "thank you. You just gave my daughters their lives back. You just gave my whole family their lives back. Thank you."

Mack smiled warmly at her. "No," she said, "your daughters *took* their lives back by being brave enough to tell someone what was going on. I just helped."

Evelyn cried more forcefully and the detective handed her a tissue. She would be dealing with her guilt for a long time, but Javier's incarceration would help her and her family heal. Mack made her excuses and left the courtroom, trusting the detective and the victim-assistance case worker to help Evelyn find out about the sentencing hearing.

The center was only a ten-minute walk from the courthouse, and Mack took the opportunity to enjoy the sunshine and the breeze. She had spent way too much time cooped up over the previous month and was looking forward to catching up on her life—and her Vitamin D intake—before the next trial started. She was surprised to find Dave, the CPS caseworker, and the kid—but no potential parents.

"Who would be late to this?" Mack asked Dave.

He shook his head and crossed his arms over his chest. "You get a verdict?"

"Guilty on all counts," Mack said.

Dave smiled. "Way to go, killer."

Mack brushed imaginary dirt off her shoulders. "Naturally," she said, grinning.

Mack had emailed James Harris and Michael Brown, James' boss, so that they would know who the suspected parents were. This was likely to be a high-profile case if, in fact, the Andersens were involved. She checked her phone at the center to see if there was any response. Nothing. Good.

At 12:02 p.m., Mack started to worry. By 12:05 p.m., she and Dave were pacing the lobby, exchanging concerned glances. Maybe someone had pretended to be the Andersens as a hoax. Maybe they'd been in a car accident. They ran through a dozen more theories, each one more improbable than the last. The kid seemed unphased—or maybe just unaware—and was peacefully drawing in an interview room off the lobby. More dragons, more princesses, and something that looked like Gollum from *The Lord of the Rings*.

It was 12:15 p.m. and they were ready to call the whole thing off when there was a flurry of activity by the door. A well-dressed blond couple in their late forties rushed into the lobby. Mack could smell the woman's perfume from twenty feet away and knew it was expensive. A Louis Vuitton tote bag hung from one narrow shoulder. They were both tall and tan, and he looked fit and strong beneath a well-tailored black suit. Neither of them had a hair out of place, and her pearl necklace and earrings were a matching set.

Dave strode toward them, his short, muscular frame looking ungainly next to the graceful couple.

"Hi, folks," he said, reaching out to shake hands, "are you the Andersens?"

The man took a subtle half-step forward so he was partially blocking his wife, and extended his hand.

"Steve Andersen," he said. "It's nice to meet you. This is my wife, Shannon."

Shannon nodded at Dave but didn't offer her hand or move from behind her husband.

"Welcome," Dave said, nodding back. He gestured Mack closer. "This is Assistant District Attorney Mackenzie Wilson."

Mack offered a smile and her hand, only to drop both when Steve stuck his hands in his pants pockets.

"Sure," he said, "sure, I know your boss. Pete and I go way back."

"I'll be the prosecutor on your daughter's case," Mack said. "Assuming we do *have* your daughter. Why don't you tell me about—I'm sorry, what's her name again?"

"Schyanne," Steve said, turning to Dave, "with an S."

"Okay," Mack said. "Can you spell that for me?"

He did, looking annoyed at the hassle.

"Got it," Mack said. "Thanks. Now, tell me about her. When did you folks notice she was missing?"

"Well, Mondays are Home Evening," Steve said. Shannon nodded behind him. "So we spent the evening together, as a family. At about nine thirty, I sent the younger kids—we have seven kids, Schyanne's the third youngest—off to bed."

"How old is Schyanne?" Mack asked.

"She turned fourteen two weeks ago," Steve said to Dave. It was the third question Mack had asked him, and the third time he had responded to Dave. Based on the spelling of their last name, Mack had assumed that the Andersens must be Latter-day Saints, but she was getting frustrated with his male superiority thing. Mack hadn't known any Mormons before moving to Arizona, but, based on her experiences in law school and as a prosecutor, had quickly decided that Mormon men didn't tend to do well with women in positions of power. Mack hoped the kid *wasn't* Schyanne, just so she wouldn't have to deal with Steve Andersen. Also, for the kid's sake, Mack hoped her name wasn't Schyanne.

"I sent Shannon to check on Sariah, Schyanne, and Shaelynn around ten thirty and—"

"—and she was in her bed like always," Shannon interjected. Mack was surprised to hear her speak. She figured the whole story would come from Steve.

Steve's jaw tightened momentarily. "Right," he said. "All the girls were in bed, and Simon and Seth were asleep in the boys' room. But this morning, when Shannon went to wake her for school, only Shaelynn and Sariah were in their room."

"What time this morning?" Mack asked.

"Schyanne, Shaelynn, and Seth all get up at five forty-five for seminary," Steve said to Dave.

"Has she ever gone missing before?" Mack asked.

"Never," Steve said. "My kids are all very well behaved."

Shannon nodded and Mack frowned. His possessiveness of his children gave her the creeps.

"Did you call the police?" Mack asked.

"Not until we saw her picture on the news," Steve said. "Shannon spent the morning calling her friends, some of the local families. We thought maybe she'd just left early without asking permission."

"Why would she need permission to leave early?" Mack asked.

Dave placed a restraining hand on her arm and Mack realized he was right. They still had no real evidence that Schyanne was the missing kid.

"Did you bring a picture of your daughter?" Mack asked Shannon.

She nodded and dug through the tote bag. She handed the photograph to Steve, who handed it to Dave. Mack's eyes narrowed. Dave, seeing that she had run out of patience, quickly shoved the picture into her hand, wrinkling one corner. They looked at it together. It was a school photo, and Schyanne was wearing what looked like her Sunday best. Her hair was long and in two braids, her face was clean, she was smiling, but it was undeniable—it was her.

"Steve, Shannon," Dave said, not smiling, "we have your daughter. Eventually, we'll need to formally interview each of you, but that can be done later. Can you give me just a moment with Ms. Wilson?"

Steve looked at his watch as Mack and Dave walked to the other side of the room.

"I don't think we should send her home with them," Dave said.

"Why not?" Mack asked.

"Because we don't know what happened to that kid, and, until we do, I'm not comfortable sending her home with people who might have been abusing her."

Mack sighed and took her glasses off. She rubbed her eyes and ran a hand through her long blond hair. She tilted her head side to side.

"Unfortunately," she finally said, "that's not the standard we have to use. You know we can't take her away from her parents unless we have reasonable grounds to believe that she's in immediate danger in their presence."

"We *do*," Dave said, keeping his voice low but obviously frustrated. "Statistically—"

Mack shook her head and held up one hand. "Look," she said, "I think this guy seems like a real asshole, too, but we have nothing. We have less than nothing. We have a politically influential guy who wants his daughter back, and no grounds to keep him from her. Do you want me to call James? Get his input?"

Dave glared at her.

"I don't like it any more than you do," Mack said. "You know how much flack CPS has been getting, though. You know we can't just take kids from parents we don't like—there's a process, and we have to follow it. Even when we don't want to."

"And if I'm right?" he asked as he walked away. "If we're sending this kid home with her abusers?"

Mack didn't respond. She watched him walk back toward the Andersens.

"Alright, folks," he said with a forced smile. "Thanks for your patience. Let's get you back with your daughter, okay?"

Steve nodded. Shannon stood quietly behind her husband. Mack was surprised by their lack of emotion. Their daughter had only been missing for six hours, sure, but it still seemed to merit more of a response than their unflappable calm.

Dave led the Andersens through the lobby toward the interview room where Schyanne sat and colored. Mack followed Shannon, who walked two steps behind Dave and Steve. The caseworker leaned toward Schyanne and said something Mack couldn't hear. Schyanne put her green crayon down and looked up, tilting her head slightly to the left. When Dave got to the door, he stepped aside for Steve to enter the room and reunite with his daughter. As he did, Schyanne let out a bloodcurdling scream. Steve froze and Shannon looked at Mack, terror in her eyes, the first emotion she had seen from the other woman during their fifteen-minute conversation.

"She's been doing that whenever a man gets too close to her," Mack said.

"I'm sure with some counseling," Dave said, "she'll be able to stop. She just needs to work through whatever happened to her in the time she was gone from your home."

"Well," Steve said, "she's going to need to knock that off but soon. I'm her father, for heaven's sake, and I won't tolerate—"

Mack walked away. Dave could handle the rest of the reunification, which would involve getting the Andersens set up with a specialized pediatric trauma counselor, scheduling an appointment for Schyanne to get the X-rays Lindsay had requested, and arranging to interview them and their other children. Mack was torn. She was thrilled that the team had been able to find the kid's parents within a day, but her interaction with Steve Andersen had left a bad taste in her mouth.

CHAPTER SIX

Wednesday and Thursday passed uneventfully as Mack caught up on emails and voice mails from defense attorneys, victims, and cops, responded to several pending motions, and completed all her outstanding charging.

On Thursday, Mack's mom, who had seen a news story about a shooting in Yuma, called to make sure her daughter had not been the victim. The fact that Mack lived hours from Yuma, and the victim had actually been named in the story, had not figured into her analysis. Mack considered pointing that out, but decided not to bother. Mothers would be mothers, after all. Her mom wondered whether Mack would be able to make it back to Cleveland sometime in the spring—maybe bring Anna, who had loved their previous trip to the Mistake on the Lake—but she knew better than to ask for a commitment so far in advance. Mack was able to avoid answering without giving a firm no.

There was another home invasion in the foothills, and the police still had no suspect. There was no word from Dave on Schyanne, other than updates regarding scheduling. Mack wondered whether the relative quiet was the calm before the storm she could not yet see, but instead decided to think of it as a blessing.

When she walked into her office Friday morning, she found an ominous note taped to her computer monitor. "See me," it read. It was unsigned, but only one person left creepy notes with orders on them—James.

Mack set down her bag and walked down the hall to his office, where the stereo was quietly playing some sort of seventies funk music. The top of James' bald head barely showed above stacks of case files.

"You summoned?" Mack asked, dropping into one of the seats in front of his desk. They had a good professional relationship, and that's just the way she wanted to keep it. Mack had no idea what his wife's name was, and James knew nothing about her childhood, but she could name ten or more defendants he had sent to prison after difficult trials and he seemed to respect her as a prosecutor. He had always given her a great deal of autonomy over her caseload, which she truly appreciated, and they stayed out of each other's personal lives.

James looked up at her, a smile on his dark-skinned face. "Morning, Mack," he said. "What's on your calendar this afternoon?"

She pulled out her phone and found her schedule.

"A couple quick telephonic meetings," she said, "but nothing all that big. Why?"

"Our presence has been cordially requested in the executive suite," he said, adjusting his tie, "to update Michael Brown and Charlie Waters on the status of the Andersen case."

Mack groaned. Charlie Waters was okay, but she couldn't *stand* Michael Brown, who had remarkably snuck through his whole career without trying a single case. This left him uniquely unqualified to oversee the office's trial attorneys, his main responsibility.

"Sorry, boss," she said, "I feel a sudden flu coming on. Can't make it today. Maybe we can reschedule for right after Mikey does his first trial."

James still smiled patiently. "We're supposed to be there at one thirty," he said.

"Well," she said, pushing herself out of the chair, "there's always the faint hope that I could die at lunch."

"Don't be late!" James called as she trudged back to her office, significantly less excited to face the day than she had been fifteen minutes earlier.

Mack spent the whole morning dreading the meeting and got very little work done as a result. It was almost a relief when James came by on his way upstairs.

"I wasn't sure you could be trusted not to get lost if left to your own devices," he said in the elevator. After being kept waiting by the administrative assistant for what seemed like hours and was probably less than five minutes, they were ushered into an ornate conference room Mack had only ever seen on television as the backdrop for Peter Campbell's monthly press conferences.

"James, Mackenzie, come on in." Michael was sitting at the head of the table with his hands folded on its surface. His brown hair was perfectly styled, as always, and Mack wondered how often he saw a barber to keep it that way. A single unused legal pad and a blue pen rested next to his right elbow. Charlie, who Mack liked despite his high-ranking position, wore rumpled jeans and a polo shirt and had his feet up on the chair next to him. He didn't look up from his phone, just waved at them with one tanned hand. Charlie always made it hard to tell whether he was working or playing *Candy Crush*, which Mack respected. She knew that being PIO for an elected official wasn't the easiest job, but Charlie kept a sense of humor about his role.

Michael, on the other hand, was one of only a handful of people at the office Mack would throw under a passing train with no hesitation. They were hired together seven years earlier and had sat next to each other during the office's Introduction to Prosecution class.

There was a happy hour on the last day of training at a bar a few blocks away. Michael's blue-and-red rep tie was loose, his curly hair in disarray, and he had leaned against the table next to Mack and her friend Lou.

"Heeeeeeey," Michael said, two beers in and already a messy drunk, "Mackenzie, right?"

"Yeah, Mike," she said. "Mackenzie. We just sat next to each other in a class of seven for three weeks."

His voice was higher than his muscular figure would have suggested. "Right, right." He nodded absently. "Do you wanna, like, have a drink with me sometime?"

Mack hoisted her bottle of Kilt Lifter, a Phoenix ale and her favorite drink in the early fall—before the pumpkin porters come out—and took a long drink.

"You know," she said, "if you think about it, Mike, we kind of *are* having a drink together."

Michael sighed loudly and hooked his left thumb in his navy-blue suspenders.

"Noooooo," he said. "A *drink. Together.*"

"Mike," she said, "are you asking me on a date?"

He smacked the table. "Yes! A date! It just seems like we could be really good together."

"I'm sorry, Mike," she said, "you seem like just a great guy and all, but five minutes ago you didn't know my name. And besides, I'm gay."

Michael stared at her in shock.

"But, but, but—" he spluttered. "You don't *look* gay!"

She rolled her eyes, drained her beer, and walked away, leaving him gaping after her.

That was the last time she spoke to Michael Brown without a supervisor present. After training, their paths quickly diverged. Either Michael knew all the right people, or Mack only knew the wrong ones, because while she had been sent out to pay her dues in misdemeanor court, Michael went directly to a felony unit downtown. Although Mack's career steadily progressed as she moved up through the ranks to her current position, Michael skyrocketed straight to the top. Now he was second-in-command of the whole office, overseeing five hundred employees and providing a layer of insulation between Campbell and the mere mortals who worked for him. Mack didn't know anyone who really got along with him, but everyone in Sex Crimes recognized that he had it in for her in a way he didn't for anyone else.

"Good afternoon, Mr. Brown," she said, sitting next to James across from Michael. It was hard for her to affect an appropriately polite tone, but she knew it had to be done.

He smiled, revealing his two slightly crooked front teeth. "Mr. Campbell and I wanted to hear from you about the Andersens' little girl," Michael said.

"Will the district attorney be joining us today?" James asked dryly. James was a master of the deadpan tone—a man who could truly play the toady and then go back to his office and call both Michael and Campbell every name in the book.

"No," Michael said, sliding the legal pad so it was directly in front of him and uncapping his pen. "Mr. Campbell is otherwise occupied this afternoon. He wants you both to know, though, how serious he believes this case to be."

"How serious is that?" Mack asked.

"Mr. Campbell and Mr. Andersen have known each other since high school," he said without batting an eye. "Anything you need in order to find out what happened to his daughter, Mr. Campbell has authorized."

"I'm sure Mr. Andersen's generous campaign donations have nothing whatsoever to do with Mr. Campbell's concern," Mack said.

James shot her a warning look.

"Now, now, Mackenzie," Michael said, running his hand over his perfect hair, "you know the important role Mr. Andersen plays in this community. He is the largest commercial real-estate developer in the state. He's a bishop in the ward both he and Mr. Campbell attend. He's served on the Tucson School Board through several election cycles."

"Oh," Mack said, "so you want the detectives working this case to actually, like, detect? The investigators to investigate? Unlike they normally do on sex crimes, you mean."

"James," Michael said, "surely you and your team know how much Mr. Campbell values the work you and your detectives do. My concern is simply for the Andersens, who are just frantic over what has befallen poor Schyanne. Our office has a duty to serve all the citizens of the Tucson area, especially those who do so much for the community."

And who do so much for Old Petie's rumored upcoming Senate campaign, Mack barely resisted the urge to say. Instead, she filled the men in on the status of the investigation. The Andersens' interviews were set for the following week. The X-rays had been sent to a pediatric forensic radiologist in North Dakota. Schyanne had met with the trauma counselor Tuesday, Wednesday, and Thursday. She still wasn't speaking but had stopped screaming when her father approached her. The swabs taken during her medical exam had been sent for analysis. Dave and his team were doing all they could, but it was likely to take a while to get any results.

Michael took copious notes as Mack spoke, and she could picture him filling in the district attorney later that day. She hoped Campbell saw just what a sycophant Michael was.

Finally, James and Mack were excused, with orders from Michael to send him a daily briefing, "Whether there's news to report or not."

James turned to Mack in the elevator. "You could have handled that better," he said.

"I know," she said. "He gets me so fired up, though. If he'd ever tried a case instead of turning himself into a little ass-kissing leech—"

"—I know your issues with Mr. Brown," James interrupted. "But you know why you do this job, and it will be very hard for you to *do* this job if you are fired for insubordination."

She hung her head, abashed. "Yes, boss."

The elevator opened to reveal Jess in the reception area. She gave Mack a thumbs up, then a thumbs down, then shrugged in an exaggerated manner. Mack subtly gave her a thumbs down.

"Go home," James said as Mack turned into her office. "And, Mack?"

"Yes, boss?"

"Consider taking this weekend off. It'll all still be here on Monday."

For once, Mack took his advice.

CHAPTER SEVEN

When Mack got to work on Monday, she was rested, refreshed, and ready to face the week ahead. She had spent Friday evening with Anna, celebrating her win with beer and nachos, and the rest of the weekend catching up on chores and errands that had fallen by the wayside during trial. She even managed to get some sun, hiking Linda Vista Trail north of town with Jess on Sunday morning.

She spent the morning cleaning her office, putting away files, and making a to-do list for the week ahead. For the first time in over two months, she had a mostly clear week—no big hearings, no trials set, and no meetings with cops or victims. She planned to take full advantage of the downtime to get ahead on upcoming motion practice and prepare for yet another trial set to start in three weeks. The matters just kept coming.

Monday afternoon, Mack had to present the case she had taken over from Jess—Benjamin Allen—to the grand jury, a group charged with determining whether probable cause exists in a case, as opposed to a trial jury's determination regarding whether the defendant is guilty or not guilty. She ate a salad at her desk as she reviewed the file, trying not to drip dressing on the police report. The detective was waiting when she got to the courtroom, impatient to get started, and they were the first ones called when the grand jury resumed for the afternoon session. She got back to her office by two, just in time to answer her desk phone.

"This is Mackenzie," she said.

"Mack, it's David Barton." He sounded tired, and Mack wondered how much overtime he had worked since Schyanne was found at the Circle K.

"What's up?"

"Just wanted to fill you in on a few things with Schyanne's case," he said. "Nothing all that exciting."

"That's a relief! At this point, not exciting is my preference."

"We have the parents scheduled for interviews tomorrow," he said.

"Why haven't they been interviewed yet?" Mack asked, surprised. It had been a week since Schyanne had gone missing, and best practice would have been to interview the family within forty-eight hours.

"Well," Dave said, "we tried to get them in earlier but Steve was unavailable. Then I got a call from my commander telling me to let them set the pace and not to rush them."

"Do you mean to tell me that the investigation into the assault on a fourteen-year-old might be compromised because Steve Andersen is friends with the district attorney? He needs to have been interviewed by now."

"Not just the district attorney, Mack. He's also friends with the chief of police, the secretary of state, and Senator Armstrong."

Mack groaned. She hoped that the special treatment Andersen was receiving wouldn't be to the detriment of his daughter's case when a defense attorney got his teeth into the delays it was causing. "Anything else I should know?" she asked.

"DNA's in progress," Dave said. "Should have some idea whether there's sperm within the next week or so. Full results will take longer."

"They always do." Mack sighed, ever frustrated by the delays at the crime lab. She had seen multiple cases resolve on the eve of trial when the DNA results had finally come in, allowing her to convince the defendant once and for all that he was sunk and should take a plea. "Are they going to run whatever they find through CODIS?" Mack asked, referring to the Combined DNA Index System—the national database containing DNA from convicted felons.

"I assume so," Dave said, "but you know they prefer known samples."

"We don't have known samples," Mack said. "To have known samples we'd need known suspects. To have known suspects, we'd need Schyanne to say what happened to her."

Dave ignored her mounting frustration, saying, "The radiologist called with some preliminary results."

"Okay," Mack said, pulling out a legal pad and grabbing a pen. "What did he find?"

"Schyanne has several healed fractures. Spiral fracture to her right humerus, her left femur, two to fingers on her left hand."

"That sounds like a lot for a fourteen-year-old," Mack said.

"That's what I said to the doc. He agreed, but none of them are absolutely the result of abuse. There might be non-abusive explanations for all of them."

"You need to get those parents interviewed," Mack said.

"Yep. You think there's any chance Dad's the guy?"

"The guy who did whatever it was that was done to Schyanne?"

"Yeah."

"I don't know," Mack said, but she remembered the creepy feeling she had gotten from Steve Andersen and shivered slightly in her overheated office. "Do you?"

"Statistically," Dave said, "he's the most likely. I just don't get that read off them, though."

"And it's totally possible," Mack said, "that she ran away to meet a boy and got in over her head."

"Sure," Dave said. "That's what happened in the Timothy Wall case—victim met him online, thought he was fifteen like she was, and he turned out to be thirty-two and a rapist."

"Exactly."

"Still," Dave said, "those injuries are suggestive."

"I think we should consider the possibility that the old injuries and whatever happened last week are unrelated."

"You mean she's been victimized by two perps?" Dave asked.

"At least two. Someone causing injuries, and someone last week."

"That's always possible," Dave said, "but I think it's more likely that it's all Andersen."

"I just don't think you should go into the interview and treat him like a suspect," Mack said. "You'll lose him."

"True. And if we lose buy-in from them—"

"—this case blows up really freaking fast," Mack interrupted.

She picked up a small plastic zombie figurine a coworker had given her for Halloween some years before and walked him across her desk, then changed the subject to another case they had in common. Dave brought her up to speed on some ongoing investigation he was doing. After five minutes or so, they had covered all the updates on Schyanne and had decided how to move forward in the other case. Before they hung up, Mack came back to the Andersens.

"Any chance you can get a swab from Steve Andersen? When he comes in for the interview?"

There was a long silence.

"I don't know," Dave said, sounding optimistic for the first time. "Maybe, if I can somehow convince him it's routine."

Mack thought about that. In Arizona, the police are allowed to lie to suspects. Was Steve Andersen a suspect? She supposed it didn't really matter, for the moment. Dave could lie to him regardless of whether he was a suspect, and if the DNA cleared him, he'd never know the difference.

"What if you swab the whole family? Tell him it's to rule out DNA that's on her from secondary transfer."

"But secondary transfer isn't real," Dave said. "That's just defense attorney nonsense."

"Exactly," Mack said. "You know that, and I know that, but Steve Andersen won't know that. If you explain that we want to make sure we account for any DNA she picked up through the laundry, he'll think we're being really diligent and won't realize what's actually going on."

Dave paused. "That might be brilliant," he said.

Mack laughed. "I try," she said. "I'll see you tomorrow at the interviews."

For the rest of the afternoon, Mack found herself seriously considering whether Steve Andersen was as upstanding a community member as he appeared. Children are much more likely to be abused by someone known to them than by a stranger, and most cases of sexual abuse are in-home. If Schyanne had been abused by her dad, the system had unwittingly sent her home with her abuser. Mack desperately hoped that her bad feeling about Andersen was unfounded.

CHAPTER EIGHT

Schyanne's case was in roughly the same position until the middle of February. Mack spent most of the intervening time occupied by other cases, including what seemed like way too much time on the foothills home invasions. After six of them, the detectives were no closer to a suspect than they'd been after the first, and the media was beginning to sound the trumpet of "Shoddy police work endangering our community!" Mack knew that the detectives were doing everything they could. Whoever this guy was, he was *really* good at not getting caught. In the most recent case, he'd even ejaculated on the homeowner, who woke up to find him masturbating over her bed. But his DNA wasn't in the CODIS system.

In Mack's continued attempts to cultivate a personal life, she went hiking with Jess each weekend, went to movies and dinners with Anna, and even went on a blind date—set up by Jess—with a very nice woman, a kindergarten teacher who Mack felt was hopelessly unprepared to talk to someone in the prosecutor's line of work. By the time the appetizers came and she'd finished her second Corona, Mack knew that their relationship was doomed to failure. The teacher had laid her hand gently on Mack's arm and told her she was doing the work of the angels. It did make for a great story to tell Jess at their next happy hour, and Mack would do just about anything for a good story.

Mack read three novels and saw two concerts and a play. Her mom had decided that if Mack couldn't spare the time to go to Cleveland, she would come to Tucson for three days. They enjoyed the sun at the desert museum and the complex pool, shopped for some new suits for Mack, and saw a movie. Anna had joined them for a drive up Mount Lemon and dinner at a Vietnamese restaurant at which she and Mack's mom had bonded years earlier.

After two weeks of relative calm, she was so bored that she volunteered to second-chair a short trial with one of the new attorneys in the unit, just for something to do. Through it all, however, Schyanne was never far from her thoughts.

The Andersens had been interviewed again, and as expected they had explanations for Schyanne's healed injuries. They all made sense and were medically feasible, but Mack was still uneasy. A single broken bone or scar could be an accident. A series was probably abuse. Dave had asked Shannon about Schyanne's malnourished state. Shannon's explanation—that Schyanne was an extremely picky eater and had wrestled with eating disorders in the past—had a hollow ring to it, but was possible.

During the interviews, Dave had swabbed both Andersen parents and all six of Schyanne's siblings for DNA. Steve bought the secondary transfer story with no hesitation. In fact, Shannon was the only one to resist, asking a number of questions about what the lab would do with the swab and how it could be helpful before eventually agreeing.

Neither Steve nor Shannon had had much to add to Steve's initial story. They couldn't explain why Schyanne's hair was so short and so choppy. Shannon had even showed a hint of actual emotion when she talked about how beautiful Schyanne's hair had been before she disappeared. She kept it in a long braid down her back, Shannon said, and every morning she tied a little ribbon around the end. Both parents seemed much more concerned with Schyanne's condition. Steve had shed a single tear when he talked about how Schyanne shrank away when he or any of her brothers entered the room.

They were keeping Schyanne home from school, they told Dave. She would keep seeing the trauma counselor four days a week until she started speaking again. They had an appointment with a neurologist, on the counselor's advice, to rule out any brain injury.

As Mack had watched the interviews from the monitoring room, she was struck by how appropriate they seemed in contrast to their first meeting a week before. They were in turn concerned, compassionate, and angry at whoever had hurt their daughter. They were perfect parents, trying to pick up the pieces after a disaster. They were candid with Dave, giving him the names and phone numbers for Schyanne's best friends and signing the release forms necessary for him to talk to the trauma counselor. Schyanne wasn't allowed to date or have social media, she didn't have a cell phone, and the only computer in the house was in the living room. Dave could take the computer, of course, if he thought there might be anything useful on it. They confirmed that, yes, Schyanne had spoken normally before she went missing. She had a beautiful singing voice.

Regardless, Mack still didn't like them. Shannon was overly submissive, often beginning her sentences with "Steve always says that..." or "Steve likes it when I..." Steve, on the other hand, remained imperious. He had mentioned his friendship with Peter Campbell no less than four times during his interview, including when Dave went to take the cheek swab. "Whatever Pete needs me to do," Steve had said. Mack groaned in exasperation.

In the weeks that followed, Mack faithfully sent her daily updates to James, Michael, and Charlie. She thought about including the Pope, just for good measure, but she was sure Michael filled him in right after he talked to Campbell. Most days, there was nothing to report. Schyanne continued to see the trauma counselor, who had her draw since she still wouldn't speak. The pictures were more of the same—dragons, princesses, the scary guy with the red eyes. Occasionally, Schyanne would make something different, usually in response to a direct request. The counselor asked for a picture of her school, for example, and Schyanne drew a red brick building that was a dead ringer for her junior high school. When asked to draw anything more personal, though, like her family, Schyanne went back to fantasy.

Dave had done some further investigation into Schyanne's life before she went missing, but it was unproductive. He made contact with the friends whose names had been provided by Steve and Shannon. All three of them—Jennifer Hayes, Jayne Harding, and Hannah Emerson—confirmed that Schyanne had no social media accounts and wasn't dating anyone. Dave pushed on the last point, asking whether she had any close male friends, any boys she'd talked about, any boys who'd even shown an interest in her, but the girls maintained that Schyanne hadn't said anything about boys to any of them. He talked to Schyanne's teachers, both at her public school and at the seminary she attended every morning. None of them had noticed any behavioral changes or any issues with Schyanne and boys.

The Andersens allowed their computer to be searched. Someone had used it to look at porn, but the police analyst couldn't tell who. There was nothing to indicate that Schyanne had secret social-media accounts, or even an email address, but Mack flagged that as an avenue for further investigation. Mostly, based on the analysis, the computer was used for homework by the kids and recipes by Shannon. Shannon's email contained a large number of family photographs that she had sent her mom and sisters back in Utah, but nothing concerning or out of the ordinary in any way.

The counselor reported to Dave that she was bothered by the relationship between Schyanne and her parents. Shannon brought Schyanne to every session, but the counselor said she never saw Shannon touch her daughter. No hugs, no pats on the back, not even a helping hand when Schyanne's short hair got a little wild. In fact, the counselor said, Shannon rarely seemed to acknowledge Schyanne at all. Schyanne was starting to talk a little bit in sessions—mostly just single-word answers to direct questions—but in front of Shannon she wouldn't say anything. When the counselor told Shannon about Schyanne's progress, she didn't get the ecstatic response she was expecting. Instead, Shannon seemed frustrated—upset, even. The counselor couldn't tell if she was frustrated by how long it was taking Schyanne to speak or upset that she was speaking at all. Either way, she found Shannon's response baffling.

She'd only met Steve twice, she told Dave. Each time, Schyanne appeared to shrink away from him, and stayed as far away from him as she could. Steve maintained she still did that with all males, including her brothers and uncles. The counselor stressed she wanted to believe him, but she had seen Schyanne around a few other males—one of her brothers, an office worker—and she didn't have the same reaction to them that she had to Steve. Steve gave the counselor the creeps, even though she didn't have a good reason to feel that way.

The most interesting thing, as far as Mack was concerned, was what the counselor had learned about Schyanne's drawings. She established, by having Schyanne respond to yes or no questions, that Schyanne was the princess who wore pink. Shaelynn, Schyanne's older sister, was the princess in purple. The dragon was the man who had hurt her. What the counselor couldn't get Schyanne to do was identify the dragon. She asked several times if the dragon was Steve, but Schyanne would never respond. She wouldn't respond to *any* questions about the dragon, in fact—whether the dragon was a grown-up or a child, had blond hair or brown, was tall or short. Any questions about the dragon caused Schyanne to shut down, and she wouldn't speak again for the rest of the session.

Dave and Mack didn't talk about it much, but it seemed to Mack like they both believed that Steve Andersen had abused Schyanne. Mack knew she did, even though she had no real evidence and no confidence that she would ever be able to prove it. She talked to James about it late one afternoon.

Mack laid out her case, which was sparse—a gut feeling, some statistics, a lack of other leads. James sat back, stroking his goatee. James was one of the very few prosecutors Mack knew who had facial hair, and the only one with a goatee. The general feeling was that facial hair on a prosecutor was sinister, made them look like the devil. Those prosecutors that chose to break that convention all seemed to go with a full beard. Not James, who had sported his neat salt-and-pepper goatee for as long as Mack had known him and looked more professorial than devilish.

"Well," he said, "your case seems to have one main problem."

"Just one?" Mack asked, surprised that he only saw one issue. "What is it?"

"It doesn't exist."

"Ah," Mack said, disappointed. "So we *are* on the same page, after all."

"Look," he said, "if Steve Andersen molested his daughter, you have my full support in going forward. You know it's not up to us, though. This case is political. Andersen has connections, and in order to convince Mr. Campbell, you are going to need a rock-solid case. Where are you on the DNA?"

Mack sighed. "I don't know. Maybe another week or two. The lab put a rush on it, but we're still looking at six weeks or so."

"Anything's better than the six months it usually takes," he said. "Come back when you have it, and we can reassess."

She left his office feeling irritated and out of options. James was right—Mack had to be patient.

CHAPTER NINE

Mack had never been very good at being patient and she was lucky that she didn't have to wait much longer. The very next Monday, as she reviewed the latest report from the string of sexually motivated home invasions, still with no suspect, her phone rang.

"Mack. Dave. We have DNA. Steve Andersen is the guy."

Her stomach dropped. Despite her suspicions about Steve Andersen, she had spent the weekend hoping that he would be exonerated by the DNA results. Now, she was faced with the reality that they had sent a little girl home with her abuser for another month.

"Break it down for me, Dave," Mack said. "What specifically do we have?"

"Sperm that matches him. Internal and external. The lab guy will say it was no more than forty-eight hours old. We have YSTR on the skin swabs, too, but those don't help us much."

YSTR DNA is passed down from father to son through the generations. It could belong to any of Andersen's three sons, his father, paternal uncles, even his brothers.

"So defense will say what?" Mack mused. "It was a male relative?"

"Probably," Dave acknowledged.

"But the sperm proves that it wasn't any of the relatives. It was definitely Andersen. So the sperm was planted? Contamination?"

"What's that old saying? If you don't have the law, argue the facts, and if you don't have the facts, attack the crime lab?"

Mack laughed. "Yeah. That old chestnut."

"I really think we have enough," Dave said.

"How good are the results on the sperm?"

"It's a match at all sixteen loci."

Mack whistled. That was impressive. It would be hard for any defense attorney to fight, but not impossible. She'd seen them successfully argue the ruse they'd used to get Andersen's swab in the first place—transfer DNA—on more than one occasion. "What's the next step?" she asked.

"I've been thinking about that," Dave said. His excitement was obvious, and Mack knew that this dedication was what made Dave a great detective. "I think we need to pull Schyanne in for another forensic interview and tell her what we've got. Meanwhile, we need to pull Steve in for a *Miranda* interview."

"Once you get Steve back in the interview room, you won't have any options. You'll have to charge it, and we can't commit to charging until we get approval from both our chains of command."

Dave groaned. "Mack, this guy molested his daughter and we sent her home with him. I don't want to give him any more access to her than he's already had."

"That's exactly my point, Dave. We need more to take up the chain. Let's get Schyanne in. See if we can get her talking. Then we decide what to do about Steve."

They hung up and Mack looked up from her scribbled notes to see Jess at her door. It was clear, from her perfect hair and manicure, that she was in trial and trying to look her best.

"You got DNA?" she asked. "I heard you on the phone."

"Yeah. It's Steve Andersen. That son of a bitch raped his

daughter, and I *know* I'll get pushback from Campbell if I try to charge him, given their friendship and political relationship."

She nodded sympathetically. "Yeah," she said, "you will. But you don't do this job to avoid pushback. You do it for kids like Schyanne. When are you going to have her interviewed?"

Jess was right, of course, and Mack knew she couldn't fixate on the political implications of charging the DA's golf buddy with raping his daughter.

"Dave's trying to get it set up for later today. We're going to have Nicole do it, since she did the first one."

"And what are you telling the parents?" Jess asked.

"I think Dave's just going to say that we have a lead based on DNA and want to try one more interview. She's been talking a bit more, so it's not so far-fetched. I hope."

Mack's email pinged. Jess came fully into the office, took off the black suit jacket she had been wearing over her red sleeveless dress, and sat in the chair that wasn't covered in files.

"It's Dave," Mack said, looking at the screen. "He has it set up for this afternoon at the center."

"That didn't take long," Jess said. "I wonder why the Andersens are being so helpful."

Mack wondered the same thing herself. Was Andersen really so arrogant as to believe that he could get away with it? It made sense that he would think he was smarter than the cops, and although Dave Barton was a fantastic police officer, Mack could understand why Andersen would think he could outsmart the unassuming detective. He had consented to a DNA sample, though. He had to have known it would come back to him.

"I have no idea," Mack said. "It's a fair question, and one that we'll hopefully learn the answer to, eventually."

Jess nodded and changed the subject to a movie that had come out the previous weekend and they'd both gone to see, but hadn't had the chance to discuss. That distracted Mack from the case until noon, when she headed over to the center to talk to Dave and Nicole before Schyanne came in for her interview.

CHAPTER TEN

Schyanne was late for her interview. Dave and Mack were worried. What if Andersen had finally realized he wasn't fooling them? What if Shannon knew what was going on and had chosen her husband over her daughter? What if Schyanne had disappeared again? Nicole tried to be the voice of reason, assuring the others that Shannon had run into traffic, or they had stopped to get some lunch, or that, really, it was unreasonable to count five minutes as "late."

After ten minutes, Nicole was proved right when Shannon and Schyanne walked into the center's lobby. Mack hadn't seen either of them in almost a month and was surprised by how different they both looked. Schyanne's hair had grown out some, and she was dressed neatly in a calf-length blue dress and a cardigan. She made eye contact with Mack and Nicole, and only drew back slightly when Dave leaned down and said hello. Where Schyanne had improved, Shannon appeared to have regressed. Her skin was pale and she looked tired. She wore no jewelry or makeup. She had lost weight and her dress hung on her gaunt frame.

"Hi, Schyanne," Nicole said, leaning down to make eye contact with the child.

"Hi," she said so softly it was almost a whisper.

"Do you remember me?" Nicole asked.

"Nicole," Schyanne said in the same quiet voice.

Mack was impressed. Clearly the work with the trauma counselor was helping.

"That's right!" Nicole said, her voice reflecting the same joy Mack felt. "I'm Nicole. Can we go talk for a while?"

Schyanne nodded, and the two walked through the lobby and toward the interview room.

Dave turned to Shannon. "You can wait here, Mrs. Andersen. Hopefully it won't take very long."

Shannon nodded disinterestedly and sat in one of the lobby's armchairs. There was a table of magazines next to her, and she probably had a smart phone in her over-sized Tory Burch purse, but she didn't reach for either. She sat stock-still, staring off into the distance.

"Do you need anything, ma'am?" Dave asked her.

She shook her head but didn't speak. Dave and Mack exchanged glances. This was a third Shannon Andersen—not the submissive wife they had met the first time or the mother reluctant to give a DNA sample at her interview. They didn't have time to give it too much thought, since they needed to get back to the monitoring room.

They watched Nicole and Schyanne get settled into the same chairs they'd occupied previously. Nicole introduced herself again and went through the rules of the interview.

"Do you remember the last time you were here?" she asked.

"Yes," Schyanne said.

Nicole pulled out Schyanne's very first picture, drawn a month earlier, the night she'd been found.

"Do you remember this?"

Schyanne nodded.

"Are you in this picture?" Nicole asked. Dave had told her that he thought Schyanne had been abused by her dad, and Nicole suggested the picture as a way to get there.

"Yes," Schyanne said. She pointed at the princess in the tower.

"Who else is in the picture?" Nicole asked.

Schyanne was silent.

"You know Dave, who you met outside?" Nicole asked.

"Yes," Schyanne said.

"Did you know he's a police officer?" Nicole asked.

Schyanne shook her head. Dave and his detectives didn't like to tell children that they were cops, because it could scare them.

"Well," Nicole said, "Dave is a police officer who has a very special job. His job is to save princesses from dragons."

Schyanne stared at her, wide-eyed.

"And you remember Mack?" Nicole asked.

Schyanne nodded.

"Well, her job is to put dragons in big stone towers where they can't hurt princesses anymore."

Schyanne looked at the picture on the table. Her eyes filled with tears.

"Schyanne," Nicole said softly, "who's the dragon?"

"I don't want to tell you," Schyanne whispered.

Dave and Mack looked at each other, surprised. That was the longest sentence they had ever heard Schyanne say.

"Why not?" Nicole asked.

"I'll get in trouble if I say," Schyanne said. "He said if I told he'd do it again."

"Who said, Schyanne?" Nicole asked. She was visibly trying to remain calm, like she was trained to do, but it was clear she was excited.

"Daddy said." Schyanne started to cry.

Nicole leaned back. Dave and Mack exhaled breaths neither of them realized they were holding. The monitoring room suddenly felt like the NASA control room when the Mars Rover landed.

"We got the bastard," Dave said.

"Not yet," Mack said. "We need specific acts for charging."

Nicole knew just what to do. She waited until Schyanne calmed down before pressing forward. Once Schyanne started talking, the words came more easily and she kept going. The interview lasted another thirty minutes, and when they were done Mack had enough specific acts of physical and sexual abuse to keep Andersen locked up for the rest of his life.

Drained, Nicole joined Mack and Dave in the monitoring room to see if either of them had any follow-up questions. They congratulated her on a job well done. They needed nothing further. Nicole had specific date ranges, locations, and detailed acts. Combined with the DNA evidence, Mack finally had enough to charge Andersen.

"Actually," she said, once Nicole had left the room, "I guess we have enough to charge anyone *other* than Andersen."

Dave rolled his eyes.

"Whether we can charge *Andersen* still depends on what his golf buddy Old Pete says. He could still tank this whole case. Just make it disappear. Andersen moves on with his life, Schyanne keeps getting victimized, like it never happened."

"I know," Dave said. He sighed and rubbed his head. "I hate the political part of this job. This is the problem with an elected official being in charge of law enforcement. The whole thing really hinges on Campbell's integrity. He's been a straight shooter so far, but the Andersen case is a little more personal for him. He warned you that your case needs to be absolutely watertight or don't even think about taking it any further, which might mean he's looking for any loophole to get this asshole off."

"You don't have to convince me," Mack said, and picked up her phone to bring James up to speed.

"You've got enough for me," he said, "but you know this one isn't up to me. You know what we need to do."

Mack sighed. "Meet with Mikey?" she asked, already feeling defeated.

"Yup," he said. "I'll set it up."

"How am I supposed to keep Schyanne safe from him in the meantime?" Mack asked.

He had to think about that. "Any reason to think Mom knows what's been going on?" he asked.

"James," Mack said, "I truly believe that she does. But I can't prove it."

"Have Dave call CPS," James finally said. "It's not the politically correct choice, but it's the right choice legally and it's the choice that protects that kid. I'll stand up for it if Mr. Campbell balks. And then get back to the office. We'll need to move fast."

CHAPTER ELEVEN

After CPS came to take custody of Schyanne, Dave went with Mack to present a united front. First, they met with James and explained the new developments in more detail. James leaned back in his chair, rubbing his head.

"So, basically, you have DNA that corroborates specific acts alleged by Schyanne?" he asked.

"Yes," Mack said. "And Schyanne was able to give the real stories behind almost all of the healed injuries. Once she was ready to talk about it, she was ready to talk about *all* of it."

"And you're sure she's not covering for a boyfriend or someone?"

"We can never be absolutely sure on that," Dave said, "but with her father's sperm inside her, we're as sure as we can be."

"Where does your commander stand?" James asked. He grabbed the stress ball on his desk and started squeezing it.

"He's on board," Dave said. "He doesn't see any other option at this point but to interview Andersen and then charge him."

"You're not going to get anything by interviewing him. At the first sign of trouble, he'll lawyer up."

"We could try a confrontation call," Dave said.

"Not anymore you can't," James said. "Shannon's called him by now. What did you tell her?"

"Just that Schyanne had started talking and based on what she was saying we couldn't let her go home," Mack said.

"That's right!" Dave said. "We never actually said it was Steve. Could be one of the sons."

"You *really* didn't go any further than that?" James asked.

"She didn't ask any follow-up questions," Mack said. "Which was really weird."

Dave's plan for the afternoon was to recruit Shannon for a confrontation call—a phone call where one side, in this case Shannon, would work with the police and agree to be recorded in conversation with a suspect, in this case Steve. The cops would suggest what she could say to encourage the suspect to make some admissions. Sometimes these calls provide powerful evidence, although the process is always risky. Sometimes the person helping the cops either intentionally or unintentionally tips off the suspect about the investigation. At that point, the suspect has to be arrested immediately before they can flee.

Dave left the room to call Shannon while James and Mack kept talking.

"I think you should let me talk in the meeting with Brown," James suggested.

"But it's my case!" Mack said. "I've been involved in this for a month. I know the facts up to this point better than anyone."

"And if there are specific factual questions," James said, "you will need to answer them. You know this meeting won't be about facts, though."

Mack sighed, knowing he was right but not wanting to admit it. Dave returned, shaking his head.

"The Andersens have already retained John Grant," he said, "and Mr. Grant conveyed, in no uncertain terms, where I could put my confrontation call."

"At least we tried," Mack said. "On a case like this, we have to try absolutely everything, right?"

James' email pinged. "They're ready for us," he said, standing and putting on a suit jacket.

Dave and Mack looked at each other and tried to smile, but neither one quite managed it. The elevator ride was tense. No one spoke. In the executive suite, the secretary showed them into the ornate conference room. At the head of the table sat the district attorney himself, flanked by Michael and Charlie—who, Mack noticed, was not playing with his phone.

James stopped short. "Mr. Campbell," he said, "I didn't realize you'd be joining us today."

"Steve Andersen has been a good friend of mine for thirty years," Campbell said. He picked a nonexistent piece of lint off his charcoal-gray suit jacket. "I want to make sure that your unit doesn't railroad an innocent man."

Mack clenched her fists and was about to retort when she felt Dave's reassuring hand on her arm.

"James, Mackenzie," Michael said, gesturing them into the room and toward the table, "and this must be…"

Dave introduced himself. Neither man appeared inclined to shake hands.

After settling in at the other end of the table from Campbell, James ran through a basic outline of how the case had developed. When he got to the DNA results, he was interrupted.

"But couldn't there be a perfectly reasonable explanation for those results?" Campbell asked, rubbing his chin with one well-manicured hand. "After all, Steve hugs his children, they share a home, their laundry is done at the same time."

Mack was shocked. That was a defense-attorney argument, not something the elected official of a large prosecution agency should ask.

"Well, sir," James said, "that's a good question. The experts we work with, however, will testify that there is no reasonable way for Steve Andersen's sperm to get inside his fourteen-year-old daughter's vagina other than sexual penetration."

"Wasn't there a case some years ago with a turkey baster?" Campbell asked.

"Yes, sir," James said, "you're right. But if Andersen's defense is the same defense as in that case—that he and his wife were trying to inseminate their daughter with his sperm in a turkey baster—then that's still a crime."

Campbell looked disgusted. Jess had long said that it was foolish to have a district attorney who had never prosecuted family crimes and therefore had no understanding of them, and Mack agreed. Campbell may well have been great with the media, and, from what Mack had heard, he had been great when he prosecuted gang crimes, but he clearly wasn't the right guy to oversee the sex-crimes unit.

"How do we know Schyanne didn't invent all this to hide some sort of boyfriend? Maybe an older man?"

Mack rolled her eyes but kept quiet.

"Sir, the DNA really eliminates that possibility," James said. Mack could tell his patience was waning. "But Sergeant Barton and his squad did investigate it. They spoke with Schyanne's friends and teachers, anyone who might have known anything about a boyfriend."

"Steve is a good man," Campbell said, "a family man. I'm sure I would have suspected something if all this were true. He's always very affectionate toward Schyanne—toward all his kids."

"As you know, sir, these crimes happen behind closed doors. You wouldn't have seen anything."

Mack wasn't sure how much more of James' indulgent behavior she could take. This was ridiculous. Any random yahoo would have been in jail by now and they wouldn't have thought twice about charging him. Because this jackass was friends with the boss and sponsored a Little League team, James was teaching Sex Crimes 101 and begging for permission for Mack and Dave to do their jobs.

"What do you propose to charge him with?" Campbell asked, rubbing his chin. "Child Abuse or something?"

James looked at Mack and nodded, but she read the warning in his eyes.

"Based on what Schyanne has disclosed, there are twenty-seven counts," Mack said, consulting her notes from the interview earlier that afternoon, "of which twelve are mandatory life counts if he's convicted at trial."

"Plus she told us some stuff about a secret laptop," Dave said, "so we want to do a search warrant to find that. We think there are likely to be more counts based on what's on the computer."

"You want to put Steve Andersen in prison for the rest of his life?" Campbell asked.

"No," Mack said, unable to contain herself. "He *deserves* to be in prison for the rest of his life for what he did to his daughter."

James ignored her outburst and turned to Campbell. "What do you think, sir? How should we proceed?"

"If they don't charge him," Charlie said, "and the media gets a hold of it, it will look like you were doing favors for a friend."

Campbell nodded, his silver hair glinting as it caught the florescent light. "Go ahead. But if you're wrong, so help me, you're all fired." He turned to Dave. "And Sergeant, I *will* have your badge."

Mack flashed a quick smile at Charlie on their way out of the room. Dave called the SWAT team from the elevator. Steve Andersen would be in custody by 5:00 p.m.

CHAPTER TWELVE

When they got back to Mack's office, Dave took over her computer to start writing warrants. He wanted to seize the secret laptop before either Andersen had time to destroy it. Mack started working on what her secretary would need to draft an indictment—the paperwork a grand jury uses to say that they have found probable cause. She also completed subpoenas for any phone calls Andersen would make or mail he would send from the jail. The best chance at intercepting a confession comes within the first week a defendant is in custody, and Mack didn't want to lose potentially valuable information because the subpoena didn't arrive in time.

By the time the SWAT team called to say they were staged and ready, Mack was riding shotgun in Dave's unmarked car, breaking speed limits as he raced to meet them with the signed warrants.

The SWAT leader wasn't happy to see them. Wasn't happy to see Mack, really. Since she wasn't carrying a gun or wearing armor, she was just a complication for him as he considered his team's safety and their mission. He politely asked her to wait in the car until the massive McMansion was cleared and Steve was in custody. Mack tried to appeal to Dave, but he just shook his head. Traitor.

Around the corner from the Andersens' house Mack made herself comfortable in Dave's car and turned on the air conditioning. She realized that she hadn't talked to Anna since the DNA results. The psychologist must have been in with a patient, so Mack settled for a detailed voice mail. She turned on Dave's department-issued radio to try to follow the SWAT team. As she fiddled with the knobs, she saw a cream-colored Mercedes pull past with the license plate "ANDERS2." Mack couldn't see the driver, but she didn't need to.

She grabbed the radio microphone and pushed the button as she had seen dozens of cops do in movies. Luckily, the movies got this one right, and she told the SWAT team that Shannon Andersen was leaving the area and needed to be stopped. As the Mercedes continued down the street toward the main road, a uniformed officer ran out from a side street and flagged it down. Two other officers jogged behind to catch up. The officers gestured to the driver to exit the vehicle, and Shannon Andersen eventually emerged. After a few minutes talking to Shannon, one of the officers waved at Mack, so she left Dave's car and walked toward them down the street. Shannon had been led away from the car and was still talking to the other two officers.

"Ma'am," the officer said, "weren't we looking for a laptop?"

"Yes," Mack said. "Is there one in the car?"

"Yes, ma'am," he said, indicating a black Toshiba on the back seat.

"What does she say about it?" Mack asked.

"Said her husband asked her to take it. She was headed to his brother's house."

"Did she say *why* her husband wanted her to take it?"

"Said he told her the police were coming and there are important business documents on it. That's all she knows."

Mack weighed her options. Given that explanation, she probably didn't have enough to charge Shannon with tampering. Not yet, at least. She quickly reviewed the search warrants in her head. Was the car covered? She didn't think so, but that would be easy to fix.

"Okay," Mack said. "Let's impound the car. She can't be let back in the house until the search warrants are executed, but you can't hold her here. Have someone stay with the car until Impound gets here."

The SWAT officer looked at Mack disbelievingly. "You want someone to miss the search of the house to stay with the car?"

"The faster you get Impound here, the faster you can rejoin your team," she exclaimed, heading back to Dave's car.

Mack's phone buzzed in her pocket.

"Hi, Charlie, what's up?"

"Mackenzie, is Barton actually executing a search warrant of the Andersens' house right now?" he asked.

"I don't think the team has made entrance yet," Mack said, "but I can't really see. It's possible that they're inside. Why?"

"Mr. Campbell is not happy. He feels like you should have waited."

"Mr. Campbell is not..." Mack's voice trailed off and she cleared her throat. "Andersen called him?"

"Unclear, but likely," Charlie said. "Look, I think you're doing the right thing, I'm just trying to do damage control. When is grand jury?"

"We're set for eight tomorrow," Mack said, "and we want him in custody before the indictment comes down. We didn't want him to get scared off and make a run for it."

Charlie laughed. "Well, it sounds like you were almost too late, based on what Campbell is saying. Good luck, Mack."

Mack couldn't believe Campbell was still fighting for his good old buddy, even after the evidence that he'd been raping his daughter for years. Mack supposed those church ties ran pretty deep.

Mack looked up to see Dave walking toward the car.

"We got him! We've still got hours to go on the search, but we got him."

"*Hours?*" Mack asked. It was after 6:00 p.m., she was hungry and tired, and she would be stranded half an hour from home for hours.

"Yeah," he said, oblivious to her plight. "I'm heading back in. I just wanted you to know. I'll see you tomorrow morning. Bright and early!"

Mack sighed and watched Dave walk back into the fading light. She picked up her phone and hit the first speed-dial number.

"Hey, doll," Anna said. "What's up? I'm sorry I missed your call earlier."

"That's okay," she said, "but I need a ride. Can you come get me?"

CHAPTER THIRTEEN

The grand jury presentation went relatively smoothly. One juror had to recuse herself because she went to church with the Andersens, but no one else seemed phased by the mention of the mogul. They indicted on all twenty-seven counts with no fuss. The only factual question they had for Dave was whether anyone had searched the laptop yet. Once they were off the record and the court reporter was no longer recording everyone, the foreman told Mack they wanted to indict Shannon as well. She told Dave as they walked back to her office.

"Do you think we have enough?" he asked.

"No," Mack said, "but I hope I'm wrong. Let's see what's on the laptop."

The computer guy assigned to Dave's squad was looking through it, but Andersen had really good encryption software. They could crack it, Dave assured Mack, but it would take some time.

Dave didn't stay to chat. Schyanne's siblings needed to be reinterviewed and two of the brothers were set for that afternoon. The picture of the second princess, who Schyanne had identified as Shaelynn, led Dave to suspect that Schyanne was not the first Andersen to be subject to abuse.

Mack sank into her desk chair, still exhausted from the previous day's excitement. She didn't bother to turn her office lights on and enjoyed the dark until Jess came rushing in.

"Holy cow," she said, flicking the switch. "Have you seen the news yet today?"

Mack blinked at her, bleary-eyed. "No," she said. "I just got back from grand jury on Andersen. They found probable cause, because of course they did. Why?"

Jess came around the desk and started typing on Mack's keyboard. The homepage for the *Arizona Daily Star* appeared on the screen. Steve Andersen's photo—probably a campaign shot—smiled back at them from the space normally reserved for governors and movie stars. Jess clicked the play button.

As Mack stared in disbelief, it took her a minute to realize what she was watching. Andersen's skin was wan against his orange jumpsuit.

"They let him give a press conference from the jail?" Mack asked.

Jess nodded.

"Many of you know me," Andersen said, "and know that I would never commit the heinous crimes I've been accused of."

"This is ridiculous," Mack said.

"Shhh," Jess said. "The best part is coming up."

"For those of you who don't know me," Andersen said, "let me assure you—I love my family, my church, and my community. I am offering a fifty-thousand-dollar reward to anyone who can find the man who actually raped my daughter and prove my innocence."

Jess laughed. "That's the part I like. If I show him the DNA, do you think he'd give me the money?"

Mack rolled her eyes and grabbed her phone to email Charlie.

"Seen it," came his terse reply, seconds later.

Mack groaned. "Can I call a technical foul on the day and go back to bed?" she asked Jess. "Maybe get a do-over?"

"Sorry, champ," she said, "no do-overs."

The Andersen story dominated the eleven, twelve, and four o'clock news cycles. It was like Mack's own personal train wreck—she just couldn't look away. Depending on which channel she watched, she was either being vilified as an anti-Mormon, an anti-Republican, a man-hating feminist, or some combination of the three. Apparently, none of the local newscasters could believe that Steve Andersen could be anything other than a hero. One channel put some of the blame on Peter Campbell, who, they said, obviously didn't know how to control his renegade prosecutors. All four of the others, however, put the blame squarely on Mack.

By the time she left that evening, Mack had gotten emails from James, Michael Brown, Charlie, Anna, her mother, and Dave. James, Anna, her mom, and Dave all offered variations on the theme of "I'm so sorry this is happening to you." Charlie informed her that Mr. Campbell would be holding his own press conference the following morning, and she should be available to answer questions by phone or email, both until then and during the conference itself. Michael said Mack should have listened to him in the first place. She found that last email surprisingly unhelpful and deleted it without responding.

Mack was back at work less than twelve hours later to prepare for hearings before meeting with the head honcho. As she looked at her calendar and determined what she had to cover and what could be handled by assigned coverage attorneys, she realized that she had never extended a plea offer to Benjamin Allen—the voyeur she had taken from Jess in January. Given that the trial date was fast approaching, Mack figured it was time.

She reviewed the police report on the Allen case, looking for anything she might have missed. Nothing. His victim, a forty-year-old woman wearing a calf-length skirt, had been bending over in the mustard aisle to grab something from the bottom shelf. She felt something brush her leg, and turned around to find Allen, squatting with cell phone still in hand. She immediately got store security, who detained Allen and called the police. Thankfully, they took his phone, so he hadn't even had the chance to delete the blurry photo before the cops came. A forensic exam of his phone revealed nothing. Allen seemed like a mopey kid who wasn't getting laid, and this was his attempt to relieve some sexual frustration. Mack wrote the coverage attorney a note instructing her to tell Allen's defense attorney that Allen could have a chance at a misdemeanor if he successfully completed five years of probation and sex-offender therapy. It was a standard offer, and Mack expected the file to come back from morning court with a status conference set in a week or two for Allen to take the plea.

By the time Mack next looked at the clock, she had to scramble to get Campbell's press conference streaming before he got too far into it. She drank her coffee and only half-listened as he talked about the case's "strong forensic underpinnings" and assured the public that the district attorney's office was not conducting witch hunts on his watch. Somehow, his speech didn't make Mack feel any better about the wringer he'd dragged her and Dave through the day before.

Finally, he excused himself with a pithy line about "getting back to fighting crime." Mack found herself contemplating, not for the first time, how challenging it was to work for a man she despised. Her phone buzzed with Dave calling.

"I hope you have good news," she said. "I just watched the press conference and can't take anything but sunshine and rainbows."

"I don't have sunshine and rainbows," he said.

Mack sighed.

"But I *do* have two more victims."

Mack could hear the smile in his voice. "You have what now?" she asked. Schyanne's sisters weren't scheduled to be interviewed until the following week, so she didn't understand how Dave could have more victims.

"They saw the news reports and called," he said. "He's been

doing this for a *long* time. We've got a cousin from when he was thirty-four and she was seven. She told her parents and they hushed it up because he went through some counseling and repented."

"Wow," Mack said.

"*And*," Dave said, "we've got a girl from his ward. He was 'counseling' her after some behavior problems at home. She was fourteen and he was showing her how to 'get right with the Lord.'"

Mack whistled. "That's incredible, Dave."

"It's not incredible, it's a goddamn miracle. Even the details match Schyanne. He said the same things, did the same things."

"When are they being interviewed?"

"We've got one coming in tomorrow and one on Saturday," he said. "You'll have the supplements on your desk Monday morning."

Mack sat back, smiling. The more victims she had that could corroborate Schyanne's story, the more likely it would be that she would get justice for all of them. Suddenly the media coverage didn't look like such a bad thing after all.

CHAPTER FOURTEEN

By Monday morning, the two additional victims had become four, and by the next Friday, with Shaelynn and now Sherrie, Steve's oldest daughter, there were seven. Some of them had been one-time incidents, but several of them, including his daughters, he'd been abusing for years. Some were girls he'd met through church, others were family members. All of them reported that he'd "counseled" them and that's when the abuse would occur. With each call from Dave, Mack's confidence in the case grew.

Unfortunately, on Monday morning, Mack found another foothills home invasion report on her desk. The guy just got bolder—during the most recent incident, the woman who owned the house woke up to find him sitting on the end of her bed, watching her as she slept. She got a better look at him than any of the previous victims and was able to give a police sketch artist a good enough description for a drawing. Detectives promptly distributed it to all the local news stations, but Mack wasn't all that optimistic. Even though the drawing was relatively detailed by police sketch standards, it still looked like around half the white men she saw on any given day. Since the guy appeared not to have any scars, deformities, or facial tattoos, she was unsure how helpful the drawing would be. Someday, she hoped, she would have an unknown rapist with his name and Social Security number tattooed on his forehead, but the home invader wasn't that guy.

On Tuesday, James and Mack met with Michael and Charlie to update them on the Andersen case. Mack was on her way out of her office when her email pinged. Linda Andrews, Benjamin Allen's attorney, was disappointed with the plea offer and thought the case really warranted a straight-up misdemeanor. She had advised her client not to take it. Mack laughed. She had never worked with Linda before, but she had heard through the grapevine that she was very whiny and inclined to believe that her clients were beautiful, if misunderstood, snowflakes. Mack replied with a very brief message saying that it was nothing personal, but the offer was what it was and wouldn't get any better. She hurried out of her office, almost five minutes late.

Luckily, she found James waiting in the lobby of the executive suite.

"Apparently," he said, looking up from his phone as Mack rushed in, "Mr. Campbell has decided to stop interfering with your case."

"An additional six victims had a cooling effect on his relationship with good old Stevie?"

He smiled. "Evidence has a funny way of doing that to people," he said. "Meanwhile, I have to meet with Charlie about one of my own cases, but he's in another meeting. You're off the hook, Mack."

"So I have the office's blessing to actually, like, prosecute the case?"

He made the sign of the cross. "Go with God, Ms. Wilson."

Mack laughed.

"It's still high profile," he said, "so you'll have to talk to me before offering a plea or doing anything drastic."

"Of course," she said. "I wouldn't have it any other way."

James smiled again and scratched his cheek. He knew Mack preferred not to bring him into her cases unless something blew up, and he respected her enough to let her chart her own course for the most part.

"Have you heard from his attorney yet?" James asked.

"Nope," Mack said, "and I'm actually really looking forward to it. I've never worked with John Grant, but I had a defendant threaten to hire him once when I was a new prosecutor. I'm curious to finally meet him!"

"He puts up a good front," James said, "but he's pretty useless. The fact is, he charges an enormous amount of money to do very little work."

"So in other words," Mack said, "he's a defense attorney."

James laughed. The conference room door opened and Charlie emerged.

"James," he said, "we're ready for you. Hey, Mack, how's it going?"

"Hey, Charlie," Mack said as she headed for the door. "No offense, but much better now that our meeting is canceled."

He frowned. "I have that effect on people," he said. "I don't know what it is."

Mack grinned all the way back to her office, but her smile faded when her phone rang and the caller ID showed Dave Barton. Over the previous weeks, calls from Dave had just meant more work—more warrants, more interviews to observe, and more time away from her other cases. This call, luckily, was good news.

"The analysis of the laptop is done," he said, "and you'll never guess what we found."

"The photos Schyanne said would be there? The ones documenting her abuse?"

"Those, and similar pictures of other victims I didn't recognize."

"All homemade?" Mack asked. "Or was he collecting?"

"A mix," Dave said, "but mostly homemade. Hundreds of images, dozens of videos."

"Any adult porn mixed in?" Mack asked, already anticipating

how Andersen's defense attorney would fight this at trial. A common ploy was arguing that any child porn was inadvertently downloaded attached to adult porn. It was ridiculous, but sometimes it fooled jurors.

"Not one damn image," Dave said. "Anyway, we're still working a few other angles. Just thought you should know the latest!"

Even though it was horrible that Andersen had memorialized the abuse of his victims, it made the case against him that much stronger. Mack got back to work, energized.

CHAPTER FIFTEEN

The tide of new victims slowed, then stopped altogether by the following week. Once the total reached eleven, Mack took the case back to grand jury to incorporate the new charges for a total of ninety-three. The presentation took most of a Thursday afternoon, and this time several jurors indicated that they had seen, heard, or read something about the case in the news. Those who had, however, promised to set that aside and base their decisions solely on the testimony presented in the courtroom.

By the time Dave got to victim number five—a friend of Sherrie's from church—two jurors were in tears and asked for a break. After a few minutes they returned, commenting that the faster they resumed, the faster they'd be done.

Dave paced the hall as he and Mack waited for the grand jury to go through the draft indictment and make their decisions. While he paced, they again discussed charging Shannon. They had talked about this several times over the previous weeks, but had never made a decision. If there was evidence that a victim's mother knew about the abuse and didn't report it or otherwise stop it, she could be charged with failing to protect the victim from abuse. Often, she could get a generous plea offer with an agreement that she would testify for the State in the abuser's trial. It didn't always work, but when it did, the testimony of a mother who turned a blind eye could be a powerful tool.

"Grant's representing her, too, right?" Mack asked.

Dave nodded.

"We'd need to get her new counsel," she said, thinking out loud. "If we got someone reasonable, though, maybe we could come up with an agreement before even filing charges."

"Would that streamline things?" Dave asked.

Mack's response was interrupted by the chimes indicating the grand jury was ready. She took a deep breath and opened the door. Scuttlebutt around the courthouse had it that some old lawyer said once that a grand jury would indict a ham sandwich, but that hadn't exactly been Mack's experience. Every once in a while, she got a panel who hated her case—or just hated her—and found that there was no probable cause. In most cases, she didn't need to worry, but since she never knew what went on when the jurors deliberated, it always felt risky to leave important decisions in the hands of sixteen random members of the community.

In this case, Mack soon realized that the worry *really* wasn't necessary. They indicted on all ninety-three charges she had suggested. As she signed the paperwork, her phone buzzed with an incoming call, a number she didn't recognize. She excused herself and stepped into the hallway.

"This is Mackenzie."

"This is Janet with Foothills Alarm Systems." Mack had had alarms installed at her condo two years earlier, after threats from a schizophrenic defendant. "Your alarm is going off," she said, "and the police have been called. Are you at home?"

Mack waved goodbye to Dave and hurried back to her office, still on the phone with the alarm company. By the time she got home thirty minutes later, a patrol car was parked next to the stairs to the condo. Mack knocked on the window to get the lone officer's attention. He rolled down the window and Mack was hit by the smell of fast-food grease and stale coffee.

"Hi, I'm Mack."

"You the one whose alarm went off?"

"Apparently!" Mack said.

The pale, heavy-set man heaved himself out of the driver's seat. Mack noticed the name plate on his chest, his shirt buttons straining over his bulletproof vest.

"Were you able to figure out why it happened, Officer Carlson?"

Carlson leaned against his car and looked Mack up and down. "It's Bobby," he said. He stuck out his hand and Mack hesitantly shook it. His palm was damp. The hairs on the back of her neck stood up.

He smiled. His teeth were yellow and he clearly hadn't had any orthodontia as a kid. "Nah," he said. "Everything looks fine. Doors and windows are locked."

"Must have been a ghost, then," she said.

"Lady," he said, "it wasn't no ghost. You got a boyfriend to keep you safe?" His eyes flicked down to her left hand. "No husband, I see." He ran a hand through his dark curls. They were long enough that Mack wondered whether he was out of regulation.

"I'll be just fine, Officer," Mack said.

"Hey," he said. "That's right. You'll be fine. Besides, you should smile. You've got Tucson's finest out here today. If there's anything to find, I'll find it."

Mack rolled her eyes. She had been willing to put up with a certain amount of chauvinism, but asking her to smile? How clichéd.

"Really, *Officer* Carlson," she said, showing him the assistant district attorney badge she kept in her work bag. "I'll be fine." It was shocking how fast his demeanor changed. He straightened up immediately, towering over Mack, and his manner went from sleazy to professional.

"Well, ma'am," he said, "it does seem that someone might have tried to force the lock. You might want to consider adding a second deadbolt." He removed a small pad of paper and a pen from his breast pocket. "Do you have any enemies?"

Mack laughed. "I have hundreds of enemies, but none who know where I live. I'm sure it was just a random burglar who got scared off when the alarm sounded."

Carlson didn't even crack a smile. "Maybe, but you should be careful, ma'am." He handed her his card. "If you need anything, feel free to call. My *personal* cell number is on the back."

Mack took the card, knowing she would never call him. She flipped the card over and noted the handwritten phone number. How many of those did he have at the ready?

"I'm the second-shift patrol for this area Tuesday through Saturday, and we're here to protect and serve."

"Thank you," she said, "but, really, I'm sure it's fine."

Carlson shrugged. "You never know. There are some real creeps out there."

The officer got in his car, but Mack could feel him watching her as she climbed the stairs and let herself into her condo. She noticed scratch marks on the door frame but couldn't recall if they had been there before. She waved and watched him drive away before she double locked the door.

Anna answered on the first ring and yawned. "Excuse me," she said.

"I think someone tried to break into my apartment," Mack said without bothering to say hello. "Can you come over?"

"Sure," she said, sounding instantly alert. "I'll even pick up dinner."

"Anna?" Mack asked before she hung up. "Bring your gun."

"You know me, boo! Never leave home without it!"

CHAPTER SIXTEEN

When Mack's alarm rang Friday morning, she scrolled through her calendar to find it was an atypically empty day. She'd already worked close to fifty hours already that week, with more to come over the weekend, so she decided to take a rare day off. Anna had no patients scheduled, so they spent the day together, with a hike in the morning and some quality time with Mack's DVR after an afternoon nap.

They went ten hours without once mentioning work. Mack almost felt like they were back together. At the beginning of their relationship, they had had so much to talk about. Not just little stuff, day-to-day minutiae, they had talked about the big questions, ideas that transcended their daily lives. Mack brought it up as they sat down for dinner that evening—leftovers from the Chinese food Anna had brought the previous night and a six-pack of San Tan IPA.

"When did we stop talking?" she asked.

Anna put down her chopsticks and looked at her. "We talk *literally* every day."

Mack played with the drawstring on her hooded Dartmouth sweatshirt. "No," she said, "I know. I mean, when did we stop talking about things other than sex crimes and people we both know and stupid stuff like celebrity gossip."

"You noticed that, too?" she asked, sitting down. "I think we stopped *really* talking when we decided we should give friendship a try. Besides, you never liked talking about the deep stuff much, anyway."

Mack shrugged, acknowledging the truth of Anna's dig. "It was really nice today," Mack said. "I liked it."

"I did, too," she said. She picked at her vegetable lo mein. "But, Mack, I don't think we should jump into bed because we spent one day—"

"—I don't, either," Mack interrupted. "I just miss it sometimes. That's all. I miss you."

Anna looked away.

They didn't talk much the rest of the meal, and Mack kicked herself for ruining the great day. Anna put a movie in the Blu-ray player and made popcorn without asking if she could stay. They settled on the couch and Mack leaned her head on Anna's shoulder.

"Thank you for coming over," Mack said.

"Of course," Anna said, pulling a blanket off the back of the couch and covering them both. "You'd be helpless if someone broke in."

"Heeeeeeey," Mack whined, lightly smacking Anna's leg. "I would not."

"What would you do?" she asked. "Throw statute books at him? Hit him with your briefcase?"

"Just because I don't believe in keeping firearms in my house doesn't mean I can't defend myself. I took three years of taekwondo as my high school P.E. requirement."

"I would believe you," she said, "*except* for the fact that you called the chick with the gun at the first sign of trouble."

Mack laughed and settled back to watch the movie. Anna hit play, and a black and white map of Africa filled the screen while "La Marseillaise" played.

Anna went home Saturday morning after spending the night on the couch, a decision that had been made mutually without discussion, and Mack dedicated the rest of the weekend to work. She had several files that needed attention, including Benjamin Allen. Linda Andrews had responded to Mack's email, saying that her client was innocent, so the current offer was unfair. Mack replied that she was, in principle, correct—someone claiming to be innocent certainly couldn't plead guilty to anything—and the case needed to go to trial. Although that sounded good in theory, in practice it meant spending the weekend getting ready. Based on Mack's preparation, she thought the trial, with a reasonable defense attorney, should be a two-day endeavor—three, with jury selection. With Linda, Mack expected it to take over a week.

It took the better part of Saturday to get the file and her trial notebook in order. Allen would almost certainly get probation after trial, but he wouldn't get the chance at a misdemeanor. For Mack, that was enough reason to go forward and spend the time necessary to get it right. No prosecutor liked to lose cases, but she was especially edgy. She was on a nineteen-case winning streak and wanted to keep it going as long as possible.

Dave called to update Mack on Schyanne's progress in therapy. Her foster parents, Curtis and Emma Potter, were LDS, but they didn't know the Andersens. They had taken in other victims over the years, so Dave knew them pretty well and thought very highly of them. Emma had taken Schyanne to her counselor's office, an hour away, every day after Schyanne got out of school. Schyanne was thriving. She had gained weight, didn't flinch from men, and was continuing to disclose more of her father's abuse.

"Will she be able to testify?" Mack asked, anticipating, as she had from the beginning, that this case would end with a jury verdict. Even though approximately ninety-five percent of Mack's cases were resolved with a plea agreement, she knew Andersen would push his case all the way to trial. He wasn't a defendant who would spare his victims from the trauma of very public testimony.

"The counselor and I both think so," Dave said, "but, more importantly, Schyanne thinks so. She told the counselor that, when trial comes, she'll be ready."

"I hope you're right!" Mack exclaimed. She had known several victims who said they were ready to face their abusers who froze when confronted with the reality. Some defense attorneys were really hard on kids, even though that was a strategy that never seemed to work in front of a jury.

When Mack checked her email Sunday afternoon, she found a message from John Grant telling her that he wanted to set a *Simpson* hearing for Andersen. Mack sighed as she read it. Andersen wasn't entitled to post a cash bond, because of the crimes he was charged with, but he *was* entitled to a hearing on the issue within seven days of asking for one. Mack hoped the hearing itself wouldn't take very long.

She was brushing her teeth that night when she heard scratching at the door. At first, she thought it was the neighborhood stray cat that sometimes came to her for food, but when she finished flossing and still heard it, she started to worry. Mack turned on the porch light and the scratching immediately stopped. It must have been the cat, after all. Still, she slept fitfully, waking often and going to the door to recheck the lock. Knowing Anna kept her phone on silent while she slept, she texted Anna around 3:30 a.m., suggesting a trip to the shooting range and asking for help buying a handgun. Then she spent forty-five minutes researching guard dogs online before deciding she couldn't keep one in her one-bedroom condo.

She finally gave up on sleep at 4:30 and decided to take advantage of the extra time before work by going for a run. When she opened her front door, she found a small manila envelope on the welcome mat. She bent down to pick it up, surprised not to see any sign of postage or an address. It had been delivered by hand.

Mack slid out three sheets of paper. The first was a photograph of her car. It took a minute for Mack to realize where it had been taken, but she finally recognized the building behind it as the bagel shop around the corner. Since she stopped there two or three times a week, she couldn't be sure of the picture's date, but she guessed it was recent. Over the previous two weeks it had finally started getting light before Mack left for work, and the image was well-lit. The second sheet was also a photograph. This one showed Anna and Mack sitting at Mack's dining room table on Thursday night. The picture was grainy, suggesting a telephoto lens. The third page was a small sheet of notebook paper with a single line of neat block letters.

I am watching.

Mack dropped the papers, cursing herself for tainting potential fingerprint evidence. She wondered when he had left the envelope—whether he saw her open it. Whether he enjoyed her reaction. She shivered in the cool morning air and took a deep breath.

She pulled her phone out of the pocket of her sweatshirt and called the police non-emergency line. She could always go for a run another time.

CHAPTER SEVENTEEN

It took almost forty minutes for police to get to the condo, and Mack was not happy to see Officer Carlson wave to her as he swung into the parking area. Mack was waiting for him on the landing, a large mug of black coffee keeping her hands warm.

"I thought you were second shift," she said, as he climbed the stairs to her door.

"I switched," he said, slightly out of breath. "I figured this way we'd have more time to get to know each other. You look good with your hair up like that."

Carlson winked.

Mack shuddered.

By the time he took the report, impounded the envelope and its contents, and let Mack get on her way, it was after nine.

She called Jess and asked her to cover the final pretrial hearing in the Allen case. When Mack assured her that all she needed to do was affirm it for trial the following week, she agreed, texting Mack minutes later that, given the extenuating circumstances, she'd even waive her usual fee of coffee and breakfast. Mack complimented her on her generosity.

Anna called while Mack was in the car, asking about her nocturnal text. She knew how anti-gun Mack was, especially after the incident with Victor Craig years earlier. Craig, a defendant Mack had prosecuted for a misdemeanor Failure to Obey count, shot an officer and threatened Mack with a gun midway through trial. Luckily, the officer was only superficially wounded and was able to shoot back, killing Craig. Since then, even the sound of gunfire in a movie made Mack flinch. She told Anna about the scraping noises and the envelope on the doorstep. Anna was horrified and insisted that Mack learn to defend herself immediately. In the light of day, though, Mack thought she had overreacted the night before. There was no reason to believe that the scratching was related to the envelope—leaving something on the doorstep didn't require scratching the door. Mack reassured Anna that, although learning to shoot might not be a terrible idea someday, that particular Monday was not the day.

The office required ADAs to report any contact with law enforcement that wasn't directly related to their jobs, and Mack's recent encounters with Officer Carlson qualified. She dreaded the unnecessary drama of telling James, but when she got to work she went straight to his office. He was concerned but rational, pointing out that Mack really had no idea what had happened with the alarm on Thursday. He also noticed that there was nothing in the envelope that specifically referenced her job.

"It could just be a random stalker," he said, which didn't make Mack feel any better. He asked if she felt like there was enough going on to warrant a security detail, but she demurred. She had been through that before and found the retired cops hired by the office as detectives to be less than reassuring in case of a real threat. James agreed with Anna that it would probably be a good idea if Mack bought a gun and learned how to shoot it. She shuddered. The more she thought about that prospect, the less appealing it seemed. James insisted that Mack keep him posted but promised not to impose a security detail on her unless and until she wanted one.

Back in her office, Mack found an email from John Grant. Based on consultation with Andersen, Grant was authorized to convey that a probation offer would be acceptable. Mack laughed so hard she had to wipe her eyes. Andersen was looking at almost a thousand years in prison after trial and the case against him was getting stronger by the day. Mack forwarded the message to James, asking him what he thought, and could hear him start chuckling in his office down the hall.

Grant's email also asked who Mack would be calling at the *Simpson* hearing. *Simpson*, the case that established that defendants who are being held without a bond are entitled to a hearing on the issue, requires the prosecutor to prove that there is ample evidence, "proof evident or presumption great" that the defendant has committed the crime. These hearings can be important tools in the defense arsenal in certain cases—those where the evidence is weak and the defendant hasn't confessed, or those where the attorney wants to show his client just how damning the evidence is. In Andersen's case, it all seemed like a waste of time. Mack could just put the photos of Andersen molesting Schyanne on the screen. The judge who conducted all *Simpson* hearings had been a sex-crimes prosecutor, so Mack was not so worried about the outcome of the hearing.

Jess came into Mack's office around noon, asking if she wanted to grab lunch. Mack agreed, and—instead of grabbing something from the café in the basement of the building—they decided to enjoy the sunshine as they walked to a sandwich place up the street. Jess reported that Judge Spears expected to start jury selection Monday morning in the Allen case and had not been happy that Mack wasn't present.

"It would appear, Ms. Lafayette," Jess drawled, doing a spot-on impression of the cantankerous old judge as she cleaned her aviator sunglasses, "that Ms. Wilson has decided she doesn't need to appear in my court any longer. Please disabuse her of that notion before Monday."

Mack groaned. "The absolute last thing I need is to *start* this trial with him mad at me."

"Don't worry about it," Jess said in her normal voice. "He'll be super-pissed at Andrews by about fifteen minutes in. He'll love you in comparison."

Mack laughed. As they walked into the sandwich shop, she noticed a man standing across the street. She didn't know what drew her attention to him—he looked like everyone else downtown that day, medium height and build, wearing slacks, a tie, and sunglasses—but she couldn't look away. He gave her a creepy feeling. Although she couldn't see his eyes behind his glasses, she would have sworn they made eye contact.

Jess called Mack's name and she turned around. When she looked back, the man was gone. She had overreacted, again, still spooked from that morning. As they ate their salads, she found herself looking over her shoulder every few minutes. She felt like she was being watched.

For the rest of that afternoon, and the rest of the week, Mack focused on getting ready for trial. She knew she wouldn't be able to give much attention to her other cases, so she worked hard to plead what she could and catch up on motions for cases she knew would eventually go to trial. Linda Andrews wanted to conduct pretrial interviews with the four officers in the Allen case, which shouldn't have taken more than two hours. It took the better part of Thursday. Andrews insisted on doing the interviews in person and asked questions well outside the anticipated testimony of each officer. This not only meant that Mack had to share a conference room with Linda and her perfume for six hours, but also see her outfit. Linda, in her early forties and not as slender as she might have been in her twenties, was notorious for dressing in very tight, very low-cut wrap dresses. That day, the dress had a blue-and-white chevron pattern, and it also had a hard time covering her substantial, sun-spotted chest. Mack knew she wore extensions because she had clearly underpaid for them—Mack could see where they attached. Her nails were long and matched her dress. It was a six-hour nightmare.

One benefit of the painful day was that Mack learned Linda's defense—the officers had taken the up-skirt photo themselves to frame her client. She focused on that during the interview of the store security guard, who, according to Linda, was also in on the plot. She asked him several times, in several different ways, if he had actually seen the photo on the phone when he had seized it. Despite his insistence that he hadn't *looked* for the photo, not wanting to disturb the phone in any way, she continued to harp on the issue. Mack assumed she'd use that as a major part of her argument at trial, and Mack believed she would be unsuccessful. For all her bravado, Linda wasn't even a mediocre attorney, and Mack wasn't worried about her trial skills. Mack decided to have some fun with her defense, to make sure that the jury found it as ludicrous as she did right from the start.

CHAPTER EIGHTEEN

"—and so, ladies and gentlemen, when you hear defense counsel tell you that her poor, innocent client was set up by the evil police officers, I want you to ask yourselves what makes more sense: that the victim, Kate Berg, the security officer, Kenneth Greene, and Officers Taylor and Mars have worked together to frame Benjamin Allen, or that he took a photo up Ms. Berg's skirt and got caught. The evidence will show that only that second explanation makes *any* sense, and once you've heard all the evidence, I will ask you to find the defendant guilty of Voyeurism. Thank you."

Mack smiled at the jurors, unbuttoned her black Monday trial jacket, and took her seat. She had rehearsed her opening statement a dozen times and had done it without notes and without stumbling. A weekend with no disturbances, either from Dave or her new mystery friend with the unsettling photographs, had left her well rested for the first time in weeks. It showed.

She carefully walked the line between what was permissible for opening statements—telling the jury what the evidence would show—and what was impermissible—making arguments. Mack wondered if she'd made the right choice warning the jury that the defense would be that Allen had been framed by the police. Even though she knew that *had* to be Linda's defense, based on the interviews with the officers, and she'd seen defense attorneys use that strategy a dozen or more times, it always felt so absurd to say the words.

Linda had objected three times. Objecting during opposing counsel's opening statement was bad form even if the objections were sustained but was especially bad form given that Judge Spears, sounding progressively more annoyed, overruled her each time. Mack picked up the styrofoam cup of water in front of her and sipped it as Linda approached the podium. She took a pad of paper with her and was obviously reading aloud as she began her opening.

"Ladies and gentlemen," she said, "I want to take this opportunity to thank you for your service here today." Mack groaned inwardly and put her pen down. She *hated* when defense attorneys—or prosecutors, for that matter—thanked the jury during openings. A waste of valuable time, it was almost always a sign that the attorney isn't comfortable enough to launch right into the case.

Instead of taking notes, Mack studied Linda's outfit. For jury selection the day before, she had opted for a beige linen skirt suit that might have been cute if it had fit. For openings, she'd chosen a red-white-and-blue wrap dress that would have been over the top at a Fourth of July orgy. She had paired it with bright-red four-inch heels. If she bent over, she'd give the courtroom a look at what her client had illegally photographed.

Finally, she got through her uncomfortable introduction, which included a three-minute segment on how "Jury duty is the most important civic responsibility in our society," and moved on to the meat of the case. As Mack expected, and had told the jury, Linda said that the evidence would show that the officers planted the photograph on the defendant's phone. Mack smiled. A better attorney would have changed course after hearing *her* opening, would have realized that the jury was already primed to think that story was ridiculous, but Linda wasn't that good. After droning on for almost fifteen minutes—Mack's own opening was long at seven—Linda gathered her notepads and sat next to her client, who immediately huddled close and started whispering to her, gesturing at the sheet of paper in front of him.

"Is the State ready to call its first witness?" Judge Spears asked, peering at Mack over his reading glasses.

"The State calls Kate Berg, Your Honor," Mack said. She smiled as Kate approached the clerk to be sworn. This was the part of being an attorney Mack most enjoyed—the performance involved in pitting her wits, preparation, and case against the opposition and convincing the jury to find in her favor.

Getting through the preliminaries was easy. Kate had spent an hour in Mack's office preparing for direct exam and Linda's cross. Mack wanted the jury to feel like they really knew her, so they could empathize with her. Mack spent substantial time letting Kate introduce herself and building toward the actual crime.

"So as you were picking up the mustard from the bottom shelf, what happened next?"

"I felt the defendant's hand hit my leg."

"Objection!" Linda said, standing.

Judge Spears tugged on his ear, which, Mack had learned during her last trial in his division, indicated he was confused. "Ms. Wilson?" he asked.

"I can clarify, Judge," Mack said. "Ms. Berg, how do you know it was the defendant's hand that hit your leg?"

"Well," she said, "I turned around as soon as I felt his hand hit my leg and he was bent over behind me with his phone out. At first I just saw his hair—it was a lot shorter then, almost like a buzz cut—but then I saw his face as I started yelling for security. He tried to race away, but I followed him. That's him in court today."

"Can you tell me where he's sitting and what he's wearing?" Mack asked.

"He's sitting over there next to his lawyer, the white guy, he's wearing a blue shirt and a patterned tie."

Mack turned around to show the jury there was no one else Kate could be talking about. "Judge, may the record reflect that the victim has identified the defendant?"

Judge Spears nodded. "It will so reflect." He crossed his arms over his chest and looked at Allen with disdain.

Mack reviewed her notes to make sure she hadn't missed anything and to allow Kate's identification of Allen to rest with the jury for a moment.

"I have no further questions at this time, Judge," Mack said. He nodded and leaned back. Mack grabbed her cross-examination notepad and sat back, ready to take detailed notes. Unfortunately, Linda let her down. She was polite to Kate, and only hinted at her conspiracy theory once, asking if Kate had ever met her client before. She asked how Kate knew that her client had taken a photo up her skirt. Mack had warned Kate that that question would probably come, and she had practiced her answer of "I had no idea what he was doing. I just knew that he had his hand between my thighs, and he didn't have my permission to be there." Linda seemed stumped by this. Mack wondered if she'd hoped to trip Kate up or get her to claim something that could later be discredited.

"Just a moment, Your Honor," Linda said, returning to her table and whispering with her client. Mack couldn't hear what he was saying, but he was pointing forcefully at his pad of paper and Linda was shaking her head. She returned to the podium in the center of the courtroom. "No further questions, Your Honor. Thank you, Ms. Berg."

In Arizona, jurors are permitted to ask questions of the witnesses. Their questions are held to the same standard as the attorneys', but they can pursue areas that neither the prosecutor nor the defense attorney have addressed. This can be a blessing or a curse. On the one hand, it means that if the witness didn't sufficiently explain something, there's another chance to clear up lingering juror confusion. On the other, it means the jurors can get distracted from the real issues in a case. Overall, Mack appreciated it. The jurors' questions tend to show what they think of the evidence.

"Had you noticed the defendant staring at you or following you around the store before he took the picture?" was the first question the jurors had for Kate, and Mack was thrilled. By the way the question called Allen "the defendant" and considered it a given that he took the picture, it looked like the jury was already adopting Mack's version of the facts.

The subsequent testimony, which lasted through Thursday afternoon, proceeded in much the same way. Allen wrote copious notes, filling at least three legal pads over the course of each day. The few juror questions indicated that they accepted Mack's theory of the case. Linda was courteous to the witnesses and brief in her questioning. Mack wondered where her change of heart had come from. The only time Mack thought she saw the old Linda was with the final witness, the officer who had looked at Allen's phone and found the blurry picture of Kate's underwear.

"You have no independent way of knowing whose underwear is in this picture, do you, Officer?" Linda asked.

"No, ma'am," Officer Mars said, "except that your client told me it was the woman from the store, and I knew that woman to be Ms. Berg."

Linda sighed and her shoulders dropped. Mack hadn't gotten any of Allen's statements out through Officer Mars—she was waiting to do that with Officer Taylor first thing Monday morning. Technically, Linda wasn't allowed to elicit her client's statements when Mack hadn't opened the door, but Mack wasn't about to object. It was better this way. Now, the jury would have his statements over the weekend, and again on Monday morning. Linda looked at Mack, but she sat impassively.

"Judge, move to strike as nonresponsive," Linda said. It was a creative approach—arguing that Officer Mars had not answered the question he had been asked, but unlikely to be successful given her question.

"Motion denied, Ms. Andrews. You elicited it."

"No further questions," Linda said, returning to her table. Allen was obviously frustrated with her. Watching him whisper-yell, Mack was glad, not for the first time, that she didn't have to represent these assholes.

"Ms. Wilson," Judge Spears said, "is this a good place to break for the weekend?"

"Yes, Judge," Mack said, grateful that he had suggested it. Judge Spears liked to start on time, and he wanted to use the full day. She had been dreading telling him that she had no further witnesses a full five minutes before they were set to break. Because Fridays are reserved for hearings on motions and other procedural matters, trials are only held Monday through Thursday. That meant the attorneys were expected to make the most of their time, rather than unnecessarily forcing a jury to come back after a weekend.

Judge Spears excused the jury and Allen half-stood to acknowledge them. He scratched his neck, leaving an angry red mark, as he continued to talk to Linda. Mack almost felt sorry for her. She really wasn't doing that bad a job, given how little she had with which to work. As Mack and Officer Mars left the courtroom, Linda was still sitting next to her client, appearing to listen patiently as he flipped through notepads and talked without pause.

CHAPTER NINETEEN

The Andersen bond hearing was set for all day that Friday, and Mack and Dave didn't have much time to talk much about it before then because they were both in trial. Andersen only had to be denied bond on one count to remain in custody, so Mack didn't have to go through the facts for each victim. They had agreed that Dave would be the only witness, and Mack would use him to admit facts he had learned from other witnesses, like the victims, who would eventually testify at trial. Hearsay evidence is admissible in *Simpson* hearings, so Mack usually called only one witness to expedite the proceedings.

In reviewing the police reports and other documents, she couldn't find any glaring mistakes in the investigation. She had never seen a "perfect" case—in the office they joked that you were as likely to see a unicorn—but Dave and his detectives had done a solid job under tough conditions. They had maintained their integrity in the face of incredible political pressure, and Mack was pleased with their results.

Dave, looking comfortable and handsome in a suit and tie, met Mack in the courtroom fifteen minutes before the hearing was set to start. They weren't the first ones there. Shannon, Steve's parents and brothers, and Steve Jr. were all sitting on the defense side. Steve Jr. glared at her as she passed. She hadn't had time to listen to Steve's phone calls, and copies of his incoming and outgoing mail since he'd been arrested were sitting in a pile on her desk, unread. Mack wondered what he was telling his family about his case. Some defendants confess in letters and calls to loved ones, while some maintain their innocence and lie, and Mack had never found a pattern. She'd even had one guy lie in the face of DNA evidence and a video of him committing the crime.

Mack settled in at the prosecution table with Dave and noticed that Andersen was already sitting in the jury box, waiting for Grant to get there. For the hundredth time, Mack found the convention of seating defendants in the same seats jurors would later occupy disgusting. She didn't understand why he wasn't permitted to sit at the defense table by himself until his attorney got there. She watched him as he sat motionless, head bowed and hands clasped in his lap. She wondered if he was praying or just tired. The few weeks in jail were clearly weighing on him. His hair was no longer cut with military precision. His tan had faded. He had lost weight. Mack hoped he wouldn't become too pathetic-looking before trial, which might make a jury sympathetic.

Grant was almost fifteen minutes late, and Judge Donoghue, impatient under the best circumstances, was not happy. When Grant finally rushed in, briefcase half open and spilling papers, tie askew, Andersen's family looked at him with dismay. He looked a lot more put together on his billboards, that was for sure. He was breathing heavily as he unpacked his bag and fastened the top button of his yellow shirt. Judge Donoghue, impatient to get started, called the case before Grant even had time to talk to his client.

Dave took the stand and got comfortable, settling into the witness chair and pulling the microphone closer without needing to be instructed. He poured himself a cup of water and smiled at Mack when he was ready to begin. She *loved* working with detectives who knew what they were doing.

Even though Mack only needed to prove one count for this hearing, she had Dave walk the judge through the basics of his investigation as a whole. Arizona has open cross-examination, so even if Dave only discussed one count on direct, Grant could ask about any count or any aspect of the investigation. It was easier just to preempt that by talking about everything. After getting an overview, Dave focused on Schyanne's disclosures from her second forensic interview. He testified that there were photographs that corroborated several of her disclosures, including one that constituted a non-bondable offense. They briefly went through the DNA results and what they meant, and as Dave explained them Judge Donoghue nodded, looking bored. Mack double-checked her notes, but she had covered everything she needed. It had taken less than forty minutes.

Grant's aggressive cross took the rest of the morning.

"My client isn't visible in the photos you were talking about, right?" he asked. His voice was deep and didn't match his compact frame.

"That's correct," Dave said.

"I see. And my client made no admissions regarding any of these acts, did he?"

"He did not," Dave said.

"Ah-ha!" He took his glasses off and put one earpiece in his mouth. Mack had never seen anyone do that in real life, and she covered a smile. "And there are no eyewitnesses to any of these alleged acts, are there?"

"Right," Dave said.

It got weirder from there. Grant questioned Dave's choice to return Schyanne to her parents before Steve was even a suspect. He questioned whether the DNA results applied to people of Scandinavian descent. He questioned the police's willingness to interview everyone who came forward claiming that they had been abused by Steve.

"You went hunting for victims, didn't you?"

"Absolutely not," Dave said, not rising to the bait.

Grant spent almost twenty minutes on the timelines in the indictment. For each count, the indictment included the basic time frame in which the crime took place, and Mack would have to prove that time frame at trial. For the eight victims that weren't family members, the time frames were easy. "It happened when I was ten," they would say, or "twelve," or "in fifth grade," and Mack could use their birthdays or information from their parents to figure out a year or two period in which the crime must have occurred. For Schyanne and her sisters, it was more challenging. Some of the offenses they could nail down with certainty, but there were a few where the indictment had to give a three-year range. Practically speaking, unless Andersen was using an alibi defense for every count, it shouldn't have mattered how long the ranges were, but lengthy time frames can be attacked and Grant did his best. He pressed Dave to narrow several of the ranges, but Dave steadfastly refused.

It was unclear whether Grant was trying to put on a show for Andersen's family or if he really believed that the investigation was of such poor quality. Either way, Mack couldn't tell if Judge Donoghue, impassive behind tinted glasses and a master of the neutral facial expression, was buying it. She hoped he wasn't. If Andersen was given a bond, Mack *knew* he would flee, and there would never be justice for his victims.

By lunch, it was clear that Dave was getting frustrated and was ready to be done, but he did a good job of politely answering Grant's questions without simply agreeing with everything he said. During the break, he and Mack walked back to her office and ran into Jess, who suggested a third option for why Grant was going on so long.

"Maybe he's trying to bore you into submission," she said to Dave.

"If he goes on much longer," Dave said, loosening his tie and pulling his shirt collar away from his neck, "he may be successful. I'm having trouble staying awake up there."

Jess went with them after lunch for moral support and to see if Grant could provoke Dave into snapping. Fortunately for all of them, Grant wrapped up after another hour or so. His final attack was on the differences between the allegations made by several different victims. It seemed like he was trying to say that since not all the crimes were committed the exact same way, they didn't happen. To Mack, that was clearly an irrational and desperate argument. She hoped Judge Donoghue felt the same way.

There was nothing Mack really needed to clean up on cross, because Grant hadn't made any killer points. Instead, she just reiterated the strongest evidence with regards to Schyanne—the photos and the DNA—and finished within ten minutes.

Grant was given the opportunity to call witnesses, but Mack wasn't surprised that he didn't have any. Any defense witnesses would be under oath and subject to cross-examination, so most defense attorneys try to avoid locking witnesses into testimony early in the process. In Mack's opinion, this was Grant's smartest decision yet.

Judge Donoghue asked for argument and gave each side five minutes. Because the obligation to prove that a defendant should be held without bond ultimately lies with the State, Mack got the first and last words. She reminded the judge of the applicable law and the standard of proof. He only had to find Andersen non-bondable as to one count. With the DNA and photos of Schyanne, the State had certainly met the burden. The court reporter shook her head at how fast Mack was talking, but she didn't tell her to slow down, so Mack took full advantage of the time allotted.

Grant, on the other hand, spoke slowly, pacing the courtroom, and wound up taking closer to seven minutes than five. He argued that the inconsistencies between how the different victims were assaulted meant that none of the assaults had actually happened. He argued that the DNA evidence didn't apply—to which Mack objected, since he was arguing facts not in evidence, but Judge Donoghue let it in anyway—and that since the photos didn't show his client's face they didn't prove anything.

When he finished, Mack stood up and was ready to speed-talk through her major points a second time. Judge Donoghue raised his hand, however, and she stopped with her mouth open.

"Ms. Wilson," he said in a monotone, "I think I've heard enough." Mack's mouth was dry and she could feel her heartbeat in her fingers. "The State has argued that I only need to find the proof is evident or that the presumption is great that the defendant committed *one* of the charged offenses." Mack nodded. "I don't find that argument particularly relevant in this case." Mack swallowed and the edges of her vision went gray. "Instead, I find that the proof is evident, and the presumption is great, as to *all* the charged offenses." Mack exhaled heavily and tried to cover her relief. "The defendant shall be held without bond." He rose from the bench without another word and disappeared into the hallway that led to his chambers.

Jess poured a cup of water from the pitcher on the prosecution table and handed it to Mack. As she gulped it down, Jess watched critically.

"I forgot how sweaty you get when you're nervous," she said. "It's gross."

Even her insult couldn't ruin Mack's good mood. They had passed the second hurdle and were in a solid position as they headed to trial and Mack headed into the weekend.

CHAPTER TWENTY

Although Mack enjoyed the challenge and the theater of being in trial, she found it exhausting. All other aspects of her life fell by the wayside, including such necessary basics as laundry and grocery shopping. She canceled dinner with Anna on Friday evening, pleading exhaustion. Instead, she stopped for Chinese food on the way home, and ate pot stickers and sautéed mixed vegetables over the sink because she hadn't had time to do dishes. Saturday and Sunday, she tried to catch up on errands, but mostly caught up on sleep.

Sunday night, she ate the rest of the Chinese food while working on her closing argument for the Allen trial the next morning. Because the State bears the burden of proof, prosecutors get to give two closing arguments—one before and one after the defense's—and she wrestled with whether to talk about the conspiracy theory in her first close or wait for Linda to bring it up. By 1:00 a.m., as the words started to blur on the computer screen, she had mostly decided to leave it for second close. That way, if Linda didn't bring it up, Mack didn't have to waste time on it.

Monday morning, Mack discovered that she had forgotten to buy coffee, milk, and cereal. Clearly, a trip to the bagel shop was in order before she went into the office. It was starting to warm up, and she didn't bother putting on her suit jacket when she left the house. She loaded her briefcase, laptop bag, purse, and lunch into the car and headed to the shop. Her phone buzzed as she pulled into the parking lot, and she sat in the car to check email and make sure it wasn't anything that required a pre-caffeine response.

Satisfied that the emails could wait, Mack grabbed her purse and got out of the car, slamming the door behind her. She realized she was not the only person who thought a bagel sounded like a great idea, viewing the long line. She could smell the fresh coffee and pastries, and was resigned to the wait. She pulled out her phone to pass the time playing mahjong.

"Mackenzie?"

She turned, surprised to see Benjamin Allen, wearing jeans and a leather motorcycle jacket, standing directly behind her. Although she had left a two-foot buffer between her and the person in front of her, Allen was standing uncomfortably close. She could smell his Axe body spray and remembered it from the popular boys in high school who also stood too close. She took a step backward, bumping into the person on the other side.

"Mr. Allen," Mack said, looking around, "you know we can't speak without your attorney present."

"Mackenzie," he said again, taking another step toward her and forcing her out of the line, "I'm just saying hello. It's not personal, right? Isn't that what you said?"

"Look," Mack said, "we can't talk. It's not allowed. It's not professional."

He stepped out of line after her. Several other patrons looked up from their phones or conversations and were watching Mack and Allen.

"Is there a problem?" asked a man who looked like a former linebacker in his sweatpants and muscle shirt.

Allen put his hands up. "No problem, I'm just trying to say hello to my friend here and she won't even talk to me."

"Doesn't look like the lady wants to be your friend," the man said, crossing his large arms over his broad chest. "Why don't you back off?"

"No, I'll go. Thank you," Mack said to the man, who watched Allen with a disapproving stare.

"But, Mackenzie!" Allen said, loudly. "I was going to buy you breakfast! It's the least I can do for an old friend who's trying to destroy my life."

Mack practically ran out of the bagel shop, fumbling with her keys to get into her car before Allen got out of the store. Her heart was racing. She was positive that Allen didn't live anywhere near her, so what was he doing at her breakfast spot on the day of closings in his trial?

Mack drove straight to the office without stopping. She wasn't hungry or tired anymore and was running on pure adrenaline. She found herself constantly scanning her mirrors, looking for Allen. Her knuckles were white as she gripped the steering wheel, praying that this wouldn't be the day when the old Saab finally gave up and died.

She was hyperventilating by the time she pulled into the secured district attorney parking lot, unsure if she had taken a full breath since seeing Allen. She started to shake, and wept, on the verge of full hysterics, until someone knocked on her window. Mack screamed and looked up, readying herself to fight.

"What the hell is wrong with you?" Jess asked, her voice muffled by the glass. She tried the door handle, but it was locked. She walked around the car and knocked on the other window. Mack unlocked the doors and her friend slid into the passenger seat, tucking the skirt of her houndstooth dress under her thigh. "You cracking up?" Her nonchalant tone belied the real concern Mack could see in Jess' eyes. "You know you're supposed to cry in your office with the door closed like a damn adult."

Mack laughed and felt herself begin to relax. She told Jess about running into Allen.

"Mack," she said, "if you let every jackass you meet in this job keep you from eating, you'd be a stick." She looked Mack up and down. "You're already rather stick-like, actually. You've lost more weight."

Mack nodded. "Between Andersen, and being in trial, and the creepy stuff going on at home…"

"I know," she said, "and now you couldn't even get a bagel. You're freaking out and that's okay. Come on. Let me buy you some stale coffee and a breakfast burrito. Mmmm, fake bacon!" She rubbed her stomach and licked her lips.

Mack laughed again. "I must look awful," she said, opening the door.

Jess met her on the driver's side. "Yup," she said, grabbing Mack's bags from the back seat and throwing her jacket over her shoulder. "You sure do. Please fix that before you go into court."

Mack stopped laughing. She had forgotten, with the stress of the morning, that she would have to face Allen in court. Ethically, she would have to tell Judge Spears and Linda what had happened. That wouldn't be fun. Plus, she had to tell James, since that morning's encounter was certainly the sort of thing he'd very explicitly told her that she must report.

Jess carried through on her promise and bought Mack awful coffee and a terrible breakfast burrito from the café in the basement. The café was run by an elderly Armenian couple, and no one could figure out where they got such an unappetizing selection of artificial pizza, imitation burritos, and fake snack food. The place was dimly lit and always smelled like fish, even though no one remembered ever seeing fish for sale. Mack tried to avoid the place whenever possible, especially since it was wildly overpriced. Her breakfast was almost ten dollars, and the tortilla was gray when she peeled away the wax paper. Still, in that moment, as her adrenaline drained, it was the best thing she had ever tasted. She didn't realize how hungry she was until she started eating, and how tired she was until she sipped the coffee.

"Would it cheer you up," Jess said, when it seemed clear that Mack was no longer on the edge of a meltdown, "to hear about my latest magical first date?"

"Absolutely! Although usually I need a beer or three before hearing these stories."

"Sobriety could be your friend, Wilson. Let's see. To start with, he's a songwriter…and a crier." She sipped her coffee and looked at Mack, straight-faced.

Mack laughed.

Jess adjusted the stack of charm bracelets adorning her right wrist. "We agreed to meet at the restaurant," she said, "and so when I get there the hostess clearly knows who I am. She leads me to this dimly-lit back corner, which has obviously been cleared of all the normal tables except the one."

Mack finished her burrito and wadded up the wax paper.

"He's strewn rose petals all around the table, so as the hostess seats me, she tells me she hopes I enjoy my anniversary. Meanwhile, he comes out from this back room holding a guitar."

"No way," Mack said.

"Way," Jess said, in a perfect Valley girl accent. "He tells me that I'm an angel because of what I do for a living, and he's written me a song."

Mack rolled her eyes.

"Meanwhile, it's important for you to know that we've exchanged a total of like five emails up to this point. Okay, so he has the guitar, and then he starts to sing." She cleared her throat dramatically. "It was like Creed ate Nickelback and decided to sing Suzanne Vega's 'Luka.' It was legitimately that bad."

"And he cried?" Mack asked. She laughed.

"Yep," Jess said. "During the song, he was so overcome with emotion he started to cry. I swear to God, Mack, the *whole* restaurant was staring at us."

"What did you do?"

"I got up and left. We had not yet ordered anything. I went straight home."

"Went straight home and drank?"

"Oh, you betchya," she said. "Heavily. Now, here's the fun part: how many times do you think he's called me since Saturday night?"

"Twice?"

"Six times. And thirteen texts. This morning, I blocked his number."

"Thirteen texts? What did he say?"

"He sent the lyrics to the song...All thirteen verses."

Mack hadn't laughed that hard in ages, and she enjoyed the ache in her side. Once she got through her first coffee, Jess sent her to the restroom to clean up while she refilled their cups. By the time they went upstairs, Mack looked mostly human. That turned out to be particularly important when she walked into James' office and found Peter Campbell.

"Ah, Mack," James said, "we were just talking about you."

"Oh?" Mack asked, hovering in the doorway.

"Sit down, Ms. Wilson," Campbell said, gesturing to the empty chair next to him.

Mack sat.

He crossed his legs and fixed the crease on his pants so it hit right at the knee. "I understand John Grant requested probation in the Andersen case," he said.

"Yes, sir," Mack said.

"And you are not granting that request, correct?" he asked.

"No, sir," Mack said. She wondered if she was destined for another infuriating pro-Andersen lecture.

"Good." He nodded. "We can't be seen granting him any favors at this point. Are you planning to make him an offer?"

Mack glanced at James. "Yes, sir," she said. "We would like to spare the victims the ordeal of trial, if possible."

"Do you have a number in mind?"

They had discussed fifty years, but she wasn't sure if James was ready to share that. He smiled, though, so Mack went for it.

"Fifty, sir."

He mulled it over for a moment.

"Okay," he said, "and if he says no?"

"Then we go to trial, sir."

He rubbed his chin thoughtfully. Mack could almost hear the wheels turning.

"Okay. You heard Grant brought in Robert Miller, right?"

Miller was one of the best trial attorneys—maybe *the* best

non-capital trial attorney—in the state. He had been an ADA for twenty years before striking out as a private defense attorney. As it happened, Mack was particularly well acquainted with Mr. Miller, since he had taught her trial-advocacy class in law school. She had also faced him in the courtroom, early in her career, on an Armed Robbery case. Mack had lost. Spectacularly. She deserved to lose, she knew that going in, but it still stung. She considered herself lucky that she hadn't crossed paths with him since. She didn't relish trying again, even on a case as strong as Andersen.

"No," James said, looking at Mack, "I don't think we did know that."

"No, s-sir," she said, her voice catching slightly.

"Well, that's what I heard at church, anyway." Campbell stood and walked to the door. "Keep up the good work, you two," he said. He tapped twice on the door frame as he left, a subconscious gesture that had been mocked during his time as a unit chief.

Mack sighed. "I'm going to ask Jess to second chair," she said.

"I think that sounds like a great idea," James said.

They sat in companionable silence for a moment before Mack broached the subject of that morning's run-in.

"Well," he said, "that's spooky, but it doesn't sound like you can prove he sought you out, right?"

"No," she said. "It's just a hunch."

"Ready for your security detail yet?" he asked.

Mack laughed and stood.

"I'll let you know when I am," she said, tapping twice on the door frame as she left his office.

CHAPTER TWENTY-ONE

By the time Mack got to Judge Spears' courtroom, she had written off the bagel shop as an unpleasant coincidence. Allen was a jerk, but there was nothing in his history to suggest that he was anything more than that. She checked his file, and his address was less than five minutes from her condo—the bagel shop was on his way downtown, too.

Mack left her purse and file cart in the courtroom and went into chambers, hoping to find the judge's judicial assistant. Since her time as a baby prosecutor, Mack had known Diana Munoz, who would usually slip her a cup of coffee and a read on Judge Spears' mood.

"How's my favorite JA this morning?" Mack asked, poking her head around the door.

The middle-aged Hispanic woman pursed her lips and raised her eyebrows. "Girl," she said, "you know I'm good. How're you, though? You haven't come to see me since this trial started."

Mack dropped into the chair in front of her desk and sighed. "I'm a mess. Just look at me."

"You look thin." She stood up and went to the office's makeshift kitchen. "Here," she said, handing Mack a mug of coffee and a chocolate chip cookie, "you need to eat. I made them myself!"

Mack smiled and accepted both items gratefully. "How's the judge this morning?"

"Same as always—cranky." They both laughed. Diana had worked with Judge Spears for over ten years, and she swore that she had only seen him smile once. "And even then," she would say, "it might have just been gas!"

"I like your outfit today," Diana said.

Mack blushed. "It's the same thing I wear every Monday," she said, running both hands through her hair.

"Oh, I know," Diana said, smiling. "But it looks good every week."

They chatted about Diana's grandson until Mack finished her coffee and walked back into the courtroom. Allen was sitting at the defense table, tapping his pen on the desk. He had changed into slacks and a dress shirt, but his curly brown hair was still a mess. Mack ignored him, and sat at her own table, jotting down some final notes on a legal pad. She still needed to tell the judge about what had happened, even with Diana's warning.

Judge Spears took the bench and cleaned his glasses as he asked if there were any issues.

"Just one, Judge," Mack said. "This morning, I saw the defendant while I was picking up breakfast. I didn't speak to him, except what was necessary to tell him that we couldn't speak. Mr. Allen did attempt to speak to me, and he told a bystander that he intended to buy my breakfast. I left immediately and didn't engage him more than absolutely necessary."

Judge Spears nodded. "Thank you for informing me," he said. "Ms. Andrews? Anything you need to add?"

Linda stood and placed her hands on the tabletop, her purple dress straining over her hips. "Judge, I think this calls for a mistrial."

"Judge!" Mack said, bumping her knee against the table in her rush to stand up. "In no way does this warrant a mistrial! The defendant spoke to me. I didn't approach him."

"Relax, Ms. Wilson," Judge Spears said, raising one hand. "I'm inclined to agree with you. Ms. Andrews, would you like to convince me that I'm wrong?"

"Your Honor," Linda said, glancing down at her client, who was smirking and nodding, "Mr. Allen assures me that Ms. Wilson approached *him* in the restaurant this morning and told him that if he bought her breakfast, she would dismiss the case against him. I have no reason to doubt his version of events. For that reason, a mistrial is warranted."

Mack was outraged and was gearing up for a scathing rebuttal when Judge Spears raised his hand.

"Ms. Wilson is an officer of the court. If she says she didn't engage your client, I believe her. Motion for mistrial is denied."

Mack closed her mouth.

"In that case, Judge," Linda said, still resting her weight on the table, "I move to withdraw. I request an *ex parte* hearing to discuss my reasons."

Linda was asking for a hearing outside Mack's presence, which was highly unusual. She had never seen a defense attorney request one. Unfortunately, she could think of nothing to prevent it. In fact, Judge Spears didn't even look at her before granting the request. Mack and Officer Taylor gathered their notebooks and left the courtroom, making themselves comfortable in the hallway. Mack emailed James and Jess, asking if they'd ever heard of such a thing. Jess wrote back, saying that Linda was probably asking to disbar Mack, immediately and without a formal hearing, for getting accosted by her client. James thought that Allen must have told Linda that he intended to lie on the stand. If Linda knew he was going to commit perjury, she would ethically have to withdraw.

Mack was inclined to think that the truth lay somewhere between Jess' and James' guesses. She suspected that Allen's move that morning had convinced Linda that he was a creep and therefore she no longer wanted to represent him. Whatever her reasons, they took a long time to explain. The clerk didn't collect Mack and the officer for almost thirty minutes.

When they walked back into the courtroom, Judge Spears had left and Linda was sitting at the defense table ignoring her client. Allen was furiously clicking the end of his ballpoint pen. Linda looked at Mack as she took her seat at the prosecution table. It was the first time Mack could remember seeing genuine emotion from her. She mouthed, "Sorry," with a pained look. Mack shrugged, unsure if she was apologizing for trying to get her disbarred, trying to mistry the case, or some other reason.

Judge Spears took the bench. Everyone stood. "Defense motion to withdraw is denied," he said. "Ms. Andrews, anything else to address before we bring the jury in?"

Linda shook her head. "No, Judge," she said, sounding tired.

The bailiff went to collect the jury. Mack could hear Allen's whispered entreaties to Linda to "at least *try*" and wondered what creative new defense she could expect. Would it surface with Officer Taylor or would Linda save it for her closing argument?

Officer Taylor's testimony—both direct and cross—went smoothly. Linda had given up. She was courteous and didn't suggest that the photo had been planted. She seemed, in fact, to have switched tactics. She asked him several times, in several different ways, how he knew that the photo was actually of Kate Berg. Ultimately, the answer was that he couldn't know for sure. Although Kate had identified her underwear as being the underwear in the picture, Officer Taylor, who had not seen Kate's underwear himself, had no direct knowledge of who had actually been photographed. Mack wondered if Linda really had the gall to argue that the woman in the photo wasn't Kate and had consented to being photographed. Even for Linda, that seemed like a stupid risk to take if she couldn't produce the woman in the picture.

When Officer Taylor was released, Mack rested.

In any trial in Arizona, following the presentation of the prosecution's case, the defense can ask for a directed verdict, which means that the judge finds that the State didn't present enough evidence for the jury to reasonably convict, and the defendant is therefore not guilty. These motions are almost never granted, but they're universally requested. Linda didn't even bother, and Mack was shocked that she was willing to concede there was sufficient evidence to go forward.

"Ms. Andrews?" Judge Spears asked.

Allen whispered furiously to Linda, tapping his foot loudly and gesticulating so much that she placed a restraining hand on his arm.

"Defense rests, Your Honor," Linda said.

CHAPTER TWENTY-TWO

Mack was thoroughly confused. If Allen wasn't going to testify, then the *ex parte* hearing hadn't made any sense. Linda was setting herself up for Allen to later claim ineffective assistance of counsel, that she hadn't done her job properly, the surest way for a case to come back for a retrial. There are only two things that a defendant has the absolute and sole right to decide—whether to go to trial and whether to testify. Allen had clearly chosen trial, but it seemed like he wasn't being offered the opportunity to choose to testify. The last thing Mack wanted was try this case twice.

"Judge, may we approach?" she asked, rising. Linda looked at her quizzically but followed when Judge Spears waved them forward. The lawyers huddled close to the bench and waited as the clerk turned on the white-noise machine that prevented the jury from hearing their conversation.

"My concern, Judge," Mack whispered, "is that the defendant is not voluntarily waiving his right to testify and this will come back on a Rule 32 claim."

"What do you suggest, Ms. Wilson?" Judge Spears asked.

Mack could smell stale coffee on his breath and wrinkled her nose. "That you conduct a short colloquy with him, outside the presence of the jury, and have him waive on the record."

"Judge," Linda said, "it is not the prosecutor's job to interfere with the defense case. I object to any colloquy with my client."

Judge Spears looked at Mack. She crossed her arms over her chest and leaned close to the microphone.

"It *is* my job to make sure we avoid a retrial if I can. Based on what I—and no doubt you and the jury—can observe of the defendant's behavior toward Ms. Andrews, I think it's necessary."

Judge Spears nodded. "I don't like it," he said, "but I'll do it. I agree with Ms. Wilson that, based on your client's behavior, Ms. Andrews, it's a valid concern."

Linda and Mack walked back to their respective tables but remained standing for the judge to dismiss the jury.

"We're going to take about a five-minute break, folks," Judge Spears said. "We'll get started again as soon as possible."

Mack heard the jury grumble as they got to their feet and were led out of the courtroom. Linda was whispering to Allen. For once, he appeared to be listening.

"Sir," Judge Spears addressed Allen, "there are some concerns that you wish to testify and are being prevented from doing so."

Allen nodded and twisted a piece of hair around his index finger. It was a surprisingly feminine gesture for a man who otherwise seemed so aggressive.

"Do you understand that you have the right to testify?" Judge Spears asked.

"She's telling me not to," Allen said.

Judge Spears paused and took a long drink from the stainless-steel water bottle he kept on the bench.

"Your attorney can advise you not to testify," he finally said, "but the final decision has to be yours."

Linda cleared her throat. "Judge," she said, "I cannot, in this case, allow my client to take the stand. If he wants to testify, he needs to represent himself for the duration of the trial."

"I see," Judge Spears said. "Well, he is entitled to do that. So, sir, I need you to tell us what you want to do—testify and represent yourself, or not testify and have Ms. Andrews continue to represent you."

Allen sat quietly for a moment. It was the first time Mack saw him be still. Throughout jury selection and trial, and even in the bagel shop, he'd constantly been taking notes, scanning the room, talking to Linda. He was unpleasant-looking, Mack decided—his too-long hair and receding hairline framing a slightly misshapen skull. His mouth was small, with thin lips pursed in a frown. His white shirt gaped against his large chest and the sleeves were tight around his arms.

"I won't testify," he said quietly, head down.

Judge Spears turned to Mack. "Satisfied, Ms. Wilson?"

"Judge, I think you probably need to go through and make a finding that he is knowingly, intelligently, and voluntarily waiving. The way it stands, he could still be waiving because of the threat of Ms. Andrews not representing him."

Judge Spears rolled his eyes, and Mack was grateful that the court reporter didn't note expressions. "Mr. Allen," he said, "has anyone threatened, coerced, or intimidated you into making this decision?"

"No," Allen said. His large hands were clasped on the table in front of him and he rhythmically squeezed and released them. The courtroom deputy stepped closer to Allen's chair.

"Thank you, Judge," Mack said. "That satisfies the State."

"Ms. Andrews?" Judge Spears asked.

"Yes, Judge," Linda said.

The jurors were brought back into the courtroom and took their seats. Judge Spears turned to Mack and told her to start her closing argument. She took a sip of water, stood, buttoned her jacket, and approached the jury. She made eye contact with each juror before she began speaking.

"Ladies and gentlemen," she said, "this case is simple. Kate Berg went to the store one day, and had her privacy violated by the defendant."

Mack's first close was brief, coming in at under twenty

minutes. She had decided not to anticipate any potential defenses and stick to the facts. The case *was* very simple, and she worried that she was overthinking it. Mack showed the jury the photo and reviewed the testimony of Kate Berg: she felt the defendant's hand hit her leg, he did not have permission to take a photo up her skirt, she recognized the underwear in the picture as the underwear she had been wearing that day. Mack thanked the jury and sat down.

Judge Spears decided it was a good time for the lunch break, and Mack was grateful. She loved that the jury had some time to consider her closing argument before they heard from defense. Plus, Mack reasoned, if the jury came back from lunch a little sleepy and didn't pay such close attention to Linda's argument, that wouldn't be the worst thing in the world.

She went back to her office to wolf down a power bar and catch up on emails and voice mails. Luckily, nothing appeared to have exploded. She ignored an email from her mom, asking when she might make it back to Cleveland for a visit. She was hit by the same pang of guilt that always hit her when she ignored maternal emails, but she couldn't make travel plans while in trial.

A stack of Steve Andersen's incoming and outgoing mail was waiting on her desk. She flipped through it idly. Most of it was correspondence with Steve Jr. and a friend who Steve seemed to know from church. Mack did find one letter that was interesting—a letter Andersen had written to the current bishop of his ward, thanking the man for his recent visit and appreciating his kindness in bringing Andersen's new calling, upon his release, to be the ward mission leader. She made a note to look up a ward mission leader's responsibilities, and whether they had much contact with minors. If Andersen's church, knowing his charges, was assigning him to a job that gave him unfettered access to children, Mack would have to— No, actually, there was nothing she *could* do, except shake her head in disbelief at the hypocrisy.

When Mack got back to the courtroom, fifteen minutes before the afternoon session, Linda was already there, sitting on a bench in the hallway. She looked old. Mack greeted her politely and checked the door. Still locked. She sat on another bench to wait, playing solitaire on her phone, and could feel Linda staring at her. After a few minutes, Mack couldn't stand it anymore.

"I'm sorry, did you need something?" she asked.

Linda immediately looked down. "Sorry," she mumbled.

They sat in silence until the bailiff unlocked the courtroom and let them in.

Linda's argument made Mack's look lengthy. She didn't bother with the conspiracy theory, or with the consensual-other-woman theory. Instead, she gave a respectable argument for a defense attorney in a hopeless case. She thanked the jury for its service, again, which was a waste of time, again. She reminded them of the incredible responsibility they bore, telling them they held her client's life in their hands. She argued that Mack had not met her burden of proving the crime beyond a reasonable doubt, and therefore the jury had to find her client not guilty. She spent very little time on the actual facts of the case, which was not a bad choice given how strong the evidence was against her client. After ten minutes or so, she sat down. She looked utterly defeated, shoulders slumped and head lowered. Her extensions looked particularly ragged, as if she'd been pulling on them or had spent a lot of time running her hands through her hair. Even her gaudy rayon dress looked wrinkled and sad.

Linda hadn't given Mack much that needed to be addressed in her second close. Mack simply addressed "beyond a reasonable doubt" and what that standard really means—not beyond all doubt, not beyond any conceivable doubt, it merely means "firmly convinced." Mack reviewed the evidence that would leave them firmly convinced of Allen's guilt, asked them to find him guilty, and sat down. Six minutes. It was her new record.

The jury retreated to the jury room. Mack looked at her watch: 2:55 p.m. She figured it would take them at least half an hour to pick a foreperson and use the restroom. That wasn't quite enough time to get back to her office, but it was more than enough to duck across the street to the coffee shop. She approached the bailiff and wrote down her cell phone number in case. She didn't think that the jury would take long to return a verdict once they got the preliminaries out of the way.

Mack ordered her favorite indulgence from the barista—a green tea latte with skim milk and artificial sweetener—and threw in a madeleine cookie as well. Win, lose, or draw, the sugar would be necessary.

She checked her email. Robert Miller had been busy already. He had filed a motion to sever each of the eleven victims. Under Arizona law, defendants are entitled to separate trials on charges that aren't necessarily related. In sex cases, this most often comes up when dealing with multiple victims who are different in some significant way: male and female, old and young. The idea is that if the charges are dissimilar, the defendant might be prejudiced by having one jury hear all the charges. Heaven forbid a jury hear all the terrible things a defendant has done— they might believe he's a bad guy!

Mack was reassured by the fact that severance isn't automatic. In cases where the evidence relating to one charge would be admissible in a trial concerning the other charges, and vice versa, the charges can stay joined under the law. Miller's motion, which Mack skimmed in the coffee shop, stated that it would be unduly prejudicial to leave the cases relating to each victim joined. Her position, in contrast, would be that evidence relating to each victim would be admissible with regards to each of the other ten victims to show that Andersen had an aberrant sexual propensity for having sex with minors. The law was probably on her side, given that all eleven of the victims were white females between eight and fourteen years old. To be safe, though, Mack knew she should get a psychologist's report stating in no uncertain terms that having sex with girls between eight and fourteen years old is aberrant, and the fact that Andersen had had sex with eleven such girls was a good indication that he had a propensity to do it.

As it happened, Mack knew just the psychologist for the job. She forwarded Miller's motion to Anna, with a note promising that her paralegal would pass along all the police reports, and a guarantee of dinner and Anna's choice of movie on completion of her report. As Mack hit send, her phone buzzed. It was Judge Spears' bailiff—the verdict was in, five minutes before Mack had expected.

CHAPTER TWENTY-THREE

"We the jury, duly empaneled, do find the defendant, Benjamin Allen, as to Count One: Voyeurism, guilty."

Mack glanced at Allen, curious to see how he took the news, but he was staring straight ahead, impassive except for his left hand, clenched tightly. At least he hadn't cried. She hated when defendants cried. She sighed, relieved. It never seemed to matter how big or small the case, when she got into trial her competitive spirit took over and the outcome became personal. Plus, this win made twenty in a row—a new unit record.

"Congrats, dude," Jess said. She had come to watch the verdict.

Mack rolled her eyes. "Thanks," she said, "but really, that would have been an embarrassing one to lose. Actually, you should have kept it! I know you need the trial practice."

Jess laughed and grabbed Mack's file cart for the walk back to the office.

Sentencing would be in a week. It bothered Mack that Allen would walk away with what was likely to be a minimal number of years on probation, but she was glad that he would have to participate in sex-offender treatment as a condition of probation. She hoped he went to someone like Anna, who might do him some good. Mack made a note in the file to recommend Anna as his treatment provider at sentencing. She knew Judge Spears was familiar with her work, since Anna had testified for Mack in a trial before him the previous year, and Mack hoped he would agree with her assessment of what would be most likely to benefit Allen.

Mack had her paralegal send Anna the police reports from the Andersen case. By then, the reports reached into the hundreds of pages, so she also sent a copy of the indictment and the summary Mack had prepared for herself to help with the grand jury and trial. Mack told Anna that, if she wanted audio recordings of the victim interviews, she could have them, but Mack didn't want to burden her unnecessarily.

The end of the day found Mack in James' office with Jess, rehashing Linda Andrews' weird behavior in trial. All three had changed into jeans after long days in court, and that—along with the softball they were tossing—gave the room a casual air. Although ADAs were not allowed to wear clothes that weren't court-appropriate in the office, James had dispensed with that policy shortly after becoming the unit chief. "I don't care what y'all wear," he had said when Mack joined the unit, "so long as I don't get any complaints from judges or victims."

James suggested that maybe Linda was dealing with a drug or alcohol problem. She certainly wouldn't be the first, on either side of the courtroom. Jess suggested mental illness but not substance abuse. Mack thought there was more to it than that. The moment that stuck with her was Linda mouthing, "Sorry" after the *ex parte* hearing. Mack couldn't figure out why she would be apologizing. Clearly she hadn't derailed the trial or called for Mack's immediate disbarring or beheading. She couldn't believe Linda would have apologized for the inconvenience of an hour's delay. Everything Mack knew about Linda indicated that she wasn't that considerate.

"While you're here," James said, "I've got a question about

the Andersen case. Any chance Schyanne had some secret social media? Maybe on a school computer?"

Mack shook her head. "We thought of that. The school's server blocks all social media and personal email. She swears up and down she had no way to stay in touch with people her parents didn't know and approve of."

"So what happens when Andersen argues that Schyanne made this all up to escape her strict parents and rendezvous with some dopey teen to be named later?"

"That's a chance I'm willing to take," Mack said resolutely. "Given all the issues in this case, if *that's* what Miller hangs it on, I'll deserve the loss."

"Listen," Jess said, "it's not that you don't need the loss. They keep you humble and God knows you could use some humility. But is this really the case to take the chance on?"

Mack caught the softball one last time and set it on James' desk. "If the entire TPD can't find anything, neither can Miller. He might be good, might be *great*, even, but on this one, I've got it."

On her way out, Mack found herself alone in an elevator with Peter Campbell, which was the last place she ever wanted to be. She readied herself for a conversation about Andersen, but it never came. It wasn't until he got off the elevator with a nod and a "Have a good night" that Mack realized the wonderful truth—he had no idea who she was.

She had never been so glad to go unrecognized.

CHAPTER TWENTY-FOUR

Anna called early Tuesday morning, confused by Mack's email.

"You want me to write a report on the Andersen case?" she asked.

"Yup," Mack said, "defense filed a motion to sever and we're in front of Judge Donoghue, so I figured it was best to rope you in."

Anna sighed. "You realize that my report will say 'it is aberrant to sleep with children, and assuming he really did sleep with eleven of them, that shows he has the aberrant propensity to sleep with them'?"

"Yup," Mack said. She dug through her desk drawers, looking for gum or caffeine.

"You realize that's stupid."

"Yup," Mack said, "but so is Donoghue. We have to spell it out for him."

"You realize your office pays me two hundred dollars an hour and this is over ten hours work?" she asked.

"Yup," Mack said. "That's why I'm counting on you to buy dinner when the hearing is over."

Anna groaned. Her voice was whiny when she spoke again. "You're calling me to testify?"

"Yup," Mack said, "so it had better be a *nice* dinner. I mean cloth napkins, Dr. Lapin. A bottle of wine that costs more than my cell phone bill."

Anna continued to grumble halfheartedly, but Mack remained firm.

"Suck it up, Doc," she said, finally finding a half-empty tin of Altoids and deciding they'd do. "This is part of your job. Sorry it's not more interesting, but this is the case I have. Besides, you know I can be counted on to rub your shoulders after a long, hard day of typing."

Mack could hear Anna choke through the phone and could picture the scene perfectly: the psychologist always started her day with a latte, and now some of that precious caffeine had gone to waste, splattered on the leather blotter that covered Anna's desk. Mack laughed.

Anna continued to complain until her next patient arrived and she had to go. She promised to get Mack a draft of the report within a week, even though the hearing on the motion to sever wasn't set until late April.

It was already late March and getting hot, soaring into the nineties in the late afternoon. Mack was sweating through her suit jackets by the end of the day and was dreading the six months of scorching temperatures to come. It seemed that her stalker friend wasn't bothered by the heat. The alarm at the condo had gone off twice more in her absence, meaning two more disconcerting encounters with Officer Carlson, and she left work one day to find that her wonderful old Saab had been keyed on both sides. Still, there was nothing concrete linking the new batch of super-creepy stuff to the envelope on her doorstep back in February.

Any time she went to lunch downtown she felt like she was being watched. Jess had taken to calling her Hoppy the Ground Squirrel, in recognition of her constantly scanning the horizon whenever she was out of the office. It seemed unwieldy, much too long for a nickname, but Jess was insistent that it would stick until Mack either calmed down or had a stress-induced heart attack.

"Whichever comes first," she would say, shrugging.

Benjamin Allen had been placed on ten years of probation, more than Mack had expected. Even better, he was ordered to register as a sex offender and participate in treatment with Dr. Anna Lapin. Mack texted her to let her know he was coming.

"Is he treatable?" she responded. Mack sent a smiley face with its tongue out. She knew Anna loved a challenge, and, based on what she had seen of Allen in trial, he was sure to provide one.

"The guy is a major jerk," Anna said, during drinks following his first group-therapy session. They had arrived at the bar— Paradise, Tucson's last remaining lesbian bar, and their favorite place to avoid the law enforcement crowd they normally ran with—early, and managed to snag seats for once. She checked her hair in the mirror above the bar before catching the young bartender's eye and ordering another Ketel and soda. "He makes my narcissists look self-sacrificing."

Mack laughed. "That bad, huh?"

"Why," she whined, stretching the word into three syllables, "did you have to recommend me to the judge?"

"You're just too darn good at what you do, Doc," Mack said, taking a deep pull of her hefeweizen.

Anna was not amused when Mack told her about her car getting keyed.

"You know," she said, nudging Mack's shoulder with her own, "I do know a little something about human behavior, and someone keying your car is not a sign of affection."

Mack frowned. "Not even if the key marks spell 'I love you'?"

"You didn't tell me that they—" she said before choking on her drink.

Mack laughed. "Just kidding, Doc. You're just too easy. I know it's not a good thing. But I have nothing to say it's related to anything else that's happened. There's just some weird stuff going on right now. It's fine."

Anna glared at Mack with her best psychologist face. It was very much an "I will accept no shenanigans" glare. Luckily, Mack was immune.

"We still need to teach you to shoot," Anna said, "and get you a gun."

Mack groaned.

"It's important that you be able to protect yourself!" she said, covering Mack's hands, systematically shredding her cocktail napkin, with her own. "I've grown quite fond of you. It would be inconvenient to me if you died at the hands of an erotomaniac."

"You've always known just what to say," Mack said, "to sweep me off my feet."

"You're easy to woo," Anna said, smiling. "A little bit of professional jargon and you melt like butter."

Mack stared at their hands and enjoyed the warmth of Anna's palms for a moment before responding. "I still don't like it. Guns are scary."

"Guns aren't scary. Bad guys with guns are scary. You"— Anna paused to take a swig of Mack's beer without asking—"are a good guy."

Mack didn't feel like a good guy the next day as she battled a hangover during a meeting with an angry mom, who couldn't understand why Mack wasn't sending her daughter's abuser to prison for the rest of his life. Mack tried to explain that her sixteen-year-old daughter had consented to sex with the twenty-year-old defendant. Since the charge—Sex Conduct with a Minor, a class six felony—wouldn't involve prison time after trial anyway, it made no sense for Mack to offer a plea that required him to go to prison. Mom didn't think that was a good enough reason, given all the damage the "rapist" had done to her daughter. *Ma'am,* Mack resisted the urge to say, *the "rapist" was a virgin until your slutty daughter seduced him.* Sometimes Mack felt like there was no way to win with parents. Half of them hated her for being too lenient, and the other half for being too harsh.

Shannon Andersen was firmly in the latter camp. The oldest Andersen daughter, Sherrie, disclosed in her forensic interview that she had told her mother what was happening to her when she was twelve. Instead of intervening, Shannon "prayed on it" and told Sherrie that she and Steve just needed some counseling through the church and to get right with God. Mack wished there was some way to get those counseling records, but that was a lost cause. She had prosecuted several other Mormon men who had "gotten right with the Lord" and continued to abuse, but she had never managed to crack the privilege that exists between clergy and parishioners. Dave and Mack reasoned that, by failing to act on Sherrie's allegations, Shannon was indirectly responsible for Schyanne and Shaelynn's abuse, and James decided that Mack should charge her with Child Abuse and Failure to Protect.

There was evidence to support that she knew the abuse had continued. Seth, one of the Andersens' sons, revealed, during his own forensic interview, that he had seen Shannon witness her husband take Shaelynn into the basement "counseling" room, and then immediately go to pray. Seth also talked about how jealous Shannon seemed of her daughters whenever Andersen paid them any attention. Their birthdays, according to Seth, were particularly difficult for her, and she would often retreat to her bedroom before the cake was served.

By filing charges against Shannon, Mack forced her hand. She and her husband couldn't both be represented by John Grant. She hired Nick Diaz, a guy Mack had met on her first day of law school and remained friendly with over the years. He was a fine defense attorney, and Mack trusted him to put Shannon's interests first. She was looking at prison after trial and Mack was offering her a chance at a misdemeanor—if she cooperated and testified against her husband at trial. Nick recognized that this was a stellar deal, and convinced Shannon to participate in a free talk. She would come into Mack's office a week before the severance hearing and be interviewed. Mack would promise, in writing, not to use what she said against her so long as she told the truth, both in the free talk and in her trial testimony. In return, after trial she would get her chance at a misdemeanor instead of five years in prison.

Nick called the day before the free talk. His voice made him sound much younger than he was, and it took Mack a moment to realize who was calling. "I just want to warn you," he said, which immediately set Mack's teeth on edge, "that it's taken her a long time to open up to me. We may need multiple sessions."

"Let me guess," Mack said. "She still loves him, even though he's cost her her kids?" She wasn't surprised, since she regularly saw moms who supported their abuser husbands or boyfriends. She just wanted to confirm what the problem was.

"It's more than love," he said. "There's some weird religious and mental health stuff going on here. I don't want to give it away, but she's got some issues."

"Of course she does."

"Mack," Nick said, "you've known me a long time. I wouldn't jerk you around. She could help your case against her husband and I think we can all agree he's the real bad guy here. You just have to be patient."

Mack thanked Nick for the call and promised that as long as it seemed like Shannon was telling the truth, she would be allowed to tell it at her own pace.

What do you think about Shannon?

CHAPTER TWENTY-FIVE

The Shannon Andersen who walked into the conference room the next day was almost unrecognizable. She'd lost at least ten pounds from her slender frame, and her cheeks were gaunt. Her skin was pale beneath her greasy, lank hair. Her long-sleeved black shirt and black yoga pants were loose and unflattering. Nick guided her in by the elbow, the handsome attorney looking even better in contrast. Picking at her cuticles, Shannon sat at the head of the table, facing the video camera Mack's paralegal had set up. She kept at it through the entire two-hour interview. Three fingers were bleeding by the end.

"This is ADA Mackenzie Wilson," Mack announced, "on the matter of State v. Shannon Andersen. I'm present with Sergeant David Barton, defense counsel, Nick Diaz, and Ms. Shannon Andersen."

"It's *Mrs.* Shannon Andersen," Shannon interjected. It was the most animated Mack had ever seen her.

"Sure," Mack said, raising her eyebrows. "*Mrs.* Shannon Andersen."

Dave and Mack had decided that he would handle the first

part of the interview, so he consulted his notes before clearing his throat.

"Shannon, tell us why you think you're here today."

"You want me to testify against Steve," she said in a monotone.

"And if you were called in the case against your husband," Dave said in a carefully neutral voice, "what would you say?"

"The truth," Shannon said.

"The truth about what?" Dave asked.

"About why he did what he did," Shannon said. "He is a good man and a wonderful father. He *had* to do it."

"Shannon, why did he have to do it?"

"I can't say. If I say, there will be trouble."

Mack looked at Nick, who mouthed, "See?" across the table.

Mack wrote *Are you sure she's competent?* on her notepad and slid it across the table to him. He read the question and nodded and scribbled a response. He passed the notepad back. *Just wait*.

"I thought you said you'd tell us the truth," Dave said, sounding frustrated.

Shannon stared at him. "I have to tell the truth, but I can't tell the truth." She broke eye contact and stared at a point just over Dave's right shoulder. "Steve *saved* me. I can't make trouble for him. I *won't*."

It continued like that for the better part of ninety minutes. Dave got her early history, and the story of her relationship with Andersen. She gave some good information and confirmed Sherrie's story about reporting having been abused. She denied, though, that she had known Andersen was abusing Shaelynn and Schyanne, and she genuinely appeared to not have known about the girls that weren't his daughters.

"He wouldn't have touched them," she said. "They weren't part of it."

Dave pressed to find out what that meant, but she wouldn't respond. Frustrated, Dave asked to take a break.

Mack excused herself to get a soda out of the vending machine. When she got back, Shannon started talking without prompting.

"Nick says it's very important that I tell you about the prophecy."

"The...prophecy?" Mack asked. She looked at Nick, who nodded and winked.

"Steve has a direct personal connection with the Lord," Shannon said in a monotone. "He received a prophecy right before Sherrie's eighth birthday."

Dave and Mack glanced at each other. He furrowed his brow and tilted his head toward Shannon, and Mack interpreted the gesture as permission to take over.

"Tell me everything about the prophecy," Mack said.

"That he was the one mighty and strong," Shannon said, "sent to restore the church to its former glory."

Dave and Mack had matching blank looks when they turned to Nick.

"The one mighty and strong," he said, "is something akin to the second coming for Latter-day Saints. Joseph Smith prophesied that the one mighty and strong would come to set God's house in order."

"I'm sorry," Dave said, "but you've lost me."

"The one mighty and strong will repair the house of God," Shannon said. "Steve had to restore the church to its magnificent glory. It was an incredibly important mission. He was very special to get such a message from the Lord."

"Okay," Mack said. "And how does that relate to what he did to the girls?"

"He didn't do anything to the girls. They weren't old enough."

"Old enough for what?" Dave asked.

"Steve was tasked with restoring the doctrine of spiritual wifery," Shannon said.

They looked at Nick, lost again.

"Better known to most people as polygamy," he said, a warning look in his eyes.

Dave coughed and took a sip of water.

"So Steve was...marrying...the girls?" he asked.

Shannon nodded. "God said that their wifely duties wouldn't

begin until they were sixteen," she said. "He told me that the sessions in the basement were spiritual education. When Sherrie told me that vile story, I was very angry with her for lying about God's plan. Steve told me he was uncomfortable with it even at sixteen, but it had to be done."

"Shannon," Mack said, trying to get her attention, "if Sherrie told you what was happening in the basement, why didn't you stop it?"

"I prayed on it," she said, "and I received a revelation of my own. God told me that Steve was only doing what he had to do. He wouldn't start touching them until they were sixteen. I would not want to be the one to argue with God."

Mack furiously jotted notes on her legal pad and the room was silent except for the scratching of the pen.

"I tried to stop it," Shannon said. Mack looked up and found the other woman staring at her. "For two years, I wouldn't give Schyanne any processed foods or cooked foods or meat or dairy."

"How would that stop it, Shannon?" Dave asked.

"If she died—"

"Let's stop here for today," Nick interjected. "Sergeant, can you show Shannon to the restroom while Mackenzie and I chat for a minute?"

Dave nodded and stood, helping Shannon with a supporting hand under her elbow. Mack waited for the door to close behind them.

"Holy hell, Nick!" she said. "Does she really believe this shit?"

"I think so," he said, "but her new shrink has put her on some medication and she's starting to come around." He made a note on his legal pad. "I'll get you her medical records—she has a long history of dependent personality disorder and schizoid personality disorder. She grew up in a deeply religious home and was abused by *her* dad as a kid."

Mack swore softly. "So Andersen picked the perfect woman to be the mother of his children," she said. She tapped her pen on the table absently and thought about what Nick had said. "Wait, I thought personality disorders couldn't be treated."

"They've got her on an antipsychotic," he said, "which is helping with a bunch of the negative symptoms of the schizoid, as well as some anti-anxiety meds, which help with some of the dependent issues."

"I've worked with women with dependent personality disorder before," Mack said, "and they've all been really manipulative. How do you know she's not faking?"

"Mack, did you see any signs of deception?"

Mack thought about each of the four times she had met Shannon. Despite her widely varying physical appearance, Mack had always noted her flat affect and her apparent lack of concern for her daughters. And now, given what she had started to say before Nick cut her off—which sounded like the beginnings of a confession of trying to starve Schyanne to death—it seemed clear that she was not lying to protect her own interests.

This changed the entire case. Mack needed all eleven of the victims to be re-interviewed about the religious component of the abuse. Had Andersen told them the same story he'd told Shannon? Had he just told his daughters? All of the girls had talked about the abuse happening in the context of religious counseling, but no one had wanted to make the Andersen case a case about religion. As a result, the detectives might have missed what Mack now suspected would be central to the whole case.

Nick and Mack agreed to reconnect after the severance hearing. He understood there was an enormous amount of follow up to do because of this new development. Dave came back into the conference room and assured Mack that his detectives would re-interview the victims as soon as possible. She was glad that he, too, saw the significance of Shannon's disclosures. In the meantime, she needed to find out more about the one mighty and strong.

CHAPTER TWENTY-SIX

To learn more about Andersen's prophecy, Mack went to her source for all Mormon knowledge: Spencer Allred, an ex-Mormon prosecutor in the violent-offenders unit. They had started with the office at the same time, and ever since Mack had found out that he and his wife had left the church many years earlier, she turned to him whenever she had a question.

He was listening to "Atlantic City" by The Band and reading a thick charging packet. He looked up when she walked into his office and raised a single finger to tell her to wait until the song finished. When it did, he paused the music, put a pen in the packet to mark his place, and turned to her with a smile.

"Sup, dawg?" he asked. Spencer was the whitest white man Mack had ever met—a transplant from St. George who treated Arizona summers like Utah winters, staying inside from the middle of May until the end of October—but he liked to pretend he was a gangster. Thankfully, he kept the act confined to his choice of greetings. With his pale skin, thick horn-rimmed glasses, and white-blond hair, he could never join the gangs he prosecuted.

"Tell me about the one mighty and strong," Mack said, taking a seat across from his desk.

He adjusted his tie and looked thoughtfully at his ceiling before answering. "Doctrine and Covenants. Section eighty-five. Seven? That might not be right."

"Tell me about the one mighty and strong in English," Mack said.

Spencer rose and walked to his bookshelf, pulling his *Book of Mormon* down. He flipped through it, cleared his throat, and began to read. "'And it shall come to pass that I, the Lord God, will send one mighty and strong, holding the scepter of power in his hand, clothed with light for a covering, whose mouth shall utter words, eternal words; while his bowels shall be a fountain of truth, to set in order the house of God, and to arrange by lot the inheritances of the saints whose names are found, and the names of their fathers, and of their children, enrolled in the book of the law of God.'" *Also next page. What does it mean.*

"So...God is going to send someone to clean house?" Mack asked.

"Basically," he said, closing the book and placing it back on the shelf.

"Who?"

"Depends on who you ask, I guess." He sat on the edge of his desk and crossed his legs. "The book doesn't name names. There are lots of different possibilities, depending on who's interpreting and why. Lots of people have claimed to be 'the one' over the years."

"So, wait, let's back up. This was something God told Joseph Smith?"

"Yeah," he said, "in 1832. It was part of a much longer revelation, but that's the part that's directly on point."

"Is 'the one' referenced anyplace else?" Mack asked.

"Not that I know of," Spencer said. "Why are you interested?"

"Steve Andersen told his wife that God told him he was the one mighty and strong."

He leaned back with his hands clasped around one knee. "Huh," he said.

"Why would she believe him, though?" Mack asked. "That's the part I don't understand. It's so obviously a crock."

"Wouldn't be obvious to her, though," Spencer said. "Personal revelation is a major part of Mormonism. It goes back to the very beginning of the church."

"So, if you're a hard-core LDS woman with some mental-health issues and someone tells you he talked to God, you automatically believe him?"

He returned to his chair, dropping lightly into it and grabbing a rubber band to stretch between his fingers. "Most likely, especially since he's her husband and priesthood holder."

"Her what now?" Mack asked.

"Her priesthood holder," he said. "It means he has some religious authority over her, including the authority to determine whether or not she gets into heaven."

"Wait, wait, wait—Andersen gets her into heaven, so she believes him when he says that as part of restoring the church, he has to marry their daughters?"

Spencer whistled and sat forward, leaning his elbows on his desk. "That's a big pill to swallow, even for an obedient LDS wife. Do you think that'll be his defense at trial? 'God told me to do it'? Or insanity?"

"No," Mack said. "I still think his defense will be that it never happened and all the girls are lying. But this is how I'm going to destroy him. I hope."

"How so?" Spencer asked.

"If he used this story with all the girls, it explains all the holes—why no one told, why the girls went back for more 'spiritual counseling,' why Shannon didn't put a stop to it. It actually unifies all my weird facts."

"You'll need to be really careful with jury selection," he said. His phone buzzed and he pulled it out of his shirt pocket to check it before continuing, "Sorry. Good Mormons *should* hate him because he's perverting their faith. But if you get Mormons who aren't totally anti-plural marriage, you hang."

"How will I be able to tell the difference?" Mack asked.

"I'm not sure yet. Let me think about that." Spencer rose again and grabbed the book off the shelf again. "You should know the next verse, too," he said. "'While that man, who was called of God and appointed, that putteth forth his hand to steady the ark of God, shall fall by the shaft of death, like as a tree that is smitten by the vivid shaft of lightning.'"

"Lost again," Mack said.

"Basically, it's about hubris," he said, closing the book. "In the Old Testament, there's a story about a guy who reaches out to steady the Ark of the Covenant, and God smites him—he didn't trust in God to keep the Ark safe. In modern LDS theology, this is interpreted as a warning against trying to change the church."

"So I need to paint Andersen as the one who tried to steady the Ark, by portraying himself as the one mighty and strong?"

He carefully put the book back and wiped the shelf with one finger, checking for dust. "Exactly," Spencer said. "That way, you'll totally get through to any good Latter-day Saints on your jury."

Mack thanked Spencer for his time and started to leave his office.

"Mack!" he said, and she turned around. "There's one more thing, and it's something that's totally none of my business."

"I trust you," she said.

"The whole country's going to be watching this one, right?" he asked.

She nodded.

"There are almost half a million Latter-day Saints in Arizona alone," he said, pulling Clorox wipes out of his desk drawer and starting to clean the bookshelf. "Almost fifteen million nationwide. You need to be very careful to separate Andersen from mainstream Mormonism, so you don't alienate that massive part of the country."

"I may need your help with that," Mack said, smiling. "You know how alienating I can be."

He laughed. "That's why I mentioned it," he said.

Mack walked back to her office, texting Anna as she went. This had the potential to bolster their argument against severance, too, and Mack wanted to give her all the forewarning she could that something big might be coming down the pike.

CHAPTER TWENTY-SEVEN

Once Dave's detectives found out about Shannon's story, they threw themselves into re-interviewing the victims. They'd completed six—all with the same results—by the time Mack called Anna the Thursday before the Tuesday severance hearing.

"So," Mack said, when she answered, "what would you think if I told you that Steve Andersen told six of his victims, as well as his wife, that his existence had been prophesied by Joseph Smith in 1832, and that in order to save the LDS church he had to sleep with children?"

Anna sniffed and cleared her throat. "I would think that's a weirdly specific hypothetical," she said.

Mack laughed. "We did a free talk with Shannon and she told us that Andersen received a revelation that he was put on Earth to set right the house of God, which included bringing back polygamy. I had the detectives follow up with the victims, and they all knew about the prophecy."

"What a great concealment technique," Anna said. "I'm almost impressed. It both normalizes the behavior and serves as a reason not to tell anyone. All your victims were raised in the church, right?"

"Absolutely," Mack said. "All in very devout and active families. Andersen himself was the bishop of his ward for a while."

"I think that's incredibly important evidence for you," she said, "especially for the severance hearing."

"That's what I think," Mack said. "If I get you the summaries of the new interviews, can you review them in time for the hearing? Maybe write a supplemental report?"

"Sure thing," she said. "Do you think he believes it?"

"Believes that he received a message from God that he needed to rape children?"

"Yeah," she said. "That."

"*No*," Mack said, "I believe he's a narcissist who used the rhetoric of his faith to abuse eleven known victims and potentially countless others."

"Good," she said, "because I was thinking the same thing."

Mack thanked her in advance for making the new information a priority and suggested they meet for dinner Friday night. When they hung up, she called Dave to make sure that the supplemental reports were sent over by the end of the day. She needed to send them to Anna, and, more importantly, to Grant and Miller. She also needed to file a supplemental response to the motion to sever and revise her notes for the hearing.

It was 9:15 p.m. by the time Mack was able to leave the office. As she did so, her phone buzzed. The screen read "No Caller ID." Even though she wasn't on call, she answered, figuring it was Dave with the latest update.

"Sex Crimes, Mackenzie."

There was no response, but she could hear the person on the other end breathing heavily.

"Hello?" she asked. "Dave?"

The heavy breathing continued.

She tried one more time before hanging up. She wondered whether she should report the call to James but decided against it. She was a professional. She could handle a crank call. It probably wasn't even a crank call, she reasoned. It was probably a robo-dialer where the robot didn't kick in. All the same, she hadn't gone to the firing range with Anna yet, and she suddenly became very aware of how exposed she was while walking to her scratched-up car. She scanned the parking lot, looking for anything out of the ordinary. Her car was the only one there, and she saw nothing that sent up alarm bells. She was willing to write it off as a coincidence. After all, she called random numbers as a kid and asked whoever answered whether their refrigerator was running. All the same, when she got home she looked at tasers online, and made a note to talk to Anna about buying one.

The hearing was set to begin at 10:00 a.m., and Mack was in the courtroom by 9:30 to set up. Jeannie Bea, the host of a legal news program for CNN, was sitting in the front row on the prosecutor's side. She had apparently decided that the hearing deserved her personal appearance in Tucson. Her signature long red curls hung loose over her suit and she was talking to the court's public information officer in a low, urgent whisper. Mack didn't watch Jeannie's show often. The woman was overbearing. A former prosecutor who seemed to show up whenever a case caught the national eye, she was quick to condemn police and prosecutors for any perceived mistakes or missteps.

Mack mostly avoided the articles and occasional news stories about the Andersen case. She knew they were out there, because she received several "Saw you on the news!" texts from her mom and some college friends, but she hadn't paid much attention. Seeing Jeannie in the courtroom was the first real sign for Mack that the case held an interest for people outside Arizona. She suspected that the latest news—the religious stuff—hadn't even hit the media yet, and she worried about the circus that was sure to result when the full extent of the scandal came out.

She texted James to let him know that Jeannie was there, and the hearing was likely to be on the national news that evening. Jess had agreed to second chair the trial, but she was in her own trial that day and wasn't planning to attend the severance hearing. As Mack watched Jeannie type furiously on a laptop, she decided that it would be less stressful to go wait in the hall.

That's where Dave, wearing the same suit he had worn to the *Simpson* hearing, found her. She was pacing the length of the courthouse and trying to decide what to do with her hair. Thankfully, she had remembered makeup that morning, so she didn't look nearly as pale and tired as she felt, but she had totally forgotten to do anything to her hair other than gather it into a low ponytail. Dave was unhelpful, and didn't seem to understand that it truly mattered, given that whatever she chose would be seen by millions of Americans that evening. She was thankful that she had put on a matching suit, rather than just slacks and a jacket.

Anna finally arrived, still five minutes early. Mack decided that a high ponytail would look better than a low one, and was in the public restroom struggling with some bobby pins when she walked in.

"Help?" Mack asked around the pins in her mouth.

Anna nodded and wordlessly plucked the pins from between Mack's lips. Her gray suit and black cashmere turtleneck sweater looked professional but not stuffy, and Mack noticed the recently added subtle red highlights. Anna gathered the younger woman's hair in her hands, and Mack took a moment to enjoy the feeling of slender fingers against her scalp. She closed her eyes and relaxed, remembering how good it used to feel when Anna would rub her head as they cuddled on Mack's couch watching old movies. For Christmas, back when they were dating, Anna had bought a massage table and gifted Mack a year of massages. In the years since their breakup, Mack had searched for a professional she liked, but no one's fingers compared to Anna's. Anna squeezed Mack's shoulders and she opened her eyes, looking into the mirror to find a perfect ponytail, not a hair out of place.

"How did you even do that?" Mack asked, turning her head side to side to admire the new style. "You haven't had long hair since you were fifteen."

"I am a voman with many skeells," Anna said in a thick Russian accent.

Mack laughed.

"You ready, champ?" Anna asked, making eye contact with Mack in the mirror and placing a warm hand on her arm. "Dave said you were freaking out a little bit."

"Jeannie Bea is here," Mack explained.

Anna's eyes lit up. "Do you think she'll sign my copy of her book?" she asked. "I could run back to the office and get it."

Mack glared at her. "Let's go. Before I lose my nerve."

They walked into the courtroom to find Andersen sitting at the defense table with both his attorneys. Miller, a tall well-built man with an expensive haircut and an even more expensive suit, was sitting as lead counsel. Mack had expected that, since he had filed the motion to sever and was the superior attorney. James was sitting directly behind the prosecution table and flashed Mack a warm smile as she walked past. Anna sat next to him and Mack could hear them exchanging pleasantries as she returned to her table and gulped water in an attempt to cure her suddenly dry mouth.

"All rise," the bailiff said, and Judge Donoghue emerged from chambers to take the bench.

The judge had the attorneys announce and asked if the State was ready.

"Yes, Your Honor," Mack said. "The State calls Dr. Anna Lapin."

Anna had always been Mack's favorite expert witness because the doctor did most of the work. As long as she knew Mack's basic direction, Mack could wind her up and let her go. Anna didn't need anyone to constantly direct her testimony. The two had worked together enough that Mack was able to get through most of it without notes, and they had spent an hour preparing for the hearing in Mack's office the previous afternoon.

As Anna got settled on the stand with her report, the materials she had relied on, and a bottle of water, Mack approached the podium. When Anna was ready, she looked up and smiled, and Mack began asking her questions. They went through her education, her experience working with sex offenders, and her research and publications. Once Mack had qualified her as an expert in the field, they moved into the substance of the Andersen case. As in *Simpson* hearings, hearsay is admissible, so Mack went through the content of the police reports with Anna, rather than needing to call Dave or his detectives. She talked about the materials she had reviewed, and which research she had used in writing her report. Last, they covered her conclusion—that, if Anna accepted as fact that Andersen had committed all of the charged acts, then the similarities in the assaults, as well as the similarities in the victims, indicated Andersen had an aberrant sexual propensity for having sexual contact with prepubescent females.

"No further questions," Mack said, returning to the prosecution table.

Miller got up to cross Anna. He shot his cuffs before he started, and Mack peered at his wrist. She was almost positive he was wearing a Breitling Chronoliner, an incredibly expensive watch that Mack coveted and would never be able to afford on her government salary. Mack had never seen Anna flustered on the stand and was looking forward to watching her stand up to the well-heeled defense attorney's questions. He was incredibly well prepared for his cross. He didn't fall into the most dangerous trap with experts, for both prosecutors and defense attorneys, but took it as a given that Anna knew more about the subject than he did. He quizzed her about several specific articles and why their conclusions did or did not apply to the Andersen case. He scored a few minor points on that topic, but Mack suspected that the worst was still to come.

"You never examined my client, correct?" he asked.

Anna folded her hands in her lap and leaned back in her chair. "That's right," she said.

"And the only statements of my client that you relied on were his statements to police before he was a suspect in the investigation into what happened to his daughter Schyanne, correct?"

"Yes," she said. She smiled, and Mack assumed that, although she herself was lost, Anna knew where he was going.

"You would agree, wouldn't you, Ms. Lapin, that there's a diagnosis that can be applied to people who have a sexual interest in children?"

"Yes, I would," she said.

"And what is that diagnosis?" Miller was clearly nearing his major point.

"Well," she said, "I suspect you're referring to pedophilia, although there are, in fact, several possibilities."

"And you haven't diagnosed my client with pedophilia, have you?"

Her smile widened. "No, I have not. That would be inappropriate under the circumstances."

"So you can't really say that my client has an aberrant sexual interest in children without having diagnosed him with pedophilia, can you?"

"My report states that your client has an aberrant sexual *propensity*, not an interest," she said calmly.

"Judge," Miller said, turning slightly to address the court, "move to strike Ms. Lapin's last statement as nonresponsive."

"Motion granted," Judge Donoghue said.

"No further questions," Miller said, taking his seat.

Mack stood, taking a last sip of water and collecting her notepad and pen.

"*Dr.* Lapin," she said, placing extra stress on her title, "can you define pedophilia?"

"It's usually thought of as a primary or exclusive sexual interest in children," she said.

Mack hoped she understood why Anna had been smiling and trusted the psychologist to help her ask the right questions to get there. "So would a true pedophile have a long-term romantic relationship with an age-appropriate person?"

Anna nodded subtly. "Not generally," she said.

"Are you familiar with any research examining the correlation between pedophilia and child molestation?" Mack asked.

"Yes," she said, unscrewing the lid of her water bottle and taking a long drink. "There have been several studies, and all of them indicate that not all perpetrators of childhood sexual abuse are pedophiles. In fact, true pedophiles are thought to be rather rare, and account for a relatively small number of child molestations, overall. This is especially true of perpetrators with in-home victims."

"So why would someone without a primary sexual interest in children engage in sexual contact with a child?"

"The research tells us that there are many reasons," Anna said, "including a desire for power, a sadistic tendency, and just plain opportunism."

"Is it necessary to diagnose someone as a pedophile in order to say that they have an aberrant sexual propensity to engage in sexual contact with children?"

"Absolutely not," she said firmly. "Calling someone a pedophile simply addresses their sexual interests. Saying someone has an aberrant sexual propensity toward sex with children addresses their likelihood to participate in certain behaviors."

"Thank you," Mack said, and sat. She winked at Anna as she left the podium.

Judge Donoghue had three questions of his own, all of which Anna had addressed already. Mack admired her patience in restating her answers for him. He was known around the courthouse for his love of demonstrating that he was the smartest person in the room, and the fact that it hadn't ever been true never seemed to stand in the way. When Anna was released, he asked for argument. Since it was a hearing on Miller's motion to sever, he got both the first and the last chance to convince the judge that, although the evidence relating to each girl might well be similar, it would still be unduly prejudicial to his client and unduly cumulative. Consequently, the counts must be severed. His first argument was eloquent.

Mack took a different tack and asked Judge Donoghue if he had any specific questions or concerns that he wanted her to address.

"Yes, Ms. Wilson," he said. "Dr. Lapin's testimony makes clear that sufficient reason exists to submit this 'aberrant sexual propensity' evidence to the jury. That doesn't overcome the undue prejudice concerns of defense, however."

Mack's stomach dropped. Donoghue was going to grant the defense motion. "Your Honor," she said, "the key here is whether it's *unduly* prejudicial. In the instant case, evidence of all eleven victims would not be *unduly* prejudicial. Arguably, evidence of *any* crime is prejudicial to the defendant, but the determination for the Court to make is whether it's unfair. Because the crimes were committed so similarly, for such similar reasons, and against such similar victims, it's not unfair for one jury to consider all the evidence."

"Can you address defense counsel's argument that evidence concerning eleven victims would be unfairly cumulative?" he asked.

"Yes, Judge. It would undoubtedly be cumulative to have eleven people testify regarding a car accident they all observed. In the instant case, however, each victim will be testifying regarding her own victimization, which was committed outside the presence—the conscious presence, I should say—of each of the other victims. It is not, therefore, cumulative."

"You've answered my questions, thank you, Ms. Wilson. Mr. Miller, you get the last word, but briefly."

As Miller stood to speak, Mack turned to James and Anna. He shrugged. Anna smiled reassuringly. Mack's phone vibrated in her pocket and she pulled it out under the table. Anna's text read *Don't worry. A judge has never not relied on my findings. You won't be the one to screw up my record.* Mack turned back and smiled.

Miller sat. Mack hadn't really listened to his final argument—there was nothing further she could do at that point, whatever he said. She was preparing herself for the reality of eleven back-to-back molest trials when Judge Donoghue looked up from his computer. He spoke in a dry monotone.

"Having considered the materials submitted to the court, the testimony of Dr. Lapin, and argument, I find that evidence regarding each victim would be admissible to show motive, absence of mistake, plan, and aberrant sexual propensity. I further find that such evidence, while prejudicial, is not unduly prejudicial, nor is it cumulative. Defendant's motion for severance is denied. All eleven victims will remain joined for trial."

Mack let out a breath she hadn't realized she was holding. Dave, sitting next to her, gave a tiny fist pump under the table. The press in the back of the courtroom murmured.

"Anything else from either party?" Judge Donoghue asked.

"No, Judge, thank you," Mack said, already starting to pack her file and notebooks into her cart.

"No, Your Honor," Miller said.

As Dave and Mack walked to meet James and Anna outside the courtroom, John Grant approached them.

"Ms. Wilson, can I have a moment of your time?" he asked.

Mack waved Dave on ahead, and the two lawyers stepped into the small workroom between the courtroom and the hallway.

Grant tossed his briefcase onto the table, trying for an air of nonchalance and instead looking like a cornered rodent. "He'll take twenty-five," Grant said.

"John," Mack replied, having expected something like this in the event that the severance hearing was unsuccessful, "the offer is fifty." She crossed her arms over her chest.

Grant rolled his eyes and huffed. "Come on, Mack, if he takes fifty he's guaranteed to die in prison. Twenty-five gives him a shot."

"Somehow," Mack said, smiling, "the thought of your client dying in prison doesn't really bother me. He doesn't deserve a shot, and he won't get one from me."

"You'd rather put those kids on the stand?" he asked. "Robert and I will tear them apart."

"Robert knows better," Mack said, "and if you think a jury won't hate you for yelling at a kid, you're delusional."

Grant glared at her.

"The fifty offer expires next week," Mack said. "Then it goes up to sixty."

She left Grant in the room, still spluttering, and joined the others outside for the walk back to the office.

"He'll take twenty-five," Mack said to James.

James smiled. "I'm sure he would. He'd only be seventy-eight when he got out of prison."

"If we wait here, can we meet Jeannie?" Anna asked.

"I don't know," Mack said, grabbing the other woman's elbow to hurry her down the hall, "and I cannot care. Come on, Doc, you're supposed to take me to dinner, and I am *starving*."

CHAPTER TWENTY-EIGHT

They stopped by Mack's office to drop off her file cart and pick up her purse before they left for dinner. Mack checked her email to find a new message from the sergeant of the sex-crimes squad. Two more home invasions. Neither woman could describe the man other than the basic "white guy, age twenty to forty, medium build" that detectives had for each of the previous eight incidents. The sketch the police had put out to the media had gone nowhere. They'd received over a hundred tips, none of which turned into promising leads.

Mack had put that investigation aside for her all-consuming focus on the Andersen case. She made a note to look through the reports stacked on a corner of her filing cabinet when she had the chance.

Anna took Mack to Café Poca Cosa, a Tucson institution. Rumor has it that, if you want to see dirty Arizona politics, you just have to grab a space at the bar at lunchtime. Mack had never seen politicians cavorting with mobsters, but she had seen a senator and several local celebrities, not to mention a married judge getting *very* close to his unmarried judicial assistant. That night, dinner was celebrity-free, but it was delicious and decadent—margaritas, guacamole, and chile rellenos. They even split a bread pudding for dessert.

The hearing wasn't discussed. Anna was planning a trip back to California to see her parents and brother, and they mostly talked about what she would do for the three days in Marina del Rey. She'd be gone during the Andersen jury selection, which made Mack anxious. She liked to sound Anna out about potential jurors but wouldn't bother her while she was with her family. Between Jess, James, and Spencer, who would assist with the Mormon angle, Mack was hopeful that she wouldn't need the psychologist's help.

By the time Anna dropped Mack off at her condo, it was late. Mack was in the front seat of Anna's Infiniti, finishing a story about the time she ran over an armadillo while she was in college, when Anna leaned over the center console and kissed her, gently, on the lips. Mack was shocked. Although short, the kiss was so familiar that her face flushed and her hand immediately moved to the other woman's thigh.

"I'm sorry," Anna said, sitting back and running both hands through her short dark hair. "I shouldn't have done that."

"Maybe I've had a little too much to drink, but, um, why not?"

"We've been doing so well as friends," she said. "I've just wanted to do that for a long time."

"We've always made a great team," Mack said. "Both in and out of the courtroom."

"That's true," Anna said. "We're unbeatable. You were great today. I like watching you be a badass lady lawyer."

Mack smiled and leaned back against the headrest. "Do you want to come up?" she asked, tipsy enough not to think the question all the way through. "I can cross...*examine* you."

Anna laughed but refused. The rejection stung a little, surprising Mack almost as much as the kiss.

Mack tripped her way up the stairs and waved as Anna drove off. She noticed a small package on her doorstep. She recognized it immediately—the signature blue of a Tiffany & Co. jewelry box tied with the standard white ribbon.

She didn't see a card. It seemed too small to contain a bomb. She shook it. It didn't explode. She tried her doorknob. It was reassuringly still locked. She dug her keys out of her purse and fumbled to get the door open, then pushed into the living room and looked around. Everything looked like it had that morning when she left, down to the half-eaten slice of toast on a paper towel on the coffee table.

She sat on the couch and stared at the box for a moment, blinking tiredly as she considered whether to open it. Finally, she picked up her phone. Anna answered on the first ring.

"Can you come back?" Mack asked.

She sighed and paused.

When she spoke again, her voice was quiet and sad. "It's not a good idea, Mack. Look, I'm sorry I did that, but we can't—"

"Oh, I'm way past that," Mack interrupted. "Someone left a jewelry box on my doorstep. I want you to come over and open it with me."

Mack heard Anna's brakes screech.

"Don't touch it," she said. "I'm calling the police and I'll be right there."

Mack sat back, letting herself sink into the cool brown leather. She covered herself with a fleece throw off the back of the couch, closing her eyes. She didn't bother to lock the door, since Anna would be there any minute.

By the time Anna got there, Mack had passed out. Anna shook her awake, muttering about how dangerous it was that the door was unlocked and there she was, sleeping, totally unprepared to protect herself in case of danger. When she saw that Mack had brought the box inside, she freaked out even more, picking it up with the paper towel that had previously held Mack's toast.

"Heeeeey," Mack said, "you'll get peanut butter on the table!"

"You can buy a new table," she said, putting the box back on the doorstep. "You cannot buy a new body if you die of ricin poisoning."

Mack adjusted the blanket so it covered her feet and was unconscious again before Anna made it back inside. When she woke for the second time, it was to the red and blue flashing lights of a patrol car shining through her front window.

Anna was standing in the doorway with Officer Carlson. Behind him, Mack could see members of the bomb squad, waving some sort of wand at the box. She gathered the blanket around her shoulders and went to the door.

"It's too small to be a bomb," she said.

"We're going to run it through the X-ray, just in case," the man closest to Mack said. His name badge announced him as Goodwin. He picked up the box, hindered by his heavy padding, and carried it carefully down to the large truck in the parking lot.

"You're a district attorney, ma'am?" his partner asked.

Mack nodded and rubbed her eyes. "Mackenzie Wilson. Sex crimes. I can find my badge if you need it."

"That's okay, ma'am." Goodwin nodded toward Anna. "Your friend has brought us up to speed on the suspicious events here at your residence. You have no idea who might be doing this?"

"Anyone I know who could hate me enough to do all *this*," she waved her hand, vaguely, "is either in jail, in prison, or dead. I really think it's just random."

"It's not random," Anna said. "Officer, this is the prosecutor on the Andersen case."

"Steve Andersen?" he asked.

"Yes," Mack said. "Are you familiar with the case?"

"Sure am," he said. "My oldest daughter went to seminary with his son." He turned to Anna. "So you think someone related to that case is targeting Ms. Wilson, here?"

Anna nodded and Mack scoffed. "The only people upset with my handling of that case are Andersen himself—who's in jail—and his wife—who is reluctantly cooperating with the State."

"They have sons, don't they?" Anna asked.

"Yes. Simon is ten, Seth is thirteen, and Steve Jr. is twenty-one."

"If Junior strongly identifies with his father…" Anna trailed off. Mack saw her point, but just couldn't believe that that nice young man had been stalking her.

Down at the truck, Mack could see the officer who had taken the box taking off his helmet and the top layer of padding.

"All clear!" he called. "It looks like it's just jewelry. A necklace, or something."

Goodwin waved him up the stairs. "Ms. Wilson," the other man said, "we're going to go ahead and impound the box, see if there are any fingerprints."

Mack shook her head. "I want to know what's in it!" she said. "What if there's a note inside and it's from someone I know and I freaked out over nothing?"

"You got a girlfriend I don't know about?" Anna asked, folding her arms across her chest and arching one dark eyebrow.

Officer Carlson scowled and scoffed under his breath.

Mack shushed Anna and watched the huddle of officers.

"Ma'am," the bomb squad guy who was still wearing his helmet said, "we'll let you open it if you wear gloves and a mask."

"Are you kidding?" Anna said. "There could be poison in there! This could be dangerous!"

"The likelihood of anything dangerous being in that box is very slim," Carlson said. "I'm sure it's just a gift, and the card fell off or went missing or something."

"That's true," Goodwin said. "The gloves and mask are precautionary." He went down to the truck. He dug through a toolbox, and returned with blue latex gloves and a surgical mask. He helped Mack get the gloves on, and put the mask on for her. Her glasses fogged when she exhaled.

"Let's go ahead and do this on your kitchen counter," his partner said, and the five of them stepped into the living room. He handed Mack the box. She crossed the room and set it down next to her record player on the breakfast bar. She pulled the end of the white ribbon and released the bow. No one in the room seemed to be breathing. Anna had a hand on Mack's lower back as she lifted the top of the box. A small white card rested on the blue leather envelope. She gingerly opened the card.

I'm still watching. Always.

Mack cringed.

Anna gasped. "It's *totally* the same guy!" she said.

Mack nodded. She opened the leather envelope and let the contents slide into one gloved hand. The officer was right—it was a necklace. A delicate silver chain linked, on either end, to a small infinity symbol.

"Always," Mack said, her voice catching.

CHAPTER TWENTY-NINE

Jury selection in the Andersen case started the next week, and Mack had been unable to sleep for more than ninety minutes at a stretch in the interim. Unfortunately, it showed—her skin was pale and her elementary concealer skills were no match for the dark circles under her eyes. She lost even more weight, and her suits were suddenly too big, hanging unattractively. Her mom called twice to alert her to sales at Tucson department stores. How her mother, in Cleveland, knew what was going on at Tucson department stores was a mystery. She had even ordered Mack a black Calvin Klein pantsuit online and had it delivered to the office.

Mack kept going on caffeine and sheer force of will, but she was starting to flag. Since they would screen five hundred jurors in hopes of finding sixteen who would be fair, impartial, and able to serve for five months until the beginning of October, she needed to be at the top of her game.

She and Jess had divided the trial as evenly as they could.

Since it was Mack's case, she would open and close, as well as handle the three main witnesses—Schyanne, Shannon, and Dr. Emilio Flores, an expert in the field of victimology. Jess would handle the DNA, since she enjoyed presenting scientific testimony and Mack found it boring. They split the remaining victims and witnesses. If Mack had to spend upward of eighty days in trial, she was glad to be spending them with Jess. She was also glad that the office hadn't tried to mandate her second chair.

The case continued to receive a massive amount of media attention. Mack heard that Jeannie Bea had reserved a suite at the downtown Hilton and would be staying for the duration. She hoped that was just a rumor, since she was sure that having her face on television every day might only encourage her friend with the necklace.

The first week was unremarkable. Each day, they brought in one hundred twenty-five people, and figured out which of them could be available until October. By the following Monday, when they started to get to the real meat of it, they were down to just over three hundred. When they released those who didn't feel they could be fair and impartial given the subject matter, they lost another hundred. After seven mind-numbing days, they were finally at the point where they would begin making their strikes and forming the final panel. Judge Donoghue announced the twenty-eight prospective jurors could be released. Before they could leave, Juror Sixty-three raised her hand. Mack flipped to her notes on her, but found very little. She was unmarried, no children, worked as a housekeeper, and had never served on a jury.

"Yes, ma'am?" the judge asked, frustrated.

The redhead stood, hugging a two-inch three-ring binder against her chest. "Yes, I'm sorry, sir, but I just cannot serve on this jury."

Mack rolled her eyes. Of course. Now that they were coming to the end of the process, there would likely be several people who came up with sudden, last-minute reasons why they couldn't serve.

"Why not, ma'am?" the judge asked.

She took a deep breath. Her dozen necklaces clanked audibly. "My monkey has liver failure."

Jess choked on the water she was sipping, and Mack struggled to keep a straight face. She had heard some crazy excuses, but none quite *this* crazy.

"Your…monkey?" Judge Donoghue asked.

"Yes, sir," she said. "I have a pigtail macaque monkey named Freckles, and he has a chronic liver condition. I can't be away from him all day every day."

"Why not?"

"He has a very strict diet, with medications every two hours. I have all the documentation right here." She raised the binder.

Judge Donoghue appeared stumped and took a moment to consider his next question.

"Who takes care of Freckles while you're at work?" he asked.

"Oh," she said, shaking her head, "I only work within a five-mile radius of my house so I can go home and give him his medications."

"What about when you go on vacation?"

"I haven't been on vacation in eleven years," she said.

"Since she got Freckles?" Mack said softly to Jess.

She nodded.

Mack didn't know or care whether this woman really had a needy pet monkey—she wasn't going to fight to keep someone who so obviously didn't want to be there. Jurors who were kept despite protests were likely to hold it against the prosecution, and Mack had enough to worry about. Judge Donoghue, however, was not so easily convinced.

"Who has been watching Freckles while you're here?" he asked.

"My sister watched him last week, but she went back to Minnesota—she's a snowbird, you know. And today he's at the vet's, but I can't afford their daycare every day."

Judge Donoghue asked the lawyers to approach and turned on the white noise machine on the bench so the panel wouldn't overhear their conversation. "I'm inclined to let her go," he said.

"Agreed, Judge," Mack said. "I don't think there's any need to look at her documentation, unless defense disagrees?" She looked at Miller and Grant.

"No objection to releasing her," Miller said.

The four lawyers returned to their tables.

"Okay, Juror Sixty-three," the judge said, "you can go. Good luck with Freckles."

Jess tapped Mack on the arm and gestured to her phone. She had done an Internet search for macaque monkeys and found an absolutely terrifying picture of a large creature with its fangs bared.

"That is *not* what I thought Freckles would look like!" she whispered. They stood as the jury filed out of the courtroom.

"Me, either," Mack said. "I was expecting something on the five-pounds-and-fluffy branch of the primate family tree."

Jess, Dave, and Mack retreated to the attorney room to make their strikes, and Spencer met them there. He had been very helpful devising questions to elicit whether the Mormons on the panel would be advantageous or not. Mack had primed the panel, when given the chance to ask questions, that religion would play into the case, and Spencer had been assessing their responses over streaming video back in his office.

"You don't want Seventy-seven," he said, as soon as the door closed behind them. "She believes in personal revelation and doesn't believe that the church has the only true interpretation of God's word."

He had two more he was sure they didn't want. Together, they made a list of who was most objectionable, who the defense would definitely strike, and a supply of maybes. They struck Juror Seventy-seven first, and Mack took the master list into the courtroom for defense. They were ready, and asked Mack to wait as they struck Juror Two-hundred-nine.

They went back and forth like that until they were left with the sixteen jurors who would decide the fate of Steve Andersen. Seven men, nine women, three Mormons, sixteen parents, two African-Americans, three Hispanics, the rest white. Mack surveyed them uneasily as Judge Donoghue called their numbers and they trudged to the jury box. Jury selection can make or break any trial, and she was especially nervous given the high stakes.

"I swear I have *never* seen some of these people," Mack said to Jess as they watched the jurors get sworn in. "They were not on our panel."

"Relax, Wilson," she whispered back. "It'll be fine. Now the fun part starts."

Since it was already after 4:00 p.m., the fun part wouldn't actually start until the next morning. She didn't sleep that night, opting instead to rehearse her opening statement, consistently clocked in at a lengthy thirty-four minutes, until her throat was raw. She spent the early morning hours drinking green tea with honey and rehearsing in a whisper in front of the mirror.

At 6:00 a.m. she watched Jeannie's show, which spent forty-two of its forty-five minutes on the Andersen case. It showed footage of the severance hearing, and all Mack could see was how bad her hair had looked, in spite of Anna's hard work with the bobby pins. Mack had been long overdue for a haircut, and her roots looked awful. She tried never to change her hair during trial but given the state of her hair and the length of the trial, she would probably have to make an exception. She made a note to call her stylist over the weekend.

Jeannie's angle appeared to be the length of time that Andersen had gotten away with abusing multiple kids. "Where," she said, in her signature Southern twang, "were these children's parents? Their church leaders? Their teachers?"

Mack turned the television off in disgust and went back to rehearsing her opening.

She was at the office at 6:30 a.m., putting final touches on materials for the day's witnesses. Jess would be starting with Jared Richardson, the first officer who responded to the Circle K the night Schyanne had been found.

Next was Dr. Flores, who would talk about the characteristics of child sexual abuse victims. They wanted him to testify before any of the victims, since his testimony would help explain any weird stuff they did on the stand, like freeze or laugh, as well as some of the weird stuff before they ever got on the stand, like not tell an adult they were being abused.

Juries think they know how victims should act. As a culture, after all, kids are taught to "No, Go, Yell, Tell!" That handy rhyme, reminding kids to say no, run away, yell as loudly as they can, and tell a trusted adult, applies moderately well in "stranger danger" situations where a kid doesn't know his or her abuser. Most kids, though, are abused by someone they know, and the rules are different.

Juries sometimes disbelieve kids who testify that they were abused for years without telling, even though the research indicates that most kids *never* disclose childhood sex abuse. As a result, Mack liked to have Dr. Flores educate jurors about what victim behaviors are normal, and she liked that education to come before they had a real live kid in front of them.

Jess figured that between openings, Richardson, and Flores, they would fill the whole first day, although unlike Spears, Donoghue wasn't a stickler for filling time. The following morning, Schyanne would take the stand. Mack's goal was to have her on and off in one day, although she realized that might be unfairly optimistic. She wasn't sure how long cross-examination would take.

At 8:30 a.m., Mack heard a gentle knock on her office door and opened it to find Anna. They hadn't spoken since the night they'd kissed in Anna's car—the night Anna had called the bomb squad, which Mack had regretted as soon as she'd seen the necklace. Mack had a feeling Anna was still mad at her for failing to take the situation seriously, and Mack was avoiding what she feared was an inevitable confrontation. She had been so caught up in trial preparation that she couldn't expend the mental energy necessary to mend fences or deal with how embarrassed she was to be caught harboring a crush on her good friend. Over the years, Mack had suspected that Anna had been seeing someone from time to time, but it had apparently never turned into something serious enough to mention. Even if Anna was single, crushes were *so* eighth grade. Mack couldn't decide what would be worse—to tell Anna how she felt and be rejected, or for Anna to reciprocate, for them to rekindle their romance, and risk losing one of her best friends when the relationship inevitably crashed and burned. Friends. Friends were safe. Mack needed friends.

"Hey," Anna said, holding up a white paper bag and a large coffee cup, "I figured you might want breakfast."

Mack smiled awkwardly and invited her in.

"You start today, right?" she asked, as Mack settled in with a breakfast sandwich and a coffee fixed just the way she liked it—lots of almond milk and sweetener.

Mack nodded.

Anna sat, hesitantly, on the edge of Mack's desk. "Can I come watch?"

"Sure," Mack said around a mouthful of sandwich.

"I brought one more thing," she said, reaching into her purse and removing a smaller bag. Mack looked at her quizzically.

"Makeup," she said, pulling out tube after unrecognizable tube. "If that's okay, I mean."

Mack nodded.

When she finished her sandwich, Anna fixed her face.

"Can't have you looking like a zombie," she said as she applied a pink-tinted gloss to Mack's lips. "Go look."

As Mack crossed her office to the mirror, Jess poked her head around the door frame. She whistled. "You go, Wilson!" she said. "You totally look ready for your close-up. I'm going to grab my file and I'll be right back."

Mack had to admit she looked better than she had in weeks. Her skin glowed against her chocolate brown suit, the dark circles under her eyes were diminished, and when she smiled she seemed almost human.

"Last step," Anna said, pulling a can of dry shampoo out of her purse.

"I *did* shower this morning," Mack said. "I am not an animal."

"I know," she said, "but this will give you some volume." She undid Mack's ponytail and sprayed her hair before brushing it back into a fresh, high ponytail. "Beautiful." She smiled. "You know," she said, "at some point we probably need to talk about—"

"No need," Mack said, blushing despite herself. "It was stupid. I clearly had too much to drink at dinner. It was my fault."

Anna reached out, gently taking Mack's hand. "But—"

"Not to ruin the sleepover," Jess said, staring at their joined hands, "but we should get moving."

It was Anna's turn to blush as she dropped Mack's hand, but Jess cackled all the way down the elevator.

CHAPTER THIRTY

"On January twelfth of this year," Mack said, "Schyanne Andersen was fourteen. She had been abused, sexually and physically, by her father since she was just eight years old. On that freezing Tuesday morning, though, Schyanne had had enough. She decided that she couldn't take one more day. So she ran away. She didn't have any clothes, she didn't have any shoes, she just ran. She trusted that *anything* would be better than living in her father's house."

Mack paused to take a sip of water and make eye contact with the three jurors she had identified as the potential foreperson.

"Ladies and gentlemen, this case is about power and control. Steve Andersen wanted to do something he wasn't supposed to—he wanted to have sex with young girls. Using the power he had gained as bishop of his ward, as an apostle in his church, and the control he had over his wife and family, the defendant found a way to get what he wanted." It was a strong start, and Mack could feel the jury's eyes on her.

"The defendant is a master manipulator," she said, "and he manipulated everyone in his life—his wife, his daughters, his church, and the eight girls he abused under the guise of 'spiritual counseling.' This case is *not* about the mainstream Mormon church. It is about the defendant's warped version of the church, which he used to serve his own perverted wishes. It is about Schyanne's bravery, which inspired ten more victims to come forward and disclose the abuse that they also suffered at the defendant's hands."

Mack went on to explain how the victimization started, when Sherrie was eight years old, and how it ended, when Schyanne had the strength and courage to run away that cold night in January. She told them about the people they'd hear testify—victims, police officers, doctors, and scientists, and the evidence they'd see, including the photographs and videos of Schyanne's abuse. They had all been warned during jury selection, but after several child-pornography trials, Mack had found that it was best to warn the jury several times before making them look at images. She had seen a juror throw up during her first pornography trial, and afterward that juror had said she'd expected photos, but it was the video that sent her over the edge.

"At the end of all that evidence," Mack said, "you folks will be asked to make a decision. You will be asked whether the defendant wins, whether his twisted version of religion gets to persevere, or whether Schyanne was right to trust that running away would put a stop to the abuse. You will be given the opportunity to tell the defendant that raping children is never okay, regardless of what he says God told him. We will ask you, at that time, to hold the defendant responsible for his crimes and find him guilty of all ninety-three counts. Thank you."

Mack returned to her table and sat down, breathing deeply and trying to calm her racing heart. Jess slipped her a piece of paper with a single word written on it. *Whoa*, it said. Mack smiled. Coming from Jess, whose trial skills Mack held in very high esteem, that was great praise.

"Mr. Miller?" Judge Donoghue asked.

"Thank you, Judge," Miller said, rising and approaching the jury box. He bypassed the podium and carried no notes, opting instead to stand before the jury with his arms raised and ready to gesture. Mack noticed that he had swapped the Breitling for a Timex. For a brief moment, she was struck by something familiar in the pose that she couldn't identify. Then she realized that it was the exact same way she stood to give her opening statements, ever since she had learned it in his trial-advocacy course.

"Ladies and gentlemen, the prosecutor is correct—this case is not about Mormonism. Steve Andersen is a proud, upstanding Mormon man." He rubbed his thumb against the first two fingers of his left hand. "This case is about money." He paused to make eye contact, and Mack hoped that the jury recognized the similarities between their presentations and thought he was copying her, rather than liking him. "This case started as a family affair. Schyanne, a troubled teenager, ran away from home. When just running away didn't work, when the police put her back with her family, she needed a story that would keep her from her loving father, who she saw as overbearing and overprotective. She came up with the worst story she could imagine—that Steve was sexually abusing her."

He returned to his table and took a drink of water, letting his words sink in for the jury. "When the media latched on to that story, other people, members of the community, saw an opportunity. An opportunity to profit." He went on to explain that Shannon had decided to leave his client and had poisoned Sherrie and Shaelynn against him. The non-family victims had come forward merely for the chance to recover civilly from Andersen's substantial fortune. Never mind the fact that no civil suits were pending.

His opening was compelling and persuasive, without crossing the line into argument. A jury could easily be swayed by him. But Mack was reminded of an old prosecutor's adage: "When you have the facts, argue the facts. When you have the law, argue the law. When you don't have either, attack the victim."

Although Miller was seemingly sympathetic to Schyanne and her attempts to get away from her "disciplinarian" father, as well as to the other minor victims, who were being manipulated by their parents, the message was clear. It was encouraging that he was resorting to attacks on the victims this early in the game, because it indicated that he thought he didn't have the facts or the law. Mack didn't think he did either.

"Lastly," he said, after going through all the "holes" in the State's case, "let's talk about Shannon Andersen. You'll hear from Shannon, and I want you to think about some things that Shannon will say when she testifies. First, she'll say that she has been diagnosed with schizoid and dependent personality disorders. Schizoid! Like schizophrenic! Second, she'll say that she knew this abuse was going on and did nothing to stop it. And third, she'll say that she was charged with Child Abuse for failing to protect her children, and she cut a deal with the State to testify against her husband in exchange for a lesser punishment. So when you hear from Shannon, you can compare the testimony of a mentally ill woman who is manipulating her children against their father, against the testimony of Steve"— he held a hand out toward his client, dressed impeccably in a gray suit with a light blue shirt and a dark blue tie—"whose only mistake was wanting to raise his children to be polite, respectful members of society."

Andersen lowered his head and shot a bashful smile at the jury. Mack rolled her eyes.

"At the close of evidence," Miller said, "you will be asked to make a decision. Did the State meet its burden? Did it prove its case beyond a reasonable doubt? When you find that they did not, we will ask you to find Steve Andersen innocent of all these charges. Thank you."

Mack turned around and saw the reporters hunched over laptops and handheld devices. Jeannie was whispering into a pocket tape recorder. Mack wondered idly if they would make the noon news, or if it would wait until evening. As Judge Donoghue announced the lunch break, she knew they were about to find out.

CHAPTER THIRTY-ONE

The whole team gathered in the conference room. Anna had ordered in sandwiches and salads, which Jess and Mack picked at restlessly. Dave turned on the TV and flipped through the network and cable news stations until he found footage from the trial. They listened to two studio commentators debating whose opening statement was more effective until Mack grew frustrated and turned it off.

James and Dave were talking about the likelihood of the Diamondbacks having a winning season when Mack's phone buzzed. The screen showed "No Caller ID," and Mack assumed it was Officer Richardson calling to say he couldn't make it in to testify that afternoon.

"Mackenzie." She swallowed the last bit of cucumber left in her mouth.

There was no response.

"Hello?"

Mack could hear the person on the other end breathing, and there was a scraping noise, like metal on wood.

"Hello? Is anyone there?"

Conversation in the room died down and four sets of eyes were on Mack. She waited a few more seconds before hanging up and going back to her salad.

"Who was that?" Anna asked.

"Wrong number, I think," Mack said, putting the lid back on the plastic bowl and preparing to throw the remainder away.

"Was it the same guy who's been causing all the trouble?" James asked.

"How would I know?" Mack snapped. She exhaled heavily. "Sorry. I don't know who it was. I have a terrible headache all of a sudden. Excuse me."

Mack left the conference room and threw her trash away on the way to her office. She closed the door behind her and collapsed into her chair, glad that the overhead light had not come on. She found a bottle of expired migraine pills in her desk drawer and took two, hoping that ten minutes in the cool darkness would be enough time for them to kick in before court. She was extraordinarily grateful that Jess would be handling the first witness.

A gentle knock at the door several minutes later pulled her from a daydream that involved a deserted beach with no cell phone but plenty of cold beer.

"Yeah," Mack said.

The door opened, revealing Anna.

Mack groaned. "Can you just give me like"—she looked at her watch and closed her eyes again—"seven more minutes? Then you can yell at me all you want."

The door closed quietly and Mack sighed. She wondered if she could relax again in the time she had left.

"I don't want to yell at you," Anna said.

Mack jumped, startled. She opened her eyes to see Anna sitting in the chair facing her desk, chewing her left thumbnail.

"Sorry," she said.

"Quit chewing your nail," Mack said. Anna blushed and put her hand in her lap. "You can stay, but you have to be quiet. I don't want to talk about it."

She nodded. Mack leaned back in her chair and tried very hard to make her jaw unclench. She didn't want Anna to know how much the call had scared her, and felt foolish for being so impacted by a stupid crank call. She'd spent seven years clawing her way up the ladder and fighting for the respect she knew she deserved as a fearless defender of truth, justice, and the American way. She simply couldn't afford to show any weakness, regardless of how frightened she was.

Silent minutes passed, interrupted only by the occasional buzz of one of the four cell phones they had between the two of them. Finally, the door opened without a warning knock.

"Yikes," Jess said, seeing them sitting in the dark, and backing quickly out of the room. "I'm *so* sorry."

"It's fine," Mack said, sitting up and stretching her arms over her head. She yawned. "You can see we're ten feet apart, right?"

Anna blushed. She picked at the cuticle she had been biting earlier.

"We should head back," Jess said.

Mack nodded and stood up, still yawning. "Ready for Richardson?"

"Oh, yeah," she said. "We went through his testimony last night. He should be fine."

Mack grabbed her jacket and followed Jess. As she passed Anna, she grabbed Mack's hand and squeezed, gently.

"I'm just worried about you," she said quietly.

Mack squeezed back. "I'm worried about me, too," she said before cracking a joke. "I'm much too pretty to be turned into a girl suit made of real girl."

Anna grimaced and Jess laughed. They shared a sick sense of humor—along with most of their colleagues—and both listed *The Silence of the Lambs* as their favorite movie.

"You two are ghouls," Anna said, standing up in answer to Mack tugging on her hand.

Jess did really well with Officer Richardson, and Mack admired, not for the first time, her ability to make direct examination more than the stereotypical "What did you do next?" on which so many prosecutors rely. She moved around the courtroom, which Mack usually found distracting, but Jess made seem natural. It gave the jury something to watch.

Mack could tell that she had prepared the officer really well, since she was able to keep him in the present tense during his entire testimony. Rather than describing what had happened that night that he contacted Schyanne, he described what was happening, minute by minute, as he arrived on scene. It was an incredibly effective way to start the trial, very exciting for the jury, and Mack especially liked the way she integrated photos of Schyanne taken that night showing her malnourished frame and her disheveled appearance. Those images would stay with the jury overnight, and the healthy, clean Schyanne they would meet in the morning would be a nice contrast.

Miller let Grant handle cross, presumably because there wasn't much to do. Richardson hadn't interviewed Schyanne. She had screamed when he approached and wouldn't talk. Grant made the points he could: that Richardson assumed she had been attacked by a stranger, that he didn't canvas the neighborhood where she was found, even though it turned out she was just three miles from home. Jess cleaned it up on redirect, although neither she nor Mack felt like Grant's points got him anywhere. The jurors had no questions for Richardson, and he was released with enough time to start Dr. Flores before the afternoon break.

Mack liked working with Flores for the same reason she liked working with Anna: he did most of the work. When Mack did her first trial with him, three months after joining the sex-crimes unit, she called him to discuss his testimony. "I have one piece of advice for you," he'd said in lightly accented English: "*Listen.*" He'd gone on to say that he had worked with too many prosecutors who were so tied up in their outlines and their scripts, that they didn't take the time to listen to his responses. "If you just listen," he'd said, "you'll find that I answer lots of questions at one time, and if you're glued to that script, I wind up repeating myself."

Mack took his words to heart. She had done almost a dozen trials with him and had never once made a script. She learned the material and the research and made a list of specific topics she wanted to be sure to cover with him but didn't tie herself to a set list of questions. That way, direct examination more closely resembled a conversation, which kept the jury engaged and—Mack always hoped—learning.

After going through his training, experience, and research, Mack introduced the material that was the heart of Flores' testimony.

"Do you know anything about the case you're here for today?" Mack asked.

"No," he said, smiling.

"Have you read the police reports or listened to any interviews?"

"No," he said again.

"Do you know how many victims there are, or what the charged crimes are?"

"I have no knowledge of anything pertaining to this case," he said.

"Well then, Doctor," Mack said, pausing to take a sip of water, "why *are* you here today?"

He waited while the jury chuckled—the jury always chuckled at that question.

"I'm here to explain generally how child sexual abuse victims behave, and to help the jury understand some common behaviors and behavioral patterns that occur related to victimization."

They talked about the five-step cycle of victimization, including how perpetrators select and groom their victims. They talked about concealment techniques, and how powerful it can be for perpetrators to make victims feel complicit in their own abuse. "A feeling of shared responsibility," Flores said, "can be a very compelling motivator." They discussed delayed disclosure, and the different ways that disclosures can occur when they do. They covered dissociation, and how the body and mind use it as a coping mechanism during traumatic incidents. "In the context of fight, flight, or freeze, dissociation is the brain's version of flight," he said. They also covered post-traumatic muteness, a topic on which neither one had much experience but which was necessary given that it had afflicted Schyanne.

They also spent considerable time preempting some of the arguments Mack knew the defense expert, Scott Stanley, with a master's degree in family counseling, would make. Flores testified that the research says not every victim exhibits behavioral changes, for example, so when Stanley testified that a lack of behavioral changes indicated an absence of victimization, the jury would be primed to disbelieve him. After ninety minutes, Mack felt like the jury knew enough to be ready to hear Schyanne's testimony without automatically rejecting it.

As expected, Miller handled cross. When Mack and Flores had met to prepare his testimony, Flores said that he had done trials with Miller both when he was a prosecutor and when he switched to defense. Based on that experience, Miller presumably knew better than to try to outsmart Flores. He did a competent, if unexciting, job of gaining the concessions that defense attorneys can always gain from so-called blind experts who don't know the facts of a particular case. No, Flores had no knowledge of whether the allegations in this case were true or not. No, it's impossible to use common behaviors as a diagnostic tool to say whether abuse did or did not occur. Yes, the second-highest incidence rate of malicious false allegations *is* in cases where teenage girls derive secondary gain from the allegations. Yes, getting away from an overly strict parent would be considered secondary gain.

There wasn't much for Mack to clean up on redirect. She just had to trust that the jurors would think back to Flores' testimony when they heard from the victims.

So ended the first day of the Andersen trial. They left the courtroom, weary but pleased with how it had gone and headed back to the office to make final preparations for the next day. Mack and Jess kept their heads down and dodged questions from Jeannie and the pack of reporters that followed in her wake. A woman asked Mack for an autograph, which made her laugh. She politely declined. They all had enough to worry about without her getting fired for improper behavior in a public forum during the first week of a five-month trial.

CHAPTER THIRTY-TWO

Mack met Schyanne and Emma, her foster mom, in the courtroom early the next morning to give Schyanne a chance to acclimate before the room was full of jurors, staff, and media—and before she had to face her father. Schyanne was obviously uncomfortable in blue capris, a pearl necklace, and a white cardigan. She looked like a little kid playing dress-up in her mother's clothes.

"Hi, Mack," she said, sounding glum.

"Hey, kiddo, how are you feeling?"

She shrugged. "Fine, I guess. I wish I didn't have to do this, though."

"I know," Mack said. "Let's get you your tour, okay?"

Mack showed her the witness stand, the tables where the attorneys sit, the jury box, and the bench. They were early enough that they even took a gamble and let her sit in the judge's chair. She saw the display gavel and picked it up.

"Order in the court!" she said, lightly tapping the bench.

While Schyanne sat in the witness chair, Mack put her through a little bit of last-minute preparation. She did a brief direct examination, focusing on the same kind of "getting to know you" questions she would use while the girl was testifying. Jess came in and volunteered to do cross. She did a good job of being tough but pleasant. Schyanne bore up admirably under the pressure.

"If you can take that," Jess said, "you can take anything."

"Can I meet the other lawyer before I testify?" Schyanne asked.

"If he gets here in time," Mack said, hoping Miller would arrive early enough to make that happen.

They got Schyanne and Emma set up in the attorney room, and Jess and Dave went to get coffee. Alone in the courtroom, Mack sat reviewing her notes on Schyanne's testimony—the crimes she had disclosed and the topics Mack wanted to make sure she addressed with her. The door to the courtroom creaked and Mack turned around. She didn't see anyone. The door was closed. All the same, her heart started beating faster and she grabbed a pen, hopeful it would be enough if she needed to defend herself. The door creaked again, and slowly began to open. Mack stood, tense and ready for action. Her vision tunneled down until she could only see the gap between the double doors.

"Mackenzie?" she heard from behind her, and she jumped, involuntarily screaming. She raised the pen to eye level, ready to bring it down into her attacker's windpipe.

Mack whipped around, in the direction of Judge Donoghue's chambers, and saw Robert Miller, carrying his briefcase and a coffee. He was staring at her with a very concerned expression. Dropping the pen, she collapsed into her chair.

"Professor Miller," she sighed, reverting to old habits in her relief. "Sorry about that."

"Mackenzie's been under some stress," Jess said, pushing through the double doors from the hallway and coming into the courtroom with Dave. "It's nothing personal, Robert." She handed Mack a coffee. "And this is why you get decaf."

Mack glared at her but accepted it without protest.

Miller didn't say anything else, just walked to his table and started unpacking his bag.

"Oh," Mack said, remembering, "Professor Miller, Schyanne would like to meet you, if that's okay. I assume you'll be the one doing cross."

He looked at Mack blankly for a moment.

"Sure," he said. "Any time."

Mack went to the attorney room and ushered Schyanne into the courtroom. "Come meet my friend Robert," she said.

"Hi, Schyanne," Miller said, offering to shake her hand. He didn't appear offended when she didn't move. "It's nice to meet you."

Schyanne looked at him intently. "You're his lawyer?" she asked.

"Yes," he said, "I represent your father."

Schyanne shuddered. "Don't call him that," she said softly.

"Any other questions for Robert?" Mack asked quickly before Miller could respond.

The girl shook her head. "Can I go back to the other room now?"

Mack showed her out and crossed paths with Jeannie Bea, laden with bags and accompanied by an eager-looking young man.

"Is this one of the Andersen girls? Can we get a statement?" she asked Mack in her syrupy drawl, before dropping into a crouch and addressing Schyanne directly. "Hi, sweetie," she said, "my name is Jeannie. What's yours?"

Schyanne looked away and they continued out of the room. When they got to the attorney room, she hugged Emma tightly.

"Do I really have to do this?" she asked.

Mack didn't answer, and they sat quietly until Jess came to get them.

When Schyanne took the stand, Mack watched her purposefully avoid looking in the direction of her father. Mack had told her that she would have to look at him once, to identify him, but that other than that she could just look straight ahead or at her foster mom, who sat in the front row on the prosecution side. Even though she had gained weight—and gone through a growth spurt—she looked very young and incredibly vulnerable sitting in a witness chair built to accommodate even the largest cops. She pulled the cuffs of her sweater down over her hands and nervously picked at the knee of her pants.

When Mack joined the sex-crimes unit, she had attended the same forensic interview training as law enforcement, and she called upon that training every time she put a child on the stand. Whenever possible, she tried to use open-ended questions that invite a narrative, rather than a yes or no answer. This elicited the most accurate information and provided the jury with a sample of what questioning a child *should* look like. Then, when the defense attorney got up and asked leading questions, or closed-choice questions, he looked like a jerk.

Mack started with rapport building, where she had Schyanne talk about school and piano lessons. This gave the jury a sense of her language skills and gave her the chance to get comfortable and settle into the routine of answering questions.

"Schyanne, do you know why you're here today?" Mack asked, when she was ready to transition into the meat of the girl's testimony.

She nodded.

"Remember, Schyanne, you need to answer out loud for the court reporter, okay?" Mack said.

The girl blushed. "Oh, right," she said. "I'm here because of him." She nodded in Andersen's direction.

"Who's 'him'?" Mack asked.

"Steve Andersen," she said.

"Okay," Mack said, surprised by her use of his full name. "And did you used to call him by a different name?"

"I used to call him Dad," she said quietly.

Mack almost applauded. She couldn't have answered better if they had rehearsed it.

After introducing the family members, which they did with the help of a family tree Mack projected onto screens for the jury, they walked through the details of the abuse. With a copy of the indictment in front of her, Mack checked off charged counts as Schyanne described them.

Jess and Mack had decided not to introduce the photos through Schyanne, even though she described them being taken.

This decision was both strategic and emotional. The computer forensics officer wasn't scheduled to testify until June, and Jess thought showing the pictures for the first time then would serve as a powerful reminder of Schyanne's testimony for the jury. More importantly, they didn't want to force Schyanne to look at pictures of her abuse in front of a group of strangers—and her abuser.

CHAPTER THIRTY-THREE

"Did the defendant ever talk to you about religion?" Mack asked, first thing after lunch. Since Schyanne had told the jury that bacon cheeseburgers were her favorite food, they had taken her to the burger place around the corner. Unfortunately, she had been so nervous about having to testify again that afternoon that she'd barely picked at her food and had thrown up in the restroom before they went back to court. Mack hadn't even tried to eat, knowing that she wouldn't be able to stomach the grease, but she did steal a few of Jess' fries and drank enough caffeinated soda to float through the afternoon.

Schyanne nodded.

"Is that a yes?" Mack asked, for the court reporter.

She smiled. "Yes," she said.

"What did he say?" Mack had practiced this question with Schyanne, and the teen knew she wasn't talking about going to church or praying before meals.

"He said God gave him a mission."

"And what was the mission?" Mack asked.

Schyanne looked down. "God told him to marry me and my sisters."

Mack took a sip of water.

"I'm sorry," Schyanne said without prompting, "there was more to it than that, but I don't really remember the rest. He would give these lectures to me and Sherrie and Shaelynn where we would have to kneel on the basement floor, but I would play the waiting games so I don't know everything he said. They might be able to tell you, though."

As it happened, "the waiting games" were next on Mack's list of topics, so she accepted the transition without trying to redirect Schyanne. Between the testimony of the other girls, Shannon, and the LDS expert who was flying in from Salt Lake in July, Mack thought even that brief account from Schyanne was enough for just then. It got the jury's attention, which was all she really needed.

"Tell the jury about the waiting games," she said.

Schyanne turned to the jury, and Mack laughed internally. Clearly, the kid had watched some court shows on television to prepare for her testimony.

"When he would do things," she said, "like lecture or hit me or the other stuff, I would play games inside my head."

"What kind of games would you play?" Mack asked.

"Well," she said, methodically folding and unfolding the tissue in her hands, "the basement ceiling has these holes in it, and so, if I could see the ceiling, I would play Count the Holes."

Mack made a note to make sure to show the jury photos of the ceiling when Dave testified and remind them of the game.

"What other games would you play?"

Schyanne shifted in her seat, and Mack couldn't tell if she was uncomfortable or just tired. "Umm, sometimes I tried to count the number of hairs on his head," she said. "And sometimes I pretended I was a princess and he was a dragon. And I played other games, too, but I can't think of any."

"How did you learn these games, Schyanne?"

She shrugged. "I didn't learn them, I just started playing them. Sometimes, I would do my multiplication tables, and those I learned in school, but otherwise…"

She talked about her other coping mechanisms, like dissociation—floating outside her body or pretending to be asleep. Out of the corner of her eye, Mack saw some of the jurors nodding as they went through topics that had been covered by Dr. Flores the day before.

"Let's talk about the night you left," Mack said.

Schyanne exhaled shakily. "I just couldn't take any more. I'd been planning to leave for weeks, but I hadn't actually gone through with it until that night. I snuck out the basement window when everyone was asleep. My plan was to go to my friend Hannah's house, but when I got out, I couldn't find it. I walked for a long time, and then I wound up at the Circle K."

"What happened that night in particular to give you the courage to leave?" They had gone through this part in trial prep, but Mack knew it was hard for her to talk about.

"It was Family Home Evening," she said, taking a deep breath, "which is this thing, in the church, that we do on Monday nights. The whole family is supposed to spend the evening together. That's when he would take one of us down to the basement for extra spiritual counseling. That night it was my turn, but he never came back down. I waited for him, because I wasn't allowed to go back upstairs, but when he never came, I decided maybe it was time to go."

"Now, Schyanne," Mack said, "the jury has heard that when you got to the Circle K, and for weeks afterward, you couldn't talk to anyone. Can you tell them about that?"

She took a long drink from the cup of water Mack had poured her when she took the stand.

"I wanted to tell Nicole that first night, but I couldn't. It's like, I would open my mouth, and I would think the words, but I couldn't make them come out. I think I was trying to tell through the drawings, but I wasn't sure if anyone understood."

"How long did you feel like you couldn't make the words come out?" Mack asked.

"A while," she said. "After a few weeks, I could say one or two words at a time, but I still couldn't talk about what happened.

Then, all at once, when I talked to Nicole the second time, I could suddenly get the words out."

They talked in more depth about her escape—having to leave without clothes or shoes, since she wasn't allowed either in the basement—and what it was like going back to her parents after she thought she'd been saved.

"Going back was the worst thing that ever happened," she said.

"Why's that?" Mack asked, genuinely curious. They hadn't covered this before.

"It felt like such a...betrayal," she said. "Even though he never touched me after that. I was finally safe, and then you guys"—she nodded at Dave and Mack—"you guys just gave me back to him."

Mack's eyes blurred with tears as she looked at her legal pad, and she blinked until they cleared. She couldn't think of any place to go from there.

"No further questions," she said quietly, smiling sadly at Schyanne before she sat down.

Mack wasn't sure how far Miller would go with Schyanne. Some defense attorneys, if the defense is "she's lying," would really push a kid to admit inconsistencies. They would try to demonstrate that the victim couldn't keep her stories straight. That approach rarely worked. Others, operating with the same defense, were very nice to the kid and then ripped the mom to shreds. That approach worked much more often, since generally the moms in these kinds of cases start out unsympathetic and get worse the longer they testify. Mack hoped, for Schyanne's sake, that Miller would choose the latter tactic.

In fact, he took a hybrid approach that Mack and Jess didn't totally understand. He started by pushing Schyanne on her failure to disclose the abuse earlier, which was to be expected.

"You had friends, right?" he asked.

"Not the kind of friends I could tell about this," she said.

"But you had friends. You told Ms. Wilson you were trying to go to your friend Hannah's house the night you left."

"Yeah, I was. I knew Hannah from seminary."

"Well," he said, stretching the word out and leaning casually on the podium, "what would you have told Hannah or her parents if you'd gotten to her house?"

"I don't know," she said. "I hadn't thought that far ahead."

He switched topics abruptly. "What about teachers?" he asked. "No teachers you trusted?"

Schyanne shook her head.

"Is that a no?" he asked.

"No," she said.

He asked her about consensual sexual partners, which she denied, but Miller wouldn't let it go. Mack wondered if Andersen had fed him some line about a boy. She made a note to let Schyanne explain *why* she hadn't had any boyfriends on redirect, since she already knew the answer: none of the Andersen girls were allowed to speak to boys outside the family. Miller then challenged specifics regarding the abuse—how, for example, did she cover the bruises that must have resulted?

"I only owned long-sleeved shirts and long skirts," she said. "No one ever saw anything."

The search team had taken photos of Schyanne's closet and dresser, and Mack added checking whether any short-sleeved shirts or shorts were visible to her list of follow up. If nothing in the pictures contradicted Schyanne, Mack would add the photos to the stack that she planned to go through with Dave.

"How's your relationship with your mom?" Miller asked, changing topics yet again.

Schyanne looked down at her hands, still clutching the tissue she'd been holding since lunch. Her shoulders started to shake gently. Luckily, Judge Donoghue noticed.

"Let's take our afternoon break," he said, smiling kindly at Schyanne.

"No," she said, "I'm okay. Please—I just want to get this over with."

"Okay," Judge Donoghue said, "but if you change your mind, just let us all know."

Schyanne squared her shoulders and looked at Miller. "She never liked me. We never really had a relationship."

"Was she abusive as well?" he asked.

She shook her head. "It wasn't the same. She would hit me sometimes, but mostly she just wouldn't feed me. I was always *so* hungry."

"So you wanted to get away from her as much as your father?" he asked, and Schyanne flinched at the words.

"No," she said, "not nearly as much. If it was just that, I would have been okay. It was the stuff he did that was the worst."

That appeared to stump Miller, and he moved on to the religious elements of the abuse. After establishing that Schyanne attended seminary every weekday and church on Sundays, and went to the temple for certain ceremonies, he asked the question toward which he was clearly building. "Did you believe your father when he told you about God's message?"

"Of course," she said. "He started telling me he was going to marry me when I was five. I knew that before I knew anything about church." Mack hadn't known that, had thought he'd told her at eight, but the fact that he'd groomed her for three years strengthened the argument about why she waited so long to disclose. "I thought everything was normal until I was thirteen."

Miller was smart enough not to follow up on that, but Mack wondered what had happened when she was thirteen that told her what was going on was not normal. Miller returned to counsel table and spoke in a whisper with Grant and Andersen. He was shaking his head in response to something Andersen was saying, but Mack wouldn't find out what it was, because Miller told Judge Donoghue he was done and sat back down.

"Let's take a break," the judge said, looking at Mack.

"Sure, Judge," she said.

After ten minutes, the jury and Schyanne were back in their seats. Miller hadn't done all that much damage yet—that would come when Shannon testified a month later. Jess had suggested calling Shannon after all the victims had testified, so that when she told the jury about the prophecy they would already be familiar with the basics. Nick Diaz was also hopeful that the additional time on her medications might lend Shannon some credibility she would otherwise lack. He was very aware that, if she fell short on her end of the deal and lied on the stand, she was looking at prison time.

"When the defendant talked about what God told him to do," Mack said, approaching the podium and smiling at Schyanne, "did he say anything about whether you were allowed to tell other people?"

"He always said not to tell," Schyanne said. She sounded exhausted, which made sense after almost seven hours testifying.

"Did he say why?" Mack asked.

"He said people wouldn't understand, and the government would get him in trouble."

"Did he say anything else?"

"He said we'd get kicked out of our church for revealing that they were on the wrong path."

"Did you believe him?" Mack asked.

"Absolutely."

"And why was that?"

Schyanne looked at Andersen. "Well, he was—he was my father."

They quickly went the timeline of the abuse. In one sense, Miller had done exactly what they expected him to do—he'd asked leading questions and confused some of the details. It was Mack's job, using narrative-inviting, open-ended questions, to clear up what he had muddied. Mack subtly checked her watch. They were fast approaching 4:30 p.m., when they would finish for the day, and Mack wanted to make sure that Schyanne didn't have to come back.

The jurors had no questions for Schyanne, and Mack wasn't sure if that was good or bad. Based on their questions she could usually get a sense of what they did or did not believe. Asking none usually meant that they either totally believed—or totally disbelieved—the witness, but it was never possible to know which. Given that jurors were nodding for her and Miller pretty equally, Mack really couldn't tell where they stood.

Schyanne pushed past Mack and Emma and bolted from the courtroom. They followed, anxious to keep Jeannie and the rest of the media jackals from intercepting her, and watched as she raced into the restroom. As Mack pushed the door open, they heard her retching.

Mack sighed. "She did a great job," she said quietly to her foster mom. "She was incredibly brave to do what she just did."

Emma nodded, her face tight. "At what cost?" she asked.

Mack had no answer.

CHAPTER THIRTY-FOUR

They were in trial on Andersen seventeen days in the month of May. Mack was drowning—she couldn't keep up with the rest of her caseload, even with all the evening and weekend hours she put in. She barely had time to work the case that was going to trial right after Andersen, let alone read three new reports discussing three new home invasions. There were now a total of twelve, and the police were no closer to solving them than they had been after the first.

Jess' cases were also suffering, and she was putting in just as much time as Mack. Saturday dinner at the Thai restaurant down the street from the office, followed by a drink or two at the bar next door, became a pleasant end to a new unpleasant weekly ritual. James did what he could, reassigning five of Mack's cases (leaving forty-six) and six of Jess' (leaving forty-seven).

It was the second Sunday in June, and Mack and Jess were at the office sharing green curry leftovers and preparing for Shannon Andersen's testimony the following morning. They had met with her and Nick Diaz twice more, once on a Friday and once on a Saturday. Each time, Shannon gave them more information about Andersen's perverted take on Mormonism, and Mack finally felt like she had a good handle on it.

In the meantime, they got Sherrie, Shaelynn, and the other eight victims on and off the stand, as well as the Andersens' middle son, Seth, forensic nurse examiner Lindsay Evans, and the crime-lab scientists who testified regarding the DNA evidence.

Miller had gotten in some good points, especially with the three victims who had turned eighteen since Andersen had abused them. He'd even gotten one to admit that she was planning a civil suit—which came as news to Mack and Jess. All in all, they were still cautiously optimistic. He may have been able to attack the motives of the victims and the delays in their disclosures, but he couldn't overcome the enormous hurdle of eleven girls, none of whom had discussed their experiences with any of the others, all of whom disclosed similar abuse at the hands of his client. Most damaging to Andersen, they had all testified regarding the prophecy.

Mack and Jess were getting through their case-in-chief, their first and primary opportunity to present witnesses to the jury, faster than they anticipated, and expected to rest in June. That would necessitate some fancy footwork, since their expert on Mormon theology, Professor Brigham Kimball—a professor at Brigham Young University who James had known for over twenty years—wasn't scheduled to fly in until after the week-long break for the Fourth of July. Luckily, he was flexible and willing to come early as a favor to James.

By 8:30 p.m., they were done preparing for Shannon and Mack was ready to go home and try to sleep. She had started using self-tanning lotions on a weekly basis to try to cover how pale she was, and she was due for a touch up before getting back in front of the cameras the next morning. She knew that Jeannie and the rest of the media, who had let up somewhat during the previous week of police witnesses, would be back in full force. Everyone expected Shannon to be the most interesting witness of the trial, unless Andersen himself decided to testify.

Mack was back at her desk by 7:15 the next morning, looking tan and more energetic than she felt. She wore her Monday trial suit, which she was sure the jury would recognize, but there was nothing to be done about it—they'd recognize any of her other suits, too. She kept meaning to buy a few more to throw into the rotation, but between her hatred of shopping and her lack of free time, this remained an idle goal.

Her mom had called the week before, asking if Mack needed her to come out and fill her freezer with easy meals. "You look so thin on the TV, Mackenzie," she said. She was the only person who really knew Mack and still called her Mackenzie. Coming from her, Mack accepted it without protest. Her dad, on the rare occasion that she talked to him, called her Knife. He loved that Bobby Darin song and had called her Mackie as a little kid. It evolved to Knife when Mack was fifteen and told him she didn't want to spend weekends at his house anymore.

"I'll even do something about your hair," her mom had said in her flat Midwestern accent.

"My hair's fine, mom," Mack said. "It looks better in person. The TV cameras wash me out. That's why I've been using the self-tanner."

Really, Mack didn't want her to visit because she would feel obliged to spend time with her, and time with her was time away from the trial—just as time grocery shopping, or sleeping, or hiking would be, if she had bothered to do any of those things since April.

Jess was already in her office, fixing her makeup in the mirror next to her door, when Mack walked in.

"You couldn't sleep?" Mack asked.

Jess yawned in lieu of answering. "You eat?" she asked.

"I haven't been to the bagel shop since the thing with Allen, and there's no place else on the way."

"No food at your house, either, huh?" She put her mascara wand down on her desk and grabbed her polka-dot Kate Spade wallet.

"When we get through Shannon, I'll go to the store," Mack said, grabbing her own wallet and following Jess down the hall.

Another routine they had developed, this one almost daily, was to grab breakfast at the café in the basement—it was the only meal of the day they could usually manage to choke down.

Fortified with oatmeal and coffee, Mack was anxious to get started and paced the hallway outside the courtroom waiting for Shannon and Nick. Spencer had emailed her some notes on how to phrase questions for Shannon that would be sympathetic without appearing to indulge her delusional beliefs. Anna had sent several articles on dependent and schizoid personality disorders, as well as a piece on the psychology of physically abusive mothers in homes where sexual abuse is also going on. They were fascinating reading, and she picked up a few more tips on how to deal with Shannon on the stand.

Jeannie and the other reporters beat Nick and Shannon to court, and Jeannie tried, once again, to get a comment from Mack.

"Just a li'l sound bite," she wheedled. "Something for your fans."

Mack laughed. "I don't have fans, and I'm not giving you a sound bite."

"Oh, you do!" she exclaimed. "We get dozens of letters every day. My viewers just *love* you. We've even gotten some proposals!"

Mack shook her head and Jeannie relented, turning on one stiletto heel and heading into the courtroom.

"She's right, you know."

Mack turned around and saw Anna leaning against the wall in knee-high brown boots and a maroon sweaterdress.

"People do love you."

Mack blushed. "What's up, Doc?" she asked. "Don't you have patients today?"

"I do," she said, "but there's this big media trial that everyone is obsessed with, and I just happen to have an in with the prosecutor. So I canceled all my sessions."

"Oh?" Mack asked. "I've always wanted an adoring fan."

Anna walked over and hugged her, and Mack breathed deeply, enjoying the scent of Dolce & Gabbana Light Blue.

She sighed with relief. Any awkwardness that might have been lingering seemed to have passed. She was clearly forgiven for the lapse in communication over the previous six weeks.

"Plus," Anna said, stepping back and winking, "I hear there's a real whack job testifying today, and that's kind of my thing."

A man cleared his throat, and Mack looked over Anna's shoulder to see Nick and Shannon standing by the courtroom door. Mack blushed. She felt guilty that they had heard Anna's comment, and embarrassed, as if she'd been caught sneaking cookies. She stammered as she introduced Anna and Nick—she didn't bother to introduce Shannon. Shannon looked better than the last couple times Mack had seen her. Mack hoped that the medications were working well enough to get her through the next two days. She had regained a bit of the weight she'd lost, and her plain blue dress and black cardigan fit nicely. She'd cut her hair, and it looked like she'd refreshed the color. She was still pale but was wearing makeup and had recently had a manicure. She almost looked like the elegant Shannon Andersen Mack had first met in the lobby of the advocacy center five months earlier.

"Ready?" Mack asked.

She shook her head and shifted her weight nervously from one foot to the other. "As I'll ever be, I guess. I haven't seen him since—"

Mack didn't know what to say to that, and let it hang in the air for a moment before clearing her throat.

"Let's head in, then," she said, "and try to get you out of here as soon as possible."

The jurors shifted uncomfortably in their seats as Shannon approached the clerk and was sworn in. One woman, a stalwart LDS mom whose youngest son was on his mission, pursed her lips and shook her head as Shannon took the stand.

As she had done with Schyanne and each of the other civilian witnesses, Mack eased Shannon into the process of testifying by asking about her family and upbringing. This had a dual purpose with Shannon—it got her comfortable, but it also laid important groundwork from which Mack could argue her knowledge of the abuse and failure to act. She testified that she was raised in the Latter-day Saint community of Orem, Utah, by very strict parents and grandparents. Her dad died when she was sixteen, and both her parents had used corporal punishment to keep her and her three younger brothers in line.

"I just idolized my daddy," she said, in a Southern accent Mack hadn't noticed during any of their earlier conversations, "and I was devastated when he passed. I was very blessed to meet Steve soon after."

Shannon wasn't looking at Mack, and it took a moment for her to realize she was looking at her husband. She wasn't just *looking* at him, though, she was batting her eyelashes at him. Mack stepped to her right, blocking Shannon's view of Andersen, sure she must have misinterpreted what she was seeing. She hadn't. Shannon leaned to one side, trying to get him back in her sight. Mack was disgusted. Any sympathy she had felt for the other woman melted.

Moving on, Mack had her describe her relationship with Andersen. They married when she was just seventeen. He was twenty-one and newly returned from his mission. They moved to the Tucson area so he could work construction for an uncle. Their oldest son, Steve Jr., wasn't born for almost six years.

"I was pregnant once three years before Stevie," she said, "but I lost the baby. I didn't have faith in God's plan for my family, and I was punished." In all the hours of preparation, Shannon had never mentioned a miscarriage, or the idea that God had been personally involved in their lives before Sherrie turned eight. Mack wanted more information, even though it would require breaking one of the cardinal rules of trial: never ask a question to which you do not already know the answer.

"How do you know that's why you lost the baby?" Mack asked, mirroring the other woman's language back to her.

"Steve told me," she said.

"So your husband was already talking to God, even back when you were in your twenties?"

"Oh, yes," she said. "He has always had a very special relationship with the Almighty. It's one of the reasons I fell for him." She smiled, and Mack suddenly felt sick. Even after all she had seen in handling abuse cases, she couldn't believe Shannon was actually flirting with her scumbag husband as she testified against him.

"Why don't you tell us about the other times he's talked to God," Mack said, following her instincts that, even though she didn't know where this line of questioning would take them, the journey would wind up helping the case.

"Sometimes the messages were about the family, like that we needed to name each of the children starting with an S," she said, "or that we needed to move to Tucson, but sometimes they were much bigger than just our little family."

"What kind of message from God would count as a 'big' message?"

Shannon batted her eyelashes and smiled. "Well, God told Steve that he needed to run for the Board of Education to spread his message more widely."

"Okay," Mack said. She was not interested in Andersen's political career. "What else?"

Shannon chewed her lower lip and glanced at Mack before looking at her husband again. "And then there's obviously the one that caused all the trouble," she said.

Bingo.

Mack turned and winked at Jess. They were back on track, and Shannon looked like a credible witness, albeit a crazy person.

"Okay, tell us about that one."

Shannon sighed. "When Sherrie was eight, God told Steve that he was the one mighty and strong."

"Tell the jury what that means," Mack said, smiling.

"God told Joseph Smith, the founder of our church, that he would send 'the one mighty and strong' to set the church in order. Steve is that one."

"And what did he have to do to set the church in order?"

"Oh, he had to do many things," she said. "He had to become a member of the First Quorum of the Seventy, and so he had to become an apostle in the church. And he had to restore the doctrine of plural marriage."

"The doctrine of plural marriage?" Mack asked.

"Righteous men must marry multiple righteous women," she said, sounding like she was reciting something long memorized, "in order to repopulate the Earth with the righteous and to attain the highest level of the heavens. This practice was abandoned by the mainstream LDS church more than a hundred years ago, and that is when the church went astray. Steve's mission was to right the course of the church."

"And how was he supposed to do that?"

"He had to marry our daughters," she said. "He didn't want to do it! We both agonized over this task, but it was ordained by God."

"So you knew that he was engaging in sexual contact with your children?"

"Objection!" Miller said, standing. "Relevance."

"Judge," Mack said, turning to face the bench, "this directly goes to Defendant's ability to get access and maintain access to his victims. It goes to opportunity and helps explain why the girls did not disclose earlier."

Judge Donoghue considered the issue. Mack could tell he was in over his head, because he assumed his thinking face, which was well-known around the courthouse. He raised his chin and squinted into the distance.

"Overruled," he said. "Mrs. Andersen, you can answer."

"What was the question?" Shannon asked.

"Did you know that your husband was engaging in sexual contact with your daughters?"

"*No*," she said, scandalized. She actually covered her heart with her hand and sat back, her expression shocked. "Their wifely duties were not to start until they were sixteen. I do not believe that Steve engaged in contact with either Schyanne or Shaelynn. He merely offered them spiritual counseling to prepare them for their role in the rejuvenation of the church."

"Mrs. Andersen, are you aware of the allegations against your husband?"

"I am, and I don't believe any of them. The only one he had sexual contact with is Sherrie, and he assures me that she was sixteen when it began. Those other girls weren't even part of the prophecy."

Mack shook her head. There was nothing to be gained from pursuing that line of questioning any further, so she moved to Shannon's physical abuse of her daughters. Shannon described it for the jury in the same flat tone she had used during that first interview in the conference room. They covered the incidents her sons had described, which indicated she had knowledge of her husband's true activities. She flat-out denied that Sherrie had disclosed the abuse to her when she was twelve, and several jurors shook their heads at that. Finally, they discussed both her plea agreement—since Mack knew that Miller would bring it up on cross—and her mental-health issues. Her own description of her illnesses was understated, at best, but Jess was calling a psychologist the next day who would testify in depth about what behaviors are typical from individuals with dependent and schizoid personality disorders. That way, Mack would be able to argue a direct connection between Shannon's mental state and her failure to intervene during her closing.

Mack had no more questions, and Judge Donoghue decided to break early for lunch rather than let Miller begin his cross.

When they reconvened, the defense attorney started fast and fierce, without so much as an introduction. "In your direct testimony, you didn't say anything about employment. Is it fair to say that you are unemployed?"

"Yes."

"In fact, you haven't worked since you and Steve got married, have you?"

"That's right. My job was to stay home and raise the children."

"Ma'am," Miller said, raising a hand, "please only answer the question you've been asked. If I want an explanation, I'll ask for one."

She nodded, chastened.

"So Steve supported you completely, right?"

"Yes."

Mack knew where he was going with that line of questioning, and he confirmed it when he started asking about the quality of her marriage. Shannon had hinted on direct that, ever since Andersen had received his big revelation, their relationship had soured, but she maintained her tone of love and reverence throughout.

"So you were tired of being married to Steve, right?"

"No, that's not what—"

"Well, you couldn't get divorced, right? That would go against your faith?"

"We're not supposed to get divorced, that's right. But I didn't want to—"

"Mrs. Andersen, please just answer the questions," Miller interjected. Mack was grudgingly impressed with both the quality of his cross and his command of the jury. If they had had even a little sympathy for Shannon, this attack would have gone very badly for Miller. He had read them right, though, and they were enjoying watching him take her down.

"So you wanted out, and you didn't want to get divorced, but you did want his money, isn't that right?"

"No, I—"

It went on like that for over two hours. He attacked her motive for testifying, even though she had already told the jury on direct that she had received a favorable plea agreement. He attacked her ability as a parent, implying one minute that she knew what was happening and did nothing to stop it, and the next that she must have believed that nothing inappropriate was happening or she would have stopped it. He attacked her willingness to reunite the family when Schyanne was returned, since at that point she knew Schyanne had been sexually abused. He attacked her willingness to believe a prophecy that was so clearly contrary to her own interests. Mack was sure he was setting up an argument to the jury that she had made up the prophecy after the fact.

Unfortunately, there wasn't much Mack could do to rehabilitate her on redirect the next morning. Shannon clarified that she was living in a shelter and getting financial help from her sister's family. Mack took a gamble and had her testify that her parental rights had been severed with regards to all her minor children. Even if she did get money from Andersen, it wouldn't include child support.

"Do you remember some talk on cross about your relationship with Schyanne?" Mack asked, hoping she could get her to repeat something she had said as they prepared her testimony.

"Yes," she said.

"And do you remember your reaction when you found out you were pregnant with Schyanne?"

Shannon looked at her husband. His head was down, hands clasped on the table in front of him. Shannon pursed her lips. "When I found out I was pregnant, I was ecstatic." She turned to the jury and smiled. None of the jurors smiled back. "When the doctor told me it was another girl, I wept."

"Why were you upset to be having another daughter?" Mack asked.

"I knew he would marry her. I knew I would have to compete with her for Steve's attention in heaven."

Mack let that sit with the jury while she checked her notes.

"You've done all you can," Jess whispered. "Stop beating the poor dead horse."

Dave shook his head. He didn't have anything else, either. Mack gave up and told the judge she had no more questions.

The jury had plenty. Jess and Mack, standing next to Miller and Grant at the bench reviewing them, exchanged surreptitious smiles at how many of them were along the same lines: *How could you put your husband and his "revelation" above the safety of your children?* Although these questions were inappropriate, they meant that a good number of the jurors believed that the girls *had* been abused. One question, however, concerned Mack: *What would you have done if Schyanne had turned sixteen and the relationship with your husband had turned physical, instead of just being spiritual?* It meant that at least one juror appeared to believe Shannon's version of events.

"If even one of these idiots believes Shannon," Jess whispered as they returned to the prosecution table, "we're sunk."

Mack nodded. She was reassured that most of the jury seemed to be on their side, but Jess was right. It only took one rogue juror to hang the case, and she still had her doubts about Juror Three.

Judge Donoghue compromised and read the most innocuous of the bunch: "If you understood the message your husband received to mean that he would marry your daughters when they turned sixteen, why did you stay with him?"

"We were an important part of God's plan," she said. "To reach the highest level of the heavens, one must make sacrifices. So I did."

CHAPTER THIRTY-FIVE

Mack stopped at the grocery store on her way home, so she was loaded down with her briefcase, purse, and three heavy plastic bags as she climbed the stairs to her condo. Even though she parked only ten feet from the base of the stairs, she refused to take multiple trips. That would be a sign of weakness. She was fumbling through her purse for her keys when she noticed the door was wide open, revealing her fully lit living room. Mack dropped the groceries and ran back down the stairs, digging her phone out of her pocket. She skipped the non-emergency line this time and called 911. The dispatcher told her to get into her car and lock it until the police got there.

Mack's next call, placed once she was safely inside the Saab, was to Anna.

"He broke into my house," she said when Anna picked up.

"Who did?" she asked, her voice thick with sleep.

"Goddamn Santa Claus," Mack said. "I don't know who. Whoever's been screwing with my life the last three months."

Anna sighed. "I'm not your enemy, here, Mack."

"Sorry," Mack said. "I'm really freaked out. Can I come stay at your place?"

"Of course," she said. "Have you eaten?"

Mack remembered the dropped groceries and wondered if the eggs had survived the fall.

"No, but I can pick something up on the way. I can take care of myself, you don't have to go out of your way. Besides, I have to wait for the cops, so it'll be a while."

"You don't need to stop. It may not be safe anywhere out there. God knows what's going on, and I'm really worried for you." Anna yawned loudly. "Let me take care of you. I'll make you a sandwich or something. Do you want me to stay on the phone until the officers get there?"

"Please," Mack said. She felt very exposed, surrounded by glass and trapped in her car. She turned so she could see the stairs to her unit. They sat quietly, Mack listening to Anna's gentle, sleepy breathing, until she saw the flashing red and blue lights coming into the complex.

"The officers are here," Mack said. "Thanks for waiting with me."

"Mhmm, 'ny time. See soon?"

Mack waited until the officer was standing outside his car before unlocking her door and getting out.

"What's the problem tonight, Mackenzie? Or did you just miss me?"

It was Officer Carlson, the sweat on his forehead gleaming under the streetlight.

"Someone broke into my condo. I didn't go inside, so I don't know what—if any—damage was done."

He nodded. "Okay," he said. "Dispatch is insisting on sending another officer to meet me here, so we'll wait for her, even though there's nothing behind that door that I couldn't take care of for you. Once we see what's going on and secure the scene, we'll get the folks from the crime lab out to take prints and photos. You got somewhere safe to stay tonight or do you need a place?"

His smile sent shivers down Mack's spine.

"That's taken care of," she said. "Thank you."

"You cold?" he asked. "You're shaking." He moved toward her slightly, raised his arms in an offer of a hug.

"Nerves," she said, and held up a hand.

He nodded and put his hands in his pockets. "Nothing to be nervous about. I'll keep you safe."

Mack pulled out her phone and pretended to text.

They waited in silence until another police car pulled into the complex and parked behind Carlson. The officer was a short African-American woman Mack didn't know.

"Mackenzie Wilson," Mack said.

"Officer Bennet." She didn't bother with a handshake. "What's the story?" she asked Carlson.

"Ms. Wilson's going to get back in her car and lock the doors," he said, "and we're going to check out her apartment."

"It's a condo," Mack said, but they were already heading up the stairs. She locked herself back in the Saab and texted James on autopilot to let him know that, yet again, she was having contact with law enforcement that wasn't work-related. He responded immediately, asking if she was okay. *Everything's fine*, she replied, *but my condo was burglarized. Police here. Will be in tomorrow.*

A knock on the window made Mack jump. Carlson was peering in at her.

"Mackenzie," he said, and Mack rolled the window down to hear him better, "no one's inside, but whoever it was tossed the place. Bennet is calling the lab techs now. We're going to take you inside so you can get some panties and whatever else you need to be comfortable tonight, okay?"

Mack nodded and got out of the car.

"We're going to need your help identifying what was stolen, if anything *was* stolen," he said, following Mack up the stairs.

"Oh, shit," Mack said, when she stepped into the living room. Carlson hadn't just been using cop slang when he said the place had been tossed: the couch was slashed, the coffee table was overturned, and the television had been thrown to the ground. Mack wandered in shock with Officer Bennet behind her. The office was a mess, with books piled haphazardly on the rug. The bathroom and bedroom were even worse. All the drawers had been pulled out and their contents strewn across the floor.

She turned to Bennet, who was patiently waiting, hands on her belt.

"I have no idea if anything was stolen," Mack said. "It will take weeks to get this cleaned up."

Bennet gently put her hand on Mack's arm. "I'm sorry," she said. "No idea who might of done this? Ex-boyfriend? Anyone?"

Mack shook her head, frustrated. "Why is that everyone's first guess? My only ex-boyfriend is Danny Peters from seventh grade, and we ended things on good terms. I have no idea who's doing this."

Bennet dropped her hand, and Mack wondered if she had suddenly lost her sympathy.

"The lock wasn't forced," she said, "so it's someone who had access to your keys."

"I don't know," Mack said. "I'm sorry. I wish I could be more helpful."

"Most home burgs never get figured out," she said. "It's a real shame."

Mack laughed. "Don't I know it," she said.

She grabbed a suitcase and a garment bag from under the bed and began packing. She took enough suits to get through to the weekend, figuring she could come back Saturday or Sunday—with Anna as backup—and get the rest. She gathered pajamas, workout clothes, and underwear, and searched the bathroom floor for allergy pills, an inhaler, migraine and anti-anxiety meds. Jewelry and toiletries joined the pile in the suitcase, and Mack noticed something that was missing from the counter and wasn't in the mess on the floor.

"Officer?" Mack said, and Carlson appeared in the doorway. "There *is* something missing. An old picture of me and a friend. I kept it in a frame on my counter here. It was just about the only photo in the house." She left out that the picture was of her only serious ex-girlfriend, Christina, who had been kidnapped and murdered when she was in law school. It was because of her that Mack had become a prosecutor, and she kept the picture handy to remind her why she did what she did. Mack was deeply uneasy at the thought that whoever had invaded her home now had that memento.

"She as good looking as you?" Carlson asked, poking through Mack's open jewelry box.

Mack forced a smile. She felt sick.

The crime-scene technicians got there just as Mack finished packing, and so did the locksmith. After they dusted the existing lock and found no fingerprints, he took over. He knelt in front of it and looked at it briefly, getting fingerprint dust on his hands.

"This wasn't picked," he said, standing up and wiping his hands on his pants. "The officers are right. Whoever it was had a key. That's good news—it's easy to re-key a lock."

"How can you tell?" Mack asked.

He pointed at the lock, which looked totally normal.

"The plug is in the right place," he said.

Mack looked at him blankly.

"If the lock had been picked, the keyhole wouldn't be straight up an' down. It would be off-center."

"Oh," she said. "That actually makes sense in English."

"So I can go ahead and re-key the lock, but I recommend adding a second deadbolt as well. That's not something I can do tonight"—he took a business card out of his shirt pocket and handed it to Mack—"but call the store tomorrow and we can get you all squared away."

He went to work and Mack realized she knew exactly how someone could have gotten her key. On her patio was a large potted cactus, and she'd hidden a spare key inside a ceramic gnome when she had first moved in, scared she'd lock herself out while on a run. She turned the gnome over. No key. Mack rolled her eyes, frustrated that she'd been so stupid as to inadvertently let a dangerous stranger into her home. How many community outreach programs had she done, advising people not to use hide-a-keys? Physician heal thyself, indeed.

Mack returned inside, curious to see what the crime-scene techs were doing. They were both in the office, dusting hardcover books. Although she had handled a number of home-burglary cases professionally, she had never been unlucky enough to experience one personally.

"Anything?" Mack asked from the doorway.

The young woman looked up and shook her head. "He probably didn't take the gloves off when he came in."

Her male partner nodded. "This isn't likely to produce anything, but it's always worth a shot."

Mack turned around and wandered back out to the landing. The locksmith was done and handed her the new key.

"Make sure to keep this safe," he said. "Don't just give out copies to everyone."

Given her foolishness with her last key, Mack didn't protest. She put the spilled groceries away—throwing away the smashed eggs—righted one of the kitchen stools and sat waiting until the techs were done. She rubbed her temples and took off her glasses, hoping she could still fight the building headache. Mack pulled out her phone. A red badge on the Gmail icon showed that she had three new messages in her personal account. The first two, a Facebook notification that her mother had mentioned her name in a post and a LinkedIn request, she ignored. But the third was from an address she didn't recognize: TPDWatcher@gmail.com. The subject line read simply "Mackenzie," and the email was time stamped nearly an hour earlier.

Sorry I missed you tonite. I thought you mite be home when I stopped by. You've been working too hard! I've been keeping up with your latest adventures—you need to take better care of yourself. I'm sure we'll see each other soon, but until then thanks for the pic. Don't forget, I'm always watching.

The email ended with a smiley face icon.

Mack stared at her phone, trying to make sense of the message. Unfortunately, it didn't seem to contain any hints as to the identity of its author. She debated showing Carlson and Bennet, or sending it to James, but quickly decided against either option. She didn't need their interference. Carlson and Bennet would want to impound her phone, and James would insist on a security detail. Not to mention how Anna would react. Mack archived the message so that she could find it again and resolved not to mention it to anyone.

It was almost midnight by the time the final officer left. She was starving and eager to leave the ruined condo. She grabbed her bags, turned out the lights, and locked her door with its brand-new key.

Officer Carlson waited until Mack was on her way before he got in his patrol car. He pulled alongside her at the complex exit and signaled her to roll her window down.

"Hopefully this is the last time, huh?" he asked. "At least under these circumstances?"

Mack gave a weak smile.

"If you ever want a drink, just call," he said. "I know you know the number by now, and I make a mean mojito." He made a left turn out of the complex, speeding off in the direction of downtown.

Anna was asleep when Mack arrived, and it took three tries before she responded to the doorbell. She had a blanket wrapped around her shoulders and her hair was sticking out in all directions. She yawned as she invited Mack in and gestured at the turkey sandwich on her kitchen table.

"Eat," she said, and pulled a cold beer from the fridge. She sat in the chair next to Mack and tried to pat down her wild hair. "Eat, and then tell me what the hell happened *this* time."

CHAPTER THIRTY-SIX

An hour later, Mack had finished her story and her sandwich, along with two beers. Anna showed her to the guest bedroom without any conversation about where Mack would be sleeping, and made sure she had clean towels. She put a key on the dresser and told Mack to stay as long as she needed, which Mack appreciated, though her plan was to be out by the weekend. She didn't want to take advantage of Anna's hospitality, and she knew it would be too easy to just fall into living in Anna's guest room indefinitely. If Anna *was* seeing someone, Mack couldn't think of a worse way to find out than running into a stranger across the breakfast table, and if she wasn't, well, Mack didn't need any more complications right now.

As Anna explained how to make the television work, Mack emailed her real-estate agent and told her she needed to sell her condo, buy a new place, and find somewhere to stay in the interim—and she needed to do all that without leaving work from 7 a.m. to 7 p.m. Monday through Friday. She also emailed her mom, telling her the condo was being fumigated and she could be reached at Anna's. No need to worry her unnecessarily.

Anna rubbed Mack's shoulder as she listlessly played with the remote. "I'm right down the hall," she said.

Mack smiled wanly. "I know."

Anna hugged Mack, and Mack sagged against her.

"You're safe here," Anna said. "This house is basically a fortress."

"Thanks," Mack said, "but I still hope your armory is limited to flaming arrows."

"There is a loaded gun in literally every room."

Mack shuddered. "God bless America."

Mack took advantage of the soft Egyptian cotton and the spacious guest bathroom and took a shower. She stayed under the hot water long after she had rinsed Anna's expensive almond conditioner from her hair. Her eyes burned, her back hurt, and she found a long scrape on her left leg. She didn't know how it had gotten there, and it stung when the water hit it. She could feel the muscles in her shoulders relaxing and didn't notice that she was crying until her sobs echoed off the tile walls.

The next morning, Mack left before Anna went for her run. Even a restless few hours of sleep was better than she had gotten in weeks, but she was still achy and tired and took a second, even hotter, shower. She left a note thanking Anna and offering to pick up dinner that night. She had forgotten how quick the drive from Anna's house to the office was, arriving a full thirty minutes earlier than Jess.

After breakfast in the basement café, Jess retreated to her office to get ready for the day ahead.

Mack headed down the hall to James' office, ready to tell him the latest in the saga of her super-fan. She found him occupied, however, with Peter Campbell.

"Come on in, Ms. Wilson," Campbell said, and gestured at an empty chair. "James has been bringing me up to speed on the problems you've been facing."

Mack glared at James, and he raised his hands in protest.

"Police reports are public records!" he said. "Someone called Charlie and asked why the prosecutor on the Andersen case has had the cops at her apartment four times in as many months."

"It's a *condo*," Mack said, still glaring.

"Who is responsible?" Campbell asked. "Is it related to Andersen?"

"I have no idea," Mack said, rubbing her forehead in an attempt to soothe the headache that hadn't faded since the night before. "I just can't believe it would be Steve Jr. I know this is clichéd, but he seems like too nice a guy. I don't think there isn't really anyone else connected with Andersen who might have it in for me, unless it's some friend of his that I don't know about. I get security alerts when people I've convicted get out of prison, but there hasn't been anyone in months. I don't know anyone else who hates me enough to do this. And, really, there's nothing to suggest it's related to my work. Maybe I smiled at the wrong barista one morning. It could be totally unrelated."

Campbell rubbed his chin as he thought about that. "All the same," he said, "can't have the prosecutor on the biggest media case this side of Casey Anthony go missing or get herself killed."

Mack rolled her eyes, hoping he wouldn't notice. James coughed and raised his eyebrows in warning.

"Have you two discussed a security team?" Campbell asked. "It seems like it might be a good investment, at this point."

"We have," James said, looking at Mack, "but Mackenzie has consistently rejected my offers. At this point, Mack, are you having any second thoughts?"

Laughing, she shook her head. "Why would I? So the security guy could have caught the eggs when I dropped the groceries? They wouldn't have been guarding my place. It still would have been burglarized. There have been no actual threats to my person."

"All the same," Campbell said, "it's something to consider. You're right, though, if there's no relationship between these *incidents* and your employment, I can't force you to accept one."

Jess approached the door. She saw Campbell and stopped, looking horrified. She pointed to her watch.

"I will consider it, sir," Mack said, rising. "I have to get to court. James, I'll talk to you later."

As she and Jess walked to the courtroom, she checked her email. Her real-estate agent said she'd do what she could, but she would expect it to take at least six weeks before Mack could be in a new place. Since Mack couldn't afford two monthly mortgage payments, she said, she needed to get the condo under contract before she could get something new, and she wasn't sure anyone would jump on a place that had *just* been burglarized. Mack forwarded the email to Anna, apologizing and asking just how much she was willing to be inconvenienced.

The morning session was filled with Jess' presentation of the remaining three police officers, all of whom had played relatively minor roles, but were necessary to give the jury the full picture of the detailed investigation.

Mack did her best to pay attention and take notes, but she was finding it hard to stay awake. In an effort not to yawn, she flipped to the back of her legal pad and made a to-do list for moving out of the condo. That done, she spent an hour going over questions for the expert on the Mormon church, who was set to fly in on Sunday. She would pick him up from the airport and they would meet Jess at the office for a full two hours of prep before taking him out to dinner and dropping him at his hotel. Professor Brigham Kimball—the most stereotypical Mormon name Mack had ever heard—seemed both charming and incredibly bright on the phone, and Mack hoped that he would present the same way to a jury. He said that he had testified before, but never in a criminal case, and never outside of Utah.

"I'm gonna need you to focus a whole lot more on *me*," Jess said quietly, fixing the lapel of her navy linen jacket as the jury left the courtroom for the lunch break, "and a whole lot less on all the stuff that isn't me."

"Sorry," Mack said, "I'm just trying to get ready for Kimball."

They camped out in the attorney room over the break, since neither of them felt like eating or running the media gauntlet.

"So what'd Campbell want?" Jess asked, when they had both finished checking their email and phones.

Mack yawned. "He'd like me not to die during trial."

"That's *so* nice of him!" she said, cracking her gum. "I'm sure it's because he cares about you, and not because, the last time a prosecutor died during a big trial, the district attorney lost his job."

Mack tried to smile but couldn't quite pull it off. She called the locksmith and arranged for a second deadbolt to be installed on Saturday. She knew Anna would be free and would come with her. Her goal was to get everything moved into a storage unit over the Fourth of July weekend, but she wanted Anna to look around with her sooner than that and see if she could spot anything missing. While they were dating she had spent almost as much time there as Mack had. Besides, she was much better at noticing visual details than Mack, a fact she never failed to emphasize when Mack couldn't find something in the refrigerator unless it was at eye level.

"You're still not paying attention to me," Jess said, interrupting Mack's concentration.

"Sorry," she said, putting her list away. "I'm all yours."

"This is still your case, after all," Jess said. "I could walk at any time, Wilson."

"Sorry," Mack said again. "I know it's my case, and I really appreciate everything you're doing. I'm just exhausted."

"You staying with Anna?" Jess asked. Mack wasn't sure if she was imagining the disapproval in her voice.

"Yeah," Mack said. "She's one of my best friends, and I have to stay somewhere. I can't afford a hotel long-term, and let's be honest, *you* would kick me out after one night."

"Sure would." She pursed her lips and looked at the ceiling, but Mack knew the conversation wasn't over. "Do you know what you're doing?"

"I think so," Mack said. "We're not getting back together or anything. We've always been really good friends. You know that."

"Yeah," she said, and shook her head, "but I never got that, either. You so obviously want to date her, and she so obviously wants you to want to date her."

"That's not fair," Mack said. "First, I don't want to date her. I want to date someone tall and blond—"

"Someone who looks just like you, in other words?" Jess interrupted. "That's a level of narcissism I find surprising even from you."

"No, no, someone two to three inches taller than I am."

Jess rolled her eyes.

"Plus," Mack said, "I'm an ash blonde, and I want to date someone more of a honey blonde."

"I'm glad you're focusing on the important stuff," Jess said, "but, seriously, folks. I worry about you."

"You and everyone else lately," Mack snapped, "but I don't need anyone to worry about me. I'm fine. Everything is fine."

Jess stared at Mack for a long moment before looking at her watch. "Let's head back in."

Mack nodded and gathered her papers and phone.

"Wilson," Jess said, as Mack was opening the door. "Pay attention to me this afternoon."

"Aye, aye, sir." Mack saluted.

CHAPTER THIRTY-SEVEN

The rest of the week went smoothly, but Mack felt like she was treading water both in and out of trial. They called the computer forensics people, and Schyanne's teacher, and the seminary instructor, and the nurse who had examined Shaelynn, all necessary pieces of the puzzle, but Mack was bored. She was ready to call Dr. Kimball and Dave and call it a day. They still didn't know if Steve planned to testify, so she didn't know if trial would last another week and a half or a full month. That was the problem with long trials: after a month or so she was ready to move on and tired of the daily slog.

Saturday's adventure at the condo proved much less exciting than she feared. The locksmith came and went, and the door looked very impressive with its second deadbolt. She and Anna cleaned up what was broken beyond repair. Only twenty or so books, out of the hundreds lining the shelves in the office, had to be tossed. She was bummed about the couch, which she had owned since starting law school, but it couldn't be salvaged. They couldn't get it out by themselves, though, so it had to wait for the movers. The real-estate agent sent her a few listings, but none of them seemed right. They were all in the wrong part of town, or too big, or didn't have a big enough kitchen.

"Maybe you're being too picky," Anna said, using her T-shirt to wipe sweat off her forehead as Mack showed her pictures of a miniscule pantry. "You don't even cook."

Mack rolled her eyes. "Not the point," she said.

"Well, what is the point?" Anna asked.

Mack thought about it.

"I just want to feel safe," she said at last, "without needing you—or anyone else—there to hold my hand."

Picking Dr. Kimball up from the airport on Sunday was easy enough, and Mack was thrilled with the man who emerged into the waiting area. Tall, with a full head of white hair above a handsome face wrinkled by sun, he matched Mack's exact mental picture of a BYU professor.

"You must be Ms. Wilson," he said, approaching her and her "Brigham Kimball" sign.

"Professor Kimball," Mack said, "it's so nice to meet you!"

"None of that 'Professor' stuff," he said, as they walked toward the car. "Brig suits me just fine."

Mack laughed. He reminded her of her grandfather, who she remembered very fondly. As they drove toward the office, he regaled her with tales from his somewhat wild life—raised in an LDS family, he had stopped believing at nineteen during his mission in Peru.

"I just saw the other side," he said, "and realized there was more to it than what I knew."

"More to it?" Mack asked.

"Life," he said.

He'd gone home at twenty and enrolled at BYU because the tuition was so cheap, eventually working his way up to a Ph.D. in Religious Studies from Yale. He'd returned to his undergraduate alma mater, where he'd taken it upon himself to educate young Mormon men and women on "being good humans, not just good Mormons."

Mack and Jess both enjoyed preparing him for court. Jess played defense counsel, and they practiced both direct and cross. They had avoided giving him any facts about the case, but they asked about basic principles and threw out some hypotheticals for him. When they dropped him off at his hotel that night Mack knew he would be an exceptional witness. He was the best conversationalist she had met in years, and he had charmed them all through dinner with stories about his travels, his research, and his students.

That night, Mack got back to Anna's and almost immediately fell into a deep and dreamless sleep, the best she'd had since the trial began.

The next morning, Brig beat Mack to court. She and Jess had gotten distracted by one of the unit's new attorneys, who wanted to ask a question about admitting other acts evidence under Rule 404(c) that he promised would be fast and wound up taking twenty minutes to fully answer. They found him sitting on a bench outside the courtroom in a brown suit and a bolo tie, his suitcase next to him so he could fly back to Utah that evening.

"I don't like to miss too many classes," he explained. "Students these days forget too easily."

As Mack reviewed his education and background for the jury, qualifying him as an expert on Mormonism, she could tell that they found him just as charming as she did. They laughed at his jokes and nodded along when he said the thing about teaching kids to be good people. His status as a BYU professor appeared to give him a great deal of credibility with the LDS jurors. When it came time to transition into the subject matter about which he'd been called to testify, Mack wasn't sure how much to cover. She wanted to keep the jury interested and engaged, without leaving anything out that she would need to argue later. She started by asking him what the church thought of personal revelation in the modern era.

"The LDS church believes that any individual can receive messages from God," he said, "so long as he or she repents, prays, obeys, and has the proper spirit." He went on to explain that a message isn't always a voice from above. Instead, it often takes the form of "promptings," or small messages from the person's own spirit, which has communicated with the larger spirit of God. "That's the 'still, small voice' talked about in the scriptures," Brig said.

"Is everyone entitled to the same sorts of revelations?" Mack asked.

"Oh, no," he said. "The church is headed by a president, and it is hierarchically organized under him. The top fourteen or so people in the church are known as 'prophets, seers, and revelators' and those fourteen men can receive revelations on matters of church-wide importance. Everyone else can receive revelations pertaining to their personal lives but are not viewed as receiving revelation regarding the church as a whole."

"Does that also apply to, for example, a father who receives a revelation about his wife and children?"

"It *can*," Brig said. "Personal revelation can pertain to anything under the responsibility of the individual. For a father, that would include his family."

"What if someone who had been a ward bishop received a revelation about the church as a whole having gone awry? Would the church endorse that as true revelation?"

"No, ma'am. It would not."

They moved on to discuss the sections of scripture Mack had learned from Spencer months earlier, starting with "the one mighty and strong." After reciting the passage from memory, Brig explained what it meant, but he went a step further than Spencer.

"The canonical interpretation of that passage," Brig said, "says it relates to the presiding bishop of Missouri in 1832. I don't want to bore you folks with the details of the history"—he nodded and smiled at the jury—"but suffice it to say that the official version of the story is that there was a threat from God that was very specific to the time period."

"So the church isn't sitting around waiting for the one mighty and strong to come set the Lord's house in order?" Mack asked.

"Not at all," he said. "Latter-day Saints very much believe in the second coming of Christ, but it will be Christ who comes—not some yahoo off the street."

"So if someone announced to his family that God told him that he was the one mighty and strong, what would the church think about that?"

"That would be kindly considered a false prophecy, and unkindly considered heresy deserving of excommunication."

"So would someone who truly believes in the LDS faith ever believe that they had received such a message?"

"In my opinion," he said, and took a sip of water, "no one who *truly* believed could possibly think that."

Mack was shocked that Miller hadn't objected to that last question. She wondered if he was lost on the religion stuff, or didn't see where she was going with it, or whether he had a card up his sleeve that she wasn't seeing. She hoped beyond hope that it was one of the first two, but she was afraid of what was coming on cross.

"Let's move on to the next verse," she said.

Brig again recited the verse verbatim, without notes. Mack wondered if he had the whole Doctrine and Covenants memorized, or if he'd specially memorized these sections for trial.

"Can you explain the story behind the discussion of someone 'steadying the Ark'?" she asked.

"Sure," he said, and took another sip of water. "During the reign of King David—so we're going really far back, at this point—a man named Uzzah is transporting the Ark of the Covenant by ox-cart. Now, an ox-cart is not the most stable of transportation methods, and at one point Uzzah reaches out and touches the Ark to keep it from tipping over. As soon as he does that, God strikes him dead."

"Why?"

"Because he had no faith in God to keep the Ark upright. Humans aren't supposed to have the hubris to believe that we can 'save' or 'right' God's kingdom through earthly efforts. That holds true in the modern day for anyone who challenges the path of the church, because challenging the church means challenging God. Anyone who does so should be careful, therefore, lest their challenge—which may well have been done with the best intentions—be used against them by God."

"Okay," Mack said, nodding. "Let's go back to the example from before. Guy says 'God told me I'm the one mighty and strong.' How does this idea of steadying the Ark play into that?"

Brig paused in contemplation before answering. "Well, to say you're the one mighty and strong presupposes that the church needs setting in order. And saying the church needs setting in order is steadying the Ark. So, theologically speaking, in order to claim to be the one mighty and strong you must necessarily be the one trying to steady the Ark. Which is probably why so many splinter groups have been founded by men claiming to be the one mighty and strong. It doesn't work to be a faithful Mormon *and* claim to be fixing the path of the church."

Mack hoped the jury had understood all that. She looked to her left and saw several of them nodding. Two appeared to be taking careful notes. She decided to leave it there and told the judge she had no further questions.

Miller wasted no time and asked his questions while seated at the defense table. "Let me get this straight," he said. "You've testified that it doesn't make sense for a good Mormon to believe that God told him he was the one mighty and strong."

"That's correct," Brig said.

"So let's think about a guy who goes on a mission, serves faithfully in his church, is the bishop of a ward, and rises to the level of apostle. He's a wealthy guy, tithes, has his temple recommend—whole nine yards."

"Sure," Brig said, "I know many men like that."

"So if there are two versions of a story, one of which has that guy claiming to be the one mighty and strong, and the other one has someone else saying 'he told me this' and that person is trying to get the guy's assets, which one would you say is more likely to be true?"

Mack saw Miller's hidden card and jumped to her feet.

"Objection!" she said. "Calls for speculation!"

"No it doesn't," Miller said, smiling. "I'm just asking this expert witness for his expert opinion."

"Overruled," Judge Donoghue said.

Brig thought about it before he answered.

"There's no way to say for sure, of course, but I'd say that the second scenario is more likely, if the man is a true believer."

"No further questions," Miller said.

Mack looked at the juror Jess had pegged as the likely foreman. He was a middle-aged engineer who identified as LDS. He was shaking his head and appeared to be crossing out notes he had previously written.

Mack looked at Jess. "Anything I can do?" she whispered.

Jess shook her head. "Sorry."

"No redirect, Your Honor," Mack said.

None of the jurors had any questions, which seemed like a very bad sign.

CHAPTER THIRTY-EIGHT

Sergeant Dave Barton was on the stand longer than any of the other witnesses, almost three days. Most of that time was spent on cross, as Miller attacked various aspects of the investigation. He started by questioning the decision to return Schyanne to her parents following her escape.

"Isn't it true, Sergeant, that your experience tells you that children are usually abused by someone they know?"

"Absolutely," Dave said, smiling pleasantly.

"In fact, if you look at girls who have been sexually abused, aren't around fifty percent of them abused by their biological fathers?"

"I don't know if it's quite that high," Dave said, "but it's a substantial number, yes."

"And yet," Miller said, leaving the podium and walking over to lean on the jury box, "you returned Schyanne to her parents, uncertain of who had abused her?"

Dave nodded.

"Is that a yes?"

"Yes," Dave said.

"Why did you do that?"

"The defendant was an upstanding member of the community," Dave said. "He was well-known and well respected. We had no evidence at that time to suggest that he had abused Schyanne, and, without reasonable grounds to believe that she was abused in-home, we couldn't by law remove her from the home. Plus we didn't know at that point about the other victims."

Miller paused to let that sink in for the jury and returned to the podium. Mack watched him draw a large check mark next to a line of text on a legal pad. She hoped the jury hadn't noticed. His next attack was on what he characterized as the police decision to release the information that Andersen had been arrested.

"Actually," Dave said, turning so he could explain to the jury rather than to the defense attorney, "that information wasn't released by police. When the media saw the arrest paperwork, which is public record, *they* put the information out."

"But your investigation benefited from the media exposure, isn't that right?" Miller asked.

"In that more victims came forward, yes," Dave said.

"Did you investigate the claims made by the ten girls and women who came forward as a result of the media exposure?"

Dave coughed. "I'm sorry," he said, "but only eight *victims* came forward as the result of the media attention. Shaelynn and Sherrie disclosed during their forensic interviews, which were conducted as a standard part of the investigation into Schyanne's case."

Miller walked back toward the jury box. He was an impressive presence in the courtroom—all eyes were on him. "The eight girls, then."

"For each victim, we confirmed that the defendant had access to them during the time periods when they reported having been abused. Most of them didn't know each other, but they disclosed very similar abusive acts and they all knew about the prophecy that the jury has heard about, which the media had not reported at that time. Because the abuse happened anywhere from two to ten years ago, we were unable to get, for example, DNA evidence in those cases."

Miller nodded and smiled. "But you followed up on things like the girls' social-media accounts?"

"No," Dave said, shaking his head and looking confused. "Social media was never a relevant part of our investigation."

"Is it not your experience that young people talk about important things happening in their lives on their social-media accounts?"

"Sometimes," Dave said.

"But you didn't check?"

"No."

"Okay," Miller said, and moved back to the podium to check something else off his list. Mack made a big note on her own pad—*SOCIAL MEDIA?!*—and underlined it twice. Jess saw what she had written and shrugged.

The defense attorney attacked the choice not to investigate Shannon's relationship with her husband, which he maintained was ending. Dave agreed that he had not looked at the family's financial records, nor did he look at the financial records of any of the other victims.

"So you don't know how much money Shannon spent in an average month?" Miller asked.

"I do not," Dave said.

"Or how much she would need to get from my client every month to maintain her lifestyle?"

"No," Dave said. Mack could tell he was itching to explain, but he resisted the urge. He knew she would give him plenty of opportunity on redirect.

Miller drew another check mark on his list and moved on. "So the police just took all comers, right?"

"No," Dave said. "We—"

"Just answer yes or no, Mr. Barton. Did anyone come forward claiming to have been abused by my client who didn't wind up as an alleged victim?"

"No," Dave said again.

"So you *did* just take all comers!"

Miller spent a bit more time on the issue of whether the police attempted to corroborate the victims' accounts, but it didn't seem like he made many points there. The sheer number of victims was corroboration enough. When combined with the DNA evidence and the photos of Schyanne being abused from Andersen's secret computer, it undercut any argument that the police should have done more.

Miller even made the seemingly bold choice to attack the portion of the investigation relating to the pornographic images of Schyanne. Even though the images were on the secret laptop, which Schyanne described as belonging to Andersen, and which contained documents relating to his business endeavors under the user account "Steve," Miller contended that the police had not proven that the laptop belonged to his client.

"You're familiar with Mr. Andersen's oldest son, right?" Miller asked.

"Steve Jr., yes," Dave said.

"And you know he's also called Steve by the family, right?"

"I did not," Dave said.

"You never asked Steve Jr. about the laptop, did you?"

"No," Dave answered.

"You never confirmed in any way that the laptop didn't belong to Steve Jr., did you?"

"The laptop was located on a rafter in the basement room where Schyanne said your client abused her. It contained documents relevant to your client's businesses, in which Steve Jr. had no involvement. It contained photographs of your client on a fishing trip Steve Jr. hadn't gone on."

"Nonresponsive," Miller said. "Move to strike."

Judge Donoghue denied his request and Mack crossed out the note she had just made to have Dave explain how they knew it was the senior Andersen's laptop.

CHAPTER THIRTY-NINE

On redirect, Dave clarified things that Miller had tried to muddy. Because Miller had gone into the number of victims who had come forward and the fact that no one *other* than the victims had come forward, Dave got to explain, again, all the similarities between the victims and their assaults. During direct, Mack had shown a chart, made by the office's IT department, which listed those similarities. Now, she took the opportunity to show it again. By the time they finished, she felt confident about how it had gone.

The jury had a number of questions, most of which had actually been answered already, but Judge Donoghue asked them again—clearly at least one juror had missed the answers. After two-and-change days of Dave's testimony, it wasn't surprising that they hadn't followed all of it. Mack had a hard time herself. A few of the jury questions indicated that they hadn't understood Dave's testimony, either because Mack hadn't asked good questions to begin with or because Miller had successfully obscured things. There were no questions, however, on the specifics of the attacks that had surfaced on cross. Mack thought that was a good sign, choosing to believe it meant that the jury had dismissed the attacks as unfounded.

Mack rested when Dave was done, midafternoon on the Thursday before the Fourth of July holiday. The jury was visibly thrilled to be released early, and with instructions not to return for a full eleven days. When they left, Miller made his motion for directed verdict. Mack settled back in her chair.

Jess and Mack had agreed that Jess would argue the motion. Actually, Mack had told her she should do it, because Mack found them annoying and Jess was the second chair, and she had grudgingly acquiesced, glaring at Mack through the whole discussion. She opened a manila folder and pulled out sheets of meticulous notes, with the evidence supporting each count laid out in detail. Mack looked at her watch and realized that, if she planned to actually cover all the material she'd prepared, there was no chance they would finish the hearing before the court staff had to leave at 4:45.

Miller, thankfully, didn't go through each count in depth. Instead, he broke them down by victim. He argued that they had presented no evidence linking the photos of Schyanne to his client—which was just plain wrong—that they had presented no evidence at all regarding the eight non-family victims—which was also wrong—and that the evidence relating to Sherrie and Shaelynn was insufficient. He asked for a directed verdict acquitting his client on all ninety-three counts.

As Jess stood, Mack sunk deeper into her chair and tried not to look as bored as she felt. She wasn't worried—she knew they had presented more than enough evidence to overcome the low bar of "no substantial evidence," and she was sure that they had hit every count in the ninety-three-count indictment. Her interest was piqued, though, when she saw Judge Donoghue raise his hand.

"I'm not granting Mr. Miller's motion, Ms. Lafayette," he said. Then he smiled for the first time since jury selection had begun. "So, unless you just really need the argument practice…"

"No, thank you, Judge," Jess said, sitting again. With a sullen expression on her face, she ran her index finger down the first page of her notes. Mack wondered exactly how many hours she'd spent on them. Not wanting all that hard work to go to waste, she grabbed them as they packed up for the long weekend.

"What's with the thievery, Wilson?" Jess asked, when she noticed they were gone.

"I'm going to use these for closing!" Mack said. "You did the hard part for me!"

Mack used the week's break for the holiday to catch up on her other cases, to meet with angry victims and even angrier defense attorneys, and to go house shopping. She decided she wanted something with a yard, just in case she got a guard dog. She was thinking that a guard chihuahua might do the job, since Dave told her that it was the bark that scares off the intruder, not the dog itself. She had spent enough time with Jess' chihuahua, The Right Honorable Sherlock Holmes—Shirley, for short— that she knew the breed was capable of fearsome barks that were disproportionate to their body size.

Mack found the perfect place—close to work, in a nice neighborhood, convenient to her favorite parts of town—but couldn't make an offer on it until she managed to sell the condo. The real-estate agent insisted that she couldn't sell the condo if it looked like a crime scene, so Mack spent every evening cleaning and packing. Anna joined her on Monday and Friday but had patients the other nights.

When she was alone, Mack worked in silence, wary that if she turned on music she would miss the sound of someone breaking in. She checked the locks every fifteen minutes. The real-estate agent had suggested putting all her personal belongings in storage but leaving the furniture. With a blanket thrown over the back of the couch, it didn't look like it had been slashed. They threw out the armchair, which was beyond saving, and the place looked pretty good by the time trial resumed Tuesday morning for Miller and Grant to start the defense case.

Technically, Mack knew, defense attorneys in Arizona have the same requirements as prosecutors when it comes to disclosing evidence they plan to use in trial. Arizona prides itself on being a state where trials are not won by secrecy and surprise attacks—both sides are supposed to know what the evidence will be before it ever comes out in front of a jury. In Mack's experience, however, judges bend over backward to accommodate defense attorneys, and ADAs rarely know what the defense case will be until it unfolds in front of them.

Therefore neither Mack nor Jess were all that shocked when they found a revised defense witness list waiting for them on Monday morning. They recognized some names—Steve Jr., for example, and a friend of one of the older victims who police had interviewed but who had not been called as a witness for the prosecution—but some were totally foreign. Two of the ones they didn't recognize had businesses listed after their names. William Landsberg worked at Verizon, and Bryce Stern worked for Citibank.

Jeannie and her team were already set up in the courtroom. "How'd y'all enjoy the break?" she asked.

Jess murmured something noncommittal and they tried to focus on getting ready for the day's testimony—a difficult task, since they had no idea what was coming.

"I went home to Atlanta," Jeannie said. "Saw my kids, my husband. Slept in my own bed. It was real nice."

Mack smiled at her but didn't respond.

"Can I get a comment from one of you?" Jeannie asked. "Just something about how it feels to be going into the defense case?"

They were saved from having to refuse by the courtroom rapidly filling with defense attorneys, James, the rest of the media, and the few members of the public.

"Professor Miller," Mack said, approaching him as he and Grant unpacked their bags, "I received your new witness list this morning. I'm going to move to preclude them all. Just so you know."

"I expected nothing less," he said, continuing to unpack.

When Judge Donoghue took the bench, Mack explained the situation and asked him to preclude all the newly noticed witnesses from testifying, since she hadn't had time to interview them or prepare any evidence or witnesses she would need to rebut their testimony. The judge turned to Miller for his explanation.

"Some of these witnesses have been known to the State since the inception of the case," Miller said. "Those that haven't are the result of recently completed investigation. They were disclosed as soon as we knew their names. I'm happy to let Ms. Wilson and Ms. Lafayette interview the new witnesses before they take the stand."

"These people are necessary for the defense case?" Judge Donoghue asked.

Miller smiled. "Yes, Your Honor," he said.

Mack knew she was sunk.

"If you give the State the chance to interview them, I don't see the problem, at this point. Ms. Wilson, if you come to a point where you need rebuttal witnesses that you don't have, you can let me know and we'll reassess."

Miller's first witness was Steve Jr., and Jess and Mack both thought they knew what his testimony would be: he'd never seen his father do anything inappropriate. Jess would handle cross. This was one of those times when Jess' five additional years of experience would be a definite asset.

Steve Jr. smiled as he introduced himself to the jury. It was a broad, friendly smile that lit up his handsome face. His blond hair was cut short, and he looked much younger than twenty-three. He described the relationship between his parents as very strong, with lots of affection when he was young, but said it became strained when he was around eleven. Mack pulled out her family tree and confirmed that when Steve was eleven, Sherrie was eight and Andersen had received his "message from God." She showed the diagram to Jess, pointing out the three-year age difference between the siblings. She nodded. Steve described his mother as changing from a warm, involved parent to cold and withdrawn. He said that she would retreat into her room for days at a time, leaving his father to feed and care for him and his siblings.

Miller asked about Andersen's relationship with his daughters. Steve said all three of his sisters adored their father and were constantly sitting on his lap and fighting for his attention. This was something Mack hadn't heard from Shannon, Seth, or any of the girls. In fact, they had all testified that Andersen discouraged lap sitting and other physical affection, claiming it was undignified. Mack wondered if Steve was intentionally lying to protect his dad or if he had subconsciously reimagined his family in an idyllic way. He testified that he never saw any inappropriate contact between his father and his sisters. He also testified that he and Sherrie were very close, and that she would have told him if she was being sexually abused.

On cross, Jess was polite. She was kind, even, as she ripped his testimony to shreds.

"You're twenty-three, now, right?"

"Yes, ma'am," Steve said. Mack could tell that the jury loved him from the way they smiled. Heck, Mack loved him herself.

"And you left home at eighteen to go on your mission?"

"Yes, ma'am, I served in Bolivia," he said.

"And when you left, Sherrie was about to turn fifteen, Shaelynn had just turned nine, and Schyanne was almost eight, is that right?"

He looked up as he tried to calculate. His lips moved as he thought.

"I think that's right," he said. "I'd have to have a piece of paper to be sure, though." He smiled, and Jess smiled back.

"And once you left on your mission, you couldn't really have much contact with your family, right?"

"That's right," he said, his smile fading. "We call home twice a year, so I only talked to them four times in the two years I was gone."

"So you and Sherrie weren't so close at that point?"

"Well," Steve said, and he paused to think, "no, I guess not. We were real close as kids, though."

"Did you stop being close when you left on your mission?" Jess asked.

"No," he said, "it was earlier than that."

"Oh, okay. When did you stop being close?"

Steve thought for a while before answering.

"I was probably twelve or thirteen."

"So Sherrie would have been somewhere in the eight to ten range?"

He shrugged and reached for the bottle of water in front of him, taking a long drink before answering. "I guess so, yeah."

Jess went on like that throughout his whole testimony. She was friendly and patient—which was so far from her natural state of being that Mack was shocked she didn't pull a muscle—and systematically discredited everything he had said on direct.

She saved the kicker for the end. "You love your dad, right?" she asked, her voice quiet and full of compassion.

"Absolutely," he said, looking at his father.

"And you don't want him to get in trouble?"

"No, ma'am."

"And you want to do *anything* you can do to help him, right?" she asked.

"Yes, ma'am."

She watched him look at his father and shook her head.

"No further questions," she said, and sighed.

Miller was brief on redirect, asking only if Steve had told the truth in testifying. No one doubted that he had told the truth, of course. He'd just gotten it wrong, out of misplaced love and respect for his father. The jurors' smiles had turned sympathetic as cross progressed, and by the end of redirect it seemed from their faces like they just felt sorry for Steve Jr. They had no questions, but Mack couldn't tell if they had really given Jess permission to tear him apart. If they hadn't, they might hold it against her and give Steve Jr.'s testimony more weight than they should.

In the afternoon, Miller called two of Andersen's friends—one from church and one from work. Jess and Mack had been given the chance to interview them over the lunch hour, so Mack took the first one and Jess took the second. Their testimony was the same: that Andersen was a great dad and a nice guy, and they just didn't believe any of the allegations. They were easy enough to discredit, since they'd never spent much time in the Andersen home and admitted that they had no idea what Steve did when he wasn't around them. Mack and Jess just had to hope that the jury understood how little the testimony was worth.

Jess was quiet as they packed up that afternoon and walked back to their building. Mack turned into her office and Jess followed, dropping into the chair across from the desk. Mack unpacked her cart and began preparing files for the next morning.

Jess stared fixedly out the window and picked at the nail polish on one thumb. "I need a drink," she said finally. "Or three. Today was exhausting."

"Which part?" Mack asked.

"Steve Jr.," she said. "I really hate shredding people whose only crime is loving someone. It's not Junior's fault his dad's a monster."

CHAPTER FORTY

Despite Miller's assurances that Mack would be able to interview his surprise witnesses, his first witness the next morning was Bryce Stern, the Citibank employee. When Mack asked Judge Donoghue for time to talk to him at least briefly before the jury came in, he denied the request.

"I don't like to keep juries waiting. If you need additional time before cross, you can raise the issue again."

Grant did direct—which was a hint, at least, that Stern had nothing catastrophic to say. He was an account executive for Citibank, where Andersen had both a checking and a savings account. "Yes," Stern said, pushing his glasses up his nose with one slender finger, "the accounts do have a co-owner—Shannon Andersen." He confirmed that he had looked at the account statements and could testify about their contents.

"Has there been any unusual activity on either of those accounts since March of this year?" Grant asked.

Jess stood immediately. "Objection, calls for speculation!" she said.

Judge Donoghue appeared to consider this. "Overruled," he said after a moment. "He can answer if he knows."

"There has," Stern said.

"Please describe it."

"Prior to this March, both accounts consistently had balances of at least fifteen thousand dollars. Starting in March, no additional deposits were recorded, but large amounts were withdrawn from each account."

"What is the current balance of each account?" Grant asked.

"Combined," Stern said, "the accounts have a balance of less than one hundred dollars."

"Other than Steve and Shannon Andersen, did anyone else have access to the accounts?"

"No," Stern said. "There were no other debit cards issued, and no other authorized users."

"So if Steve Andersen hasn't accessed the account since the beginning of March, who made the withdrawals?" Grant asked.

"Objection! Calls for speculation!" Jess said, rising again.

"Overruled," Judge Donoghue said without hesitation.

"Shannon Andersen," Stern said.

"No further questions." Grant returned to the defense table.

"Were any of the withdrawals made in person?" Jess asked, without bothering to say good morning.

"No," Stern said, flipping through the documents in front of him, "they were all made through the website, transferring the money into other accounts at other banks."

"Do you know the name of the account holder at the other banks?"

"No," Stern said.

"Generally speaking, how does a user verify his or her identity on the website?"

"They're supposed to enter a password," Stern said, "but many people actually store the password on their computers."

"Was the Andersens' password stored on their computer?" Jess asked.

"I don't know," Stern said.

"Did anyone else have access to the Andersens' computer?"

"I don't know," Stern said again, shifting in his seat.

"So how can you be sure Shannon Andersen was the one using the computer?"

"She's the only other authorized user on the account," Stern said.

"I understand that, Mr. Stern," Jess said, her tone hardening the slightest amount. "What I don't understand is how you were able to testify with such certainty on direct that Shannon Andersen made these withdrawals."

Stern stared at her for a moment. "I guess I shouldn't of been so certain," he said.

Jess had no more questions. Grant, in a surprising display of restraint, decided not to try to clean it up, and the jury didn't have anything, either. Stern was on, neutralized, and off the stand with time to spare before lunch. Miller asked Judge Donoghue if they could break early, since his next witness wasn't expected until 1:00 p.m.

"Who's the witness?" the judge asked.

"Defense is recalling Melinda Young, Your Honor," Miller said.

CHAPTER FORTY-ONE

Melinda Young—Mellie, as she had introduced herself to the jury when called to testify a month earlier—had been victim number six. She had been abused by Andersen on two occasions. She knew the Andersen family from church, as did all the victims, but her father was also friends with Andersen from work. Mellie had been ten years old when Andersen pulled her aside after Sunday school one week. He had explained to her that she would play a very important role in the coming of the New Jerusalem. Then he had abused her. He did it again the next week. After that, Mellie was careful never to be alone with the ward bishop again.

Twenty when she disclosed the abuse for the first time to one of the female detectives on Dave's squad, Mellie was a chain-smoking Waffle House waitress with a four-year-old son. When Jess and Mack had met with her to prepare for trial, she had sported bright purple hair, a neck tattoo, and a large bar through her septum. She told them how deeply the abuse she'd suffered had affected her, and how she blamed Andersen for what had become of her life. She had cut off all contact with her family and her church. It was clear, even from two hours spent in her company, how much anger and betrayal she still felt over the events of a decade earlier.

They were both surprised and impressed by the Mellie who had arrived at court just over a month earlier. She had dyed her hair an almost-natural color, taken out the nose piercing, and was wearing jeans and a turtleneck sweater. Her anger was still intact. It clearly impacted the jurors, but there was no way to be sure whether they believed her.

During the lunch break, Jess and Mack speculated as to why Mellie was being recalled. Jess—who had handled her testimony the first time—tried calling the last good cell phone number she had for her, but the government-issued pay-as-you-go phone was out of minutes. Neither Jess nor Mack could think of anything that had discredited Mellie's testimony, but they knew Miller wouldn't recall a victim for no reason. James suggested that maybe he just wanted to remind the jury of Mellie's anger in order to discredit her earlier testimony. Jess suspected there was more to it than that, and they dreaded going back to court for the afternoon session.

An email from Mack's real-estate agent said that three prospective buyers had looked at the condo that morning. She was hopeful that one of them would make an offer, but she wasn't sure it would be high enough. Mack replied that she was much more concerned with selling quickly than with getting the right price. She skimmed the rest of her emails, seeing something from her mom commenting on the color of her blouse in trial the day before, which she had seen on the news, from the sergeant in charge of the home invasion task force, asking her opinion on the idea of doing a neighborhood canvas, from two different defense attorneys, both asking for plea offers, and from Judge Spears' judicial assistant, asking to reset a hearing in another case. She didn't have time to respond to any of them, though, because Jess was already waiting outside her door.

Mellie was sitting outside the courtroom when they got there. She was fidgeting with the cuffs of her long-sleeve white thermal shirt and looked ready to throw up. Mack wondered how long it had been since she'd had a cigarette, or if she'd been using something stronger. Her hair was stop-sign red and cut in a jagged pixie. Her nose piercing was back in place. She had lost weight over the last several weeks and looked very pale.

"I thought I was done after last time!" she said, as they approached. "You guys told me I was done!"

"We thought you *were* done," Jess said, sitting next to her and trying without success to maintain eye contact. "Defense counsel is the one who had you come back. Do you know why?"

"I don't know nothing," she said, still picking at her cuffs. "A guy came and told me I had to come back. He didn't tell me who he was or why or nothing."

Jess looked at Mack. From the way Mellie was talking, it seemed clear that she was not sober. She certainly wouldn't be the first witness who had showed up to court high for either of them.

"Mellie," Jess said, trying once again to make eye contact with the younger woman, "are you on something right now?"

"What?" she asked. "No. I even quit smoking. I'm just really nervous. You said I was done."

They sat quietly, Mellie fidgeting, until it was time to go into the courtroom.

Miller got Mellie on the stand, and the jurors were as confused as Mack and Jess. They started whispering to each other as soon as he said her name, and their whispering only intensified when they got a look at her. Once Mellie stated and spelled her name for the court reporter, Miller jumped right in.

"You have a Facebook account, correct?" he asked, approaching the podium.

Mellie rolled her eyes. "Yeah," she said. "Everyone has a Facebook account."

"Is your account open or do people have to be friends with you to see your posts?"

"It's open," she said. "I've never had a problem with people I don't know looking at stuff."

"Do you remember when you found out that my client had been arrested?"

Mellie thought for a moment. "Sometime in March, I think. It was on the news at the diner."

"And how long after that did you call police?" Miller asked.

"The next day? Maybe two days after."

"If I told you that you called police on March fourteenth of this year, would you have any reason to doubt me?"

"No," Mellie said, "that sounds about right."

"And do you remember what you posted on Facebook on March *thirteenth* of this year?"

Mellie stiffened. She looked at Jess pleadingly, her eyes widened. "I—I don't—I'm not sure, exactly—"

"Would it refresh your recollection to see a printout of your Facebook wall?" Miller asked.

"Maybe," Mellie said.

Miller walked to the witness stand and handed Mellie a sheet of paper. "Does that help?" he asked from his new position near the jury box.

Mellie nodded.

"Please answer out loud, Ms. Young," he said, a bit of an edge in his voice now.

"Yes, I—I remember now."

"Can you tell the jury what you posted that day, the day before you called police?"

Mellie cleared her throat. "I've been waiting for this day a long time," she read in a low voice. "He will pay."

"No further questions," Miller said, returning to his table.

Jess and Mack sat in stunned silence for a moment before Jess recovered and rose for cross-examination.

"Melinda," she said, "do you remember what that post was about?"

Mellie nodded.

"Is that a yes?"

"Yes," Mellie said automatically.

"Tell the jury what the post was about."

Mellie turned to face the sixteen men and women in the jury box. Some stared at her with open disdain, while others averted their eyes.

"It *was* about Steve Andersen," she admitted, "but I didn't mean pay with money."

"What did you mean?" Jess asked.

"I meant he'd go to jail!" Mellie said. "He'd pay for what he did to me! For how—fuc—messed up everything got after he came into my life!" She reached for the box of tissues in front of her and started crying.

Jess watched her, face impassive, until she stopped.

"Did you have any intention, in March of this year, of trying to get money from Steve Andersen or his family?" Jess asked. It was a huge gamble—Jess did not know the answer to the question before she asked it—but Mack trusted Jess' sense of the girl on the stand. Clearly, she had faith in Mellie's motives in coming forward.

"*No*," Mellie said. "Not then, and not now. I want justice, not money."

"No further questions," Jess said.

The jury was not so easily satisfied. They wanted to know why she had used those words if she wasn't talking about money. They wanted to know why she had said she'd been "waiting for the day," but hadn't gone to police about it earlier. They wanted to know why she was posting something like that to a public Facebook page at all. These were all valid questions, and Mack also wanted to hear the answers.

Unfortunately, Mellie's answers weren't great. She didn't put much thought into the words she used, she said. She didn't want to go to the police by herself, because she knew that if it were her word against Andersen's, he'd win every time. She posted lots of things to Facebook. There were sonograms of her son, complaints about her job, the kind of things that most twenty-year-olds put online for the world to see. The average age of the jurors was fifty-seven, though, and they seemed particularly unconvinced by that last explanation.

Andersen was smirking as Mellie left the stand. Mack wondered if their whole case had just been undermined by a twenty-year-old with no sense of what should be kept off the Internet.

CHAPTER FORTY-TWO

Scott Stanley, the "expert" Miller brought in to discredit Dr. Flores, was the next defense witness, and his testimony took the rest of the day. Jess and Mack had each gone up against him several times, but their opinions differed. Mack saw Stanley as the typical defense whore who would testify to anything for the right price, while Jess maintained that, if asked the right questions in the right way, he could wind up being a basically harmless—and perhaps even helpful—witness for the State.

They had interviewed him back in April, when they were gearing up for trial, and Mack knew that Jess had spent much of the long break preparing for his testimony. As they expected, Stanley spent a lot of time on the reasons for malicious false accusations in sex-abuse cases, including the common motive of secondary gain. Following Mellie's disastrous trip back to the stand that morning, it seemed like this line of testimony was particularly likely to resonate with the jury. Stanley also discussed behavior changes in abuse victims, and issues related to disclosure—reporting their abuse. Unlike Dr. Flores, who relied on the prevailing research and testified that most victims *never* disclose, and for those who do, there is usually some delay, Stanley indicated that most victims disclose right away.

Overall, Jess seemed to be right—on cross, he agreed with most of her points, and often bolstered Dr. Flores' testimony. Jess even asked him about Flores' research, and he agreed that it was based on valid methodology and came to seemingly accurate conclusions. Thankfully the jury seemed to remember Flores' testimony well enough to recognize that in many ways Stanley was just repeating what they'd heard from Flores. Several of their questions began with "Dr. Flores said" and asked for Stanley's opinion on specific points. This showed that they had taken good notes through Flores' testimony and that, in spite of the points Miller had scored against Shannon and Mellie, they still believed Flores.

When Stanley was done, Judge Donoghue asked Miller who the next defense witness would be.

"May we approach?"

Judge Donoghue sighed, waved the lawyers forward, and turned on the white noise machine.

"Judge," Miller said, "our client has not yet decided if he wants to testify. I'd ask that we come back tomorrow morning and he can either testify or we can rest."

The judge looked at Mack.

"That's fine, Judge," she said. She wondered what had happened to the Verizon guy, but she knew better than to tempt fate by asking.

For once, Mack left work at a reasonable hour. She offered to pick up dinner as an apology for her long stay and for being cranky during trial and had chicken burritos on the table waiting for Anna, who was going to come back to the house to eat before her evening sessions. Mack had done all the preparation she could for Andersen's cross and couldn't stand to look at her notes for another minute. She was slumped on the couch in shorts and a T-shirt, too tired to change after going for a run, flipping aimlessly through the channels, when she noticed the file on the coffee table. It was on top of a stack of patient files Anna had brought home sometime in the last couple of days, the patients' names written in Anna's neat block letters on the tabs. "Allen, Benjamin," it read.

Mack knew she shouldn't pick it up, but she couldn't resist. She sat, weighing the file in her hands. She wanted desperately to open it but couldn't bring herself to violate Anna's trust.

"What the hell are you doing?" Anna yelled, walking into the room. Mack had been so absorbed in her dilemma, she hadn't heard the door from the garage close. Mack jumped and dropped the file back onto the coffee table.

"You're reading my patient files?" Anna asked, picking up Allen's file. "You're violating confidentiality?"

"I wasn't reading it," Mack said, "honest. I was just holding it." It sounded lame, even to Mack.

Anna stared at her in disbelief and shook her head. "I think you need to go, Mack."

"Anna," Mack said, "I swear I wasn't reading the file. I'm so sorry for even picking it up, but I never opened it."

"I believe that you're sorry," she said, "but I think you're sorry because you got caught. You need to go. You violated my ability to keep work documents in my own living room."

Mack looked at her, weighing whether she could argue her way out of the situation, but it seemed clear that Anna wouldn't be swayed.

"Let me get my stuff," Mack said, rising from the couch.

Anna didn't follow her to the guest room. It took her less than ten minutes to pack, and when she left, Anna was still standing by the coffee table, staring at the stack of files. It wasn't until she got to her car that she realized she didn't know where she was going. She tried calling Jess, but she didn't answer. Mack was surprised, scrolling through her phone, that there was no one else she could call for a last-minute place to stay. A pang of loneliness hit her.

She headed back to her condo, using the fifteen-minute drive to run through the argument with Anna and give it a series of better outcomes. The idea of spending a night in a motel was unappealing, and Mack tried not to think about whether she was doing something stupid by going home—she just wanted to lick her wounds in peace now that the new deadbolt would keep out any unwanted visitors.

Even under these circumstances, it was nice to be back. She paused by the front door to enjoy the familiar smell and the quiet of the empty condo before locking the deadbolts behind her. It was cleaner than it had been in some time. She had even had the carpets steam cleaned. She kicked her sandals off and dropped her bags by the door.

Mack hadn't taken her burrito with her when she fled Anna's house and she could feel her stomach rumbling. There was no food in the kitchen, of course, except for a yogurt that was a month past its expiration date and not worth trying. When they had packed up the kitchen earlier in the month, though, she had left her collection of delivery menus in a drawer and a bottle of white wine in the pantry. She decided on Chinese food and called in an order of soup, scallion pancakes, and an egg roll.

She had canceled her satellite TV and Internet service and couldn't stand the idea of working on Andersen's cross. Her stereo system was still in the living room, though, and she hooked her phone up to the speakers. Soon, a playlist of female singer-songwriters filled the room. She found a novel she had been meaning to read in a drawer of one of the nightstands and settled down to open it.

By the time the doorbell rang, she was fifty pages into the novel and halfway through the Riesling. Thanks to a surprising bit of luck, she had enough cash in her wallet to pay the bill *and* tip the delivery guy. She juggled her wallet and the bags, kicking the door shut behind her. Mack hurriedly made herself comfortable on the couch to enjoy what promised to be the best meal—and the first junk food—she had had in a week. Her phone buzzed on the table, but when she saw that it was Anna she let it go to voicemail. She wasn't in the mood to get yelled at again that night. She wondered if that friendship was over. She hoped not, but she wasn't sure how long she could avoid Anna without consequences.

Mack was halfway through her soup and had just turned up

the volume on a Tegan and Sara song when the unlocked door opened. She didn't even see him until he was standing in front of her. By then, it was too late. He was already raising the gun above his head.

CHAPTER FORTY-THREE

When Mack woke up, she couldn't move her arms or legs. She was tied to something—her desk chair, based on the cushioned seat and high back. Her head ached and she could taste the metallic tang of blood around the fabric stuffed in her mouth. She gingerly tipped her head from side to side, trying to figure out if there was a position in which it didn't hurt. There wasn't.

She tried opening her eyes, which made the headache worse, but she blinked a few times, and the blurriness began to fade. She was still in the living room, facing the counter that divided the living room from the kitchen. On the counter were items that had not been there before: a roll of duct tape, a coil of rope, a silver revolver with a black handle, a very long, very sharp knife, and the framed photograph of her and Christina that had been stolen from the condo.

It took her a moment to recognize the man standing at the sink, filling a glass with water. His hair was shorter, and he was wearing a black hoodie, even in the summer heat. Mack blinked again, forcing her mind to clear along with her eyes. She hadn't seen him in over a month. Since sentencing.

Benjamin Allen was in her kitchen.

Mack recoiled when he looked at her. He smiled, but looked cruel and angry. "Welcome back, Mackenzie," he said. "I wasn't sure when you'd wake up. I've been waiting for you."

Mack tried unsuccessfully to speak against the gag.

"No," he said, turning off the faucet and setting down the glass, "you've said enough." He picked up the knife and walked closer, crouching in front of her. She tried to move the chair backward but couldn't quite get enough purchase with her bare feet.

"Ah, ah, ah!" he cautioned in a singsong voice. "I think you should stay right there." He reached out a single gloved finger and ran it down Mack's cheek. She shuddered. "I've been waiting for this opportunity for a *long* time. Since I first saw you, really. That day in court."

He raised the knife and used the tip to trace the path his finger had just taken. Mack felt hot blood trickle over her freezing skin.

"You're a beautiful woman, you know that, Mackenzie?" he asked as he ran his finger through the blood and raised it to his lips. "Inside and out." He put his finger in his mouth and smiled.

Mack shook her head, trying again to speak. He stood and backhanded her across the face, sending blood flying from her cheek, and making her head throb even more. She could hardly breathe. Her nose was running, and from the taste as it dripped into the corner of her mouth, it was a mix of blood and snot.

Allen turned her chair to face the couch and walked to her bags, still sitting where she had dropped them by the door. He unzipped the rolling carry-on bag and dug into it. He pulled out a T-shirt, which he used to wipe the blood from his knife.

"I've been practicing," he said, sitting on the couch and putting his feet up on the coffee table. He looked surprisingly casual for someone who had already guaranteed himself a life behind bars. Mack wondered if he planned to kill her—he had nothing to lose at this point. "I've been getting ready for you. At first, I didn't know it was for you. I just knew I was getting ready. But when I saw *you*—"

Mack's phone buzzed. From the way it lit up on the coffee table, again and again, she could tell it was receiving a series of texts. Allen picked up the phone.

"It's our friend Dr. Lapin," he said gleefully. "Let's see what the doctor has to say. Just finished session with Allen," he read, "and got results of latest poly." He paused. "My, my," he said, "Dr. Lapin should know better than to share confidential patient information with an assistant district attorney."

"Allen is responsible for the foothills home invasions," he read. "He's obsessed with you." He put the phone back on the table. "She's right, you know," he said. "About the home invasions. But I wouldn't call my interest in you an obsession. That's Dr. Lapin editorializing. Of course, either way, the information comes a bit late for you."

Mack struggled uselessly against the ropes tying her to the chair.

Allen picked up the knife, bringing the handle down full force on Mack's phone and shattering the screen.

"I think we've heard enough from the doctor," he said. "Don't you?" He looked inside the Chinese delivery bag. "Why, you got me an egg roll!" he said, removing it and the accompanying duck sauce from the bag. "And scallion pancakes!" He took a bite of the egg roll. Head pounding, Mack didn't want to take her eyes off of him for even a second. When he finished, he wiped his hands on his pants.

"I've been thinking about this for a long time," he said, putting his feet on the floor and leaning forward, hands clasped in his lap. "I've been close before. That woman who did the sketch for the police? I was very close with her, but it just never seemed right. *This* seems very right." He stared at Mack.

He stood and pulled off his sweatshirt, revealing a black T-shirt that was tight against his muscled chest. He had been working out since his conviction. Thick veins stood out on his forearms and the slight paunch he had during the trial was replaced by six-pack abs that were visible through his flimsy shirt. He grabbed the knife and walked toward Mack. He leaned down, his lips very close to her ear, which was still ringing from the slap.

"I'm very excited," he said softly. "I hope you're excited, too."

Mack moaned against the gag and struggled again, but stopped when he held the knife to her throat.

"That's better," he said, lowering the knife, but she could feel warm blood ooze down over her collarbone. He slid the knife under the collar of her Arizona State T-shirt and slit the seam down one sleeve. He withdrew the knife and did the same on the other side, and the shirt pooled around her waist. She hunched her shoulders, trying to cover herself, but the cords holding her bit into her wrists and she had to arch her back to relieve the pressure.

"Don't hide from me," he said. "Don't you know I'm the only one who sees you as you really are?"

Mack shook her head.

"You're so strong," he said, trailing a finger down her chest, "but you don't have to be strong for me. It's your weakness I find most appealing."

Mack shuddered under his finger.

"I loved seeing your face in the bagel shop that day," he said. "You looked so"—he paused and pursed his lips as he searched for the right word—"vulnerable." He turned around and walked back to the kitchen, picking up the glass of water and drinking it in one long swallow. "I loved seeing your face the other times, too," he said, "with the necklace, and when I keyed your car."

He picked up the handgun. "I know you don't know much about guns," he said, "because I've been reading your emails with the dear beloved doctor. But you recognize this, don't you?"

Mack nodded.

Allen approached her, carrying the gun. He leaned down so they were making eye contact. "I'm going to take the gag out," he said, "so we can talk. If you scream, I *will* kill you. Do you understand?"

Mack nodded again, and he smiled. He set the gun on the table and reached behind her head. The gag came off suddenly and she gasped, breathing deeply for the first time since she came to in the chair.

"So, Mackenzie, what is this?" he asked.

"R-revolver," she rasped. Blood was dripping down her throat. She wondered if her nose was broken.

"Very good!" he said. He manipulated the gun and the cylinder swung open. "What do you see?" he asked.

"No bullets," she said. Her throat hurt and the room was beginning to spin.

"Exactly," he said. "Let's fix that, shall we?" He reached into his pocket and drew out a single bullet. He inserted it into one chamber, loaded the cylinder, and spun the barrel.

He lowered the gun and cocked his head. "What's that?" he asked, striding toward the front door. He stood at the window and opened the blinds. After a moment, he turned back to Mack. "Do you hear that, Mackenzie?"

"I don't hear anything," she said.

"It sounded like a siren," he said, returning to stand in front of her, "but it went away. Now, where were we?"

He pointed the gun at her left hand and pulled the trigger. There was a hollow click. She started to cry.

"No crying!" he said. "Mackenzie, this is just a game. I don't want to hurt you!" He laughed. "I love you, Mackenzie. I just want to play some games, okay?"

Mack bit her lip and tried to stay very still. She wondered if she could negotiate her way out of this. If there might be a way to survive. He grabbed her chin and tilted her face upward until she was looking right at him.

"Are you ready to play more games?" he asked.

Mack didn't answer.

He dropped her chin and punched her very hard in the right side. She gasped and the pain hit her like a knife. She cried harder.

"Stop crying!" he said. "You can't cry during game time! You can cry later."

Mack saw motion outside the window, out of the corner of her eye, but she couldn't focus enough to tell what it was. Allen spun the barrel a second time. It was pointed at her right hand when Mack saw the top of his head fly off in a spray of red mist.

CHAPTER FORTY-FOUR

The top of Allen's head hadn't blown off, exactly. The sniper's bullet had just grazed his scalp, knocking him off-balance long enough for the SWAT team to burst into the condo and put him in cuffs. Anna told Mack that they tased him a couple times as well, just to make sure he didn't resist arrest. All relatively minor wounds—especially compared to the number he'd done on Mack.

Anna had rushed in with the SWAT team. She had convinced someone to give her a bulletproof vest and a helmet, and she was untying Mack's arms and legs when Mack vomited all over her and passed out for the second time that night. She woke up in the ambulance, and Anna was right there, holding her hand and muttering apologies.

The CT scan was clear, but she had a mild concussion. It didn't feel mild, especially since they wouldn't give her anything stronger than Tylenol for the pain. Wouldn't even let her have a cup of coffee. The doctors assured Mack that her nose wasn't broken, but she did have two black eyes and a split lip. The cuts on her cheek and neck would heal but she might need plastic surgery to keep from scarring. She had rope burns on her wrists and ankles, a fractured left ulna, two broken ribs, and a few other miscellaneous bumps and bruises she couldn't account for. She didn't know what Allen had done while she was passed out.

Just to be safe, they did a rape kit, but they didn't volunteer the results and Mack didn't ask. She wordlessly accepted the STD prophylactics, swallowing them with water that tasted like the wax on the paper cup.

They made her stay in the hospital both Monday and Tuesday nights, despite her protests. Anna refused to leave, so Mack had her call Jess and tell her she would be alone for trial Tuesday morning. Jess didn't appreciate a call from Anna at 3:00 a.m., but when she heard what had happened, the timing was forgiven.

"He did *what*?" she said, loudly enough that Mack could hear it from her hospital bed a few feet away from Anna. She promised to tell Judge Donoghue what had happened and to delay the Andersen trial as long as she could to give Mack time to recover.

Mack asked Anna not to worry her mom, but when Mack was asleep, and unable to downplay the gravity of what had happened, the psychologist made the call. Mack's mom was horrified and promised she'd be on the next plane.

The nurses woke Mack every hour or so. She wasn't allowed to read or watch television. Allen had destroyed her phone, but they wouldn't have let her use it anyway, so it wasn't such a loss. She tried to apologize to Anna, again, for picking up Allen's file.

"Please don't say you're sorry," she said, rubbing Mack's shoulder over her hospital gown. "I should be the one apologizing to you."

"For what?" Mack asked, her eyes starting to close. "You didn't know what he'd do. Plus, you were right to be angry—even though I really didn't read it."

Anna chewed on the cuticle of her left thumb until Mack pulled her hand away.

"I should have known he was obsessed with you. The signs were all there."

Mack drifted off, Anna's hand firmly in her own. When the nurse next came by to wake her, Anna was still sitting on the edge of her bed.

"He would talk about the woman who got him into this, but I thought he meant the victim. He never used her name, but he never used your name, either. He was all wrapped up in this big conspiracy theory, and at first I just thought he was just a typical paranoid weirdo."

Mack's head hurt, but she was curious. She stifled a yawn. "What changed your mind?" she asked.

Anna sighed. "I finally got his polygraph results," she said, "and I saw that he had told the polygrapher that he had broken into a couple houses. He said they were all intended to be rapes, but he always got caught before he went through with it. I remembered you talking about the home invasion cases and wondered if he was the guy responsible. After I went back to work that night, he was one of my evening patients. I asked him outright. He denied it but knew a lot about the cases for someone with no involvement."

"Like what?"

"He knew you were the prosecutor assigned to the investigation," she said. "It was the first time we'd ever talked specifically about you. The venom in his voice bothered me."

"So he was really going to—"

Mack couldn't bring herself to ask the question. She wasn't sure she really wanted the answer.

Anna cleared her throat. "When he was getting ready to leave my office," she said, "he said something about knowing you didn't like guns, but that you should be careful because someone was always watching." She squeezed Mack's hand.

"Like the note!" Mack said. As she did, she discovered that speaking in anything louder than a whisper made her head throb. Mack fell back to sleep.

The nurse woke her an hour later. "How do you feel?" she asked.

Mack groaned.

"Yeah," she said, taking Mack's pulse, "that's going to last a week or so."

Anna laughed and stood from the uncomfortable chair. Someone must have brought her a clean set of clothes, since she had changed from the black slacks and sweater she had worn the night of the attack to gray yoga pants and a blue hooded sweatshirt. She stretched, and Mack envied her ability to move without hurting. She crossed to the bed and sat.

"A few minutes after Allen left, it suddenly clicked for me. *You* were the woman he was talking about. I tried calling you, but you didn't pick up."

Mack blushed and looked away. "I thought you were calling to yell at me."

"I am *so* sorry," Anna said through tears.

Mack patted her arm gently, trying not to dislodge the IV in her hand or the oximeter on her finger.

"When you didn't respond to my texts, I called the police and started driving."

"I'm surprised they responded," Mack said. "You really didn't have much to go on."

Anna smiled sheepishly. "I *might* have told them that if anything bad happened to you they could be held liable in civil court."

Mack laughed, which made her face hurt, but it also made Anna smile, so it almost felt worth it.

When the doctor made her rounds on Wednesday morning, she agreed that Mack could go home. She hauled herself out of the bed, pausing once she was upright to make sure her feet would hold her. Anna had brought a clean pair of sweats, which Mack had already changed into. She was eager to get back to the office.

"You need to take it easy, though," the doctor said.

Mack nodded earnestly and winced from the pain. "Absolutely, Doctor," she said.

Anna laughed and pushed her hair behind one ear. "Doctor, Mackenzie Wilson does not know the meaning of 'take it easy.'"

"I got this," Mack said. "No marathons, no gun fights, no driving. Easy."

The doctor stared at her for a moment and turned to Anna. "You'll make sure?" she asked.

Anna nodded. "Scout's honor. No gun fights."

The doctor sighed, but she signed the discharge papers.

They insisted on wheeling Mack out to Anna's car, and she appreciated the brief opportunity to rest. She knew the day ahead would be long and painful. Anna didn't even ask where they were headed. She just drove Mack to her house.

The bright sun hurt Mack's eyes, but she resisted the urge to close them. She was afraid she would fall asleep. "Don't you have to work?" she asked, already planning her escape.

Anna smiled. "I took the day off," she said. "I assume you're planning to go in?"

Mack blushed. "Yeah."

"Come on," she said, and led Mack to her bedroom. "I'll help you wash your hair."

"Thank you," Mack said. "No makeup, though. I want to milk the facial injuries for all they're worth."

CHAPTER FORTY-FIVE

Once Mack was clean and dressed in her loosest, most comfortable suit, Anna drove her to the office.

"You have my purse, right?" Mack asked.

"Yeah," she said. "I grabbed it when the paramedics were getting you ready to go."

"I don't want to go back there," Mack said. "I don't want the furniture anymore. Don't want the boxes."

"Okay," she said, and she looked at Mack out of the corner of her eye.

"I wish I hadn't gotten the carpet steamed," Mack said. "Now it probably needs to be cleaned again."

They drove in silence and Mack watched four mile-markers pass.

"You don't have to go in," Anna said, sounding worried. "I haven't heard back from Jess."

Mack ran her fingers over the gauze pad on her cheek. It had taken six stitches to close the cut. The adhesive was starting to itch. So was the cast on her left arm. She leaned her head against the window and wished she had sunglasses.

"I do, though," she said. "This is my case." She wondered when she would be allowed to have coffee again and settled for a sip from Anna's water bottle. "Besides," Mack said, "I have to get a new phone, and I have to tell James what happened."

Anna cleared her throat and turned down the radio. "Detective Wood actually already called James," she said.

Mack sat up and turned to face her fully, exhaling heavily as her ribs protested the move. "Debbie Wood?" she asked.

Anna nodded.

Mack groaned. "*She's* the assigned detective? I've known Debbie for five years. I don't want to be interviewed by Debbie."

"She's the best detective on the adult sex-crimes squad," Anna said. "You've told me that yourself."

"But she's *Debbie*," Mack said.

Anna laughed.

Mack sighed. "Do I have an appointment?" she asked.

"You're supposed to call when you get the new phone. She knows you're in trial, so she said she'd come down to your office if that works better."

"Did you talk to her?"

"Yeah," Anna said. "She came to the hospital while you were asleep. The nurses wouldn't have let her interview you, anyway. So she interviewed me, and we talked about scheduling."

Mack considered that. "So, what's the deal?" she finally asked. "Are you my minder until my mom gets here? Do you just feel guilty?"

Anna's hands tightened on the steering wheel, but she didn't respond to Mack's sudden anger.

They pulled up to the gate leading into the district attorney parking lot. Barry, the gatekeeper, peered into the car, not recognizing Anna.

"Ms. Wilson!" he cried. "What happened to you?"

"I had an attack of the clumsies," Mack said, not wanting to get into it.

He shook his head and opened the gate.

"You feel better," he said as they drove past.

Usually, Mack could walk from her car to her office in less than five minutes, even accounting for a wait at the elevator. That morning, however, the trip took closer to fifteen. She had to stop twice because she was dizzy, and she was breathless by the time they arrived outside James' door.

"Jesus, Mack," he said, standing and crossing the office to help Anna get Mack into a chair. "He really did a number on you."

"You should see the other guy!" Mack said wryly. "Not a scratch on him!"

James didn't smile. "He's *never* going to get out, Mack," he said. "I promise you that."

Mack sighed and tilted her head from side to side, trying to relieve the stiffness in her neck. "You can't promise that, James," she said, "no one can. We know that better than anyone."

Anna pulled a piece of paper out of her purse and handed it to James. "These are the responding officers," she said. "Her phone was smashed, and they impounded it."

"It's been like three days since I checked my email," Mack said. "I think I'm going through withdrawal."

"Why do I hear Wilson's voice?" Jess called from the hall. Mack glanced up at James' clock; it was close to 11:00 and Jess should have been in trial. She appeared in the doorway, in jeans, carrying a large stuffed monkey.

"A pigtailed macaque for the invalid!" she said, handing him to Mack. "I was going to bring him to the hospital, but you beat me to it."

"Freckles!" Mack said. She smiled and accepted the gift. "What's going on?" she asked.

Jess threw herself into the other chair and pulled her hair into a ponytail. "What's going on is that Steve Andersen is not testifying."

"Did they call anyone else?" Mack asked.

"Of course not," she said. "We called off the jury. Tomorrow morning, they'll rest on the record and we'll do closings, unless you want to call Shannon in rebuttal."

They hadn't even talked about rebuttal. They were both so sure that Andersen would testify that when they parted on Monday afternoon they assumed they'd have a week to plan.

"For the bank records, you mean?" Mack asked.

Jess nodded.

"I think I just argue it," Mack said. "You discredited the guy, and I think putting Shannon back on just reminds the jury that she's awful."

"I agree," Jess said. "Plus, we don't actually know that Shannon *didn't* empty that account. Unless you asked her?"

"I didn't ask her," Mack said. "Maybe it doesn't matter. I think it's one of those things that we'll just never know the answer to, like who cut Schyanne's hair."

"That's so frustrating!" Jess exclaimed. "If Shannon took the money, who could blame her—she has to support herself and obviously has no income—but it could just as easily have been Andersen himself. Or someone he told to do it, I guess. If we knew, I could explain it to the jury. As it stands, he gets to make a point and I have nothing."

"Plus," Mack said, "I can't do closings tomorrow! I won't be able to do something that strenuous until next week, at least."

Anna folded her arms across her chest and leaned against James' bookshelf. "She speaks the truth," she said, shaking her head. "Hour-long impassioned speeches are not 'taking it easy.'"

"Will Donoghue give you more time?" James asked, tilting back in his chair.

"Not a chance," Jess said. "He was very clear. No more delays."

"Can I give closing argument while seated?" Mack asked.

"Don't be ridiculous," Anna said. "Jess *has* to do it."

Mack sighed. She knew Anna was right, but she was devastated. She had been working toward this single day of argument for months. This was the biggest case of her career. She didn't want to give up control this late in the game, even though she wasn't strong enough to put up much more of a fight.

"If you give me your notes," Jess said, "I'll do my best to give the closing you wanted to give. I'll even use your PowerPoint."

It was a nice gesture and Mack appreciated her sensitivity, but she still wasn't happy. "Maybe Donoghue will be swayed by my pathetic appearance," she said, "and let me have more time after all." This was met by three blank faces. She sighed again. "Oh, fine."

Before leaving for the day, Mack was able to check her email. Anna said she shouldn't spend more than fifteen minutes looking at a computer screen, but that was more than enough time to make sure the world wasn't exploding. Mostly messages from colleagues and defense attorneys. Her new phone wouldn't be ready until the next day, so any emerging disasters would just have to wait.

"Did I get media or something?" she asked Anna, who was checking her own email and waiting for Mack to finish.

"Hit the Internet that night when Allen's booking paperwork went up. Was on the news this morning."

"Plus," Mack said, "James is a gossip and so are cops."

She smiled. "That probably helped," she said. "The media reports didn't give your name."

"And yet somehow people figured it out," Mack said, feigning surprise. She picked up her desk phone. She had fourteen voice mails, thirteen of which were from concerned defense attorneys and police officers. The fourteenth was Linda Andrews—Allen's attorney in the Voyeurism trial.

"Mackenzie," she said, "this is Linda. Linda Andrews. Benjamin Allen's attorney?" Her voice was muffled and hard to understand. "I'm so sorry to hear what happened. I'd like to talk to you about it, when you're up for it." She gave her cell phone number.

"That's weird," Mack said, hanging up the phone. "Linda Andrews wants to talk to me about what happened."

"Do you think she knew how he felt about you?" Anna asked.

Mack shrugged, sending a wave of pain through her ribs. "No idea," she said. "Can we go home now?"

As Anna took her arm to help her stand, Mack realized that "home" meant Anna's house, which she'd always found comfortable and inviting. It was the only place other than her own where Mack could consistently get a good night's sleep, and Mack suspected that it wasn't just the thread count of the sheets. She couldn't look at that too closely. Instead, she closed her eyes and leaned against the slender brunette, willing the dull ache behind her eyes to clear.

CHAPTER FORTY-SIX

By the time Mack got to court the following morning, carrying only a pad of paper and accompanied by her mother, who actually *had* gotten on a plane from Cleveland and wanted to see a bit of the trial, the bruises on her face had darkened and she looked and felt really awful. For once, though, she wasn't in a hurry to cover it up. She wanted Judge Donoghue to realize that forcing them to move forward—even though they were almost two months ahead of schedule—was unfair.

Jeannie gasped as Mack walked past. "So it's true?" she asked.

"Ignore her," Mack whispered to her mom, who looked like she wanted to respond.

"I heard you were attacked in your home by a man you prosecuted. Would you like to comment?"

Jeannie was persistent. Mack had to give her that.

Mack and her mother headed into the attorney room to avoid further questioning. They had picked up her new phone that morning, and she texted Jess to hurry.

"In the elevator," she responded almost immediately.

When they returned to the courtroom, this time with Jess and Dave, they found Emma Potter, Schyanne's foster mom, sitting in the front row. She hadn't attended every day of trial but had tried to be there for the important witnesses. Mack was glad she'd come for closings, since the more people the jury saw on the prosecution side of the courtroom, the better. Sherrie Andersen was also there, along with two parents of other victims, and James. They stopped to say hello to all of them.

"What happened to you?" Sherrie asked, gesturing at Mack's face.

With Jeannie hovering on the edge of their tight little circle, Mack decided to deflect the question.

"Lost a fight with a javelina," she said.

The defense side of the courtroom, routinely occupied by Andersen's parents and siblings, was empty except for Steve Jr. His dedication to his father was heartbreaking. Mack shot him a tight smile and nodded when she caught his eye.

"What do you think?" she asked Jess. "Does Junior know what Daddy did?"

Jess studied him for a moment. With his short hair and round, red cheeks, he looked very young and very alone.

"I think he does," she said, turning away. "He just doesn't want to admit it."

When Judge Donoghue took the bench, Andersen and his attorneys were settled in at the defense table. Andersen's suit was now too big for him and his shirt gaped around his neck. Throughout the trial, he had looked calm and confident whenever Mack happened to glance at him. Today, as they all prepared to hand the case to the jury, he was biting his lip and drumming his fingers on the table in front of him.

"Any issues before we bring the jury in?" Judge Donoghue asked. He nodded in Mack's direction. "Ms. Wilson, thank you for joining us."

Mack stood, trying to make it look effortless and failing, and leaned on the table with her good arm.

"Judge, the State is asking to delay closings until next week. I was diagnosed with a concussion and will need that time before I am able to argue."

The judge was unmoved. "That's why you have co-counsel, Ms. Wilson. I'm sure Ms. Lafayette will do a thoroughly competent job. Anything from defense?"

Mack's shoulders slumped. She stayed standing as the jury came in, moving no more than necessary. When everyone was seated, Judge Donoghue nodded at Jess and she stood, hitting a button on the computer remote in her hand. Schyanne's school picture filled the screens around the courtroom.

"Schyanne Andersen lived through six years of hell," she said, approaching the jury box with her hands behind her back. She made eye contact with several of the jurors and watched as the rest looked at Schyanne's picture. "From the time she was eight years old, the defendant, Steve Andersen, Schyanne's father, abused her sexually and physically." The image on the screen changed to show Schyanne the morning after she escaped—dirty face, matted hair, vacant expression. "Schyanne went through hell because the defendant told her that he was her ticket to heaven."

As promised, Jess used Mack's PowerPoint and notes. Sort of. Mack had to admit, though, that what she presented was better than any closing Mack had ever given. She wove together the stories of all eleven victims, differentiating the ways in which their lives had been changed by Andersen's crimes. As she discussed each of them, she showed their school pictures from the time they were victimized as well as present-day photos, so that the jury would remember all of them. She reviewed the DNA evidence and the computer forensics—all the physical evidence that supported Schyanne's testimony.

She summarized the testimony of Dr. Flores and demonstrated to the jury how and where it applied to each of the victims. She reminded them of Brig's explanation of the religious aspects of the case, and all the evidence that fit in with Andersen's perverse religiosity. She even managed to keep the jury engaged through the boring parts—the breakdown of each count and what evidence supported it. For that part, she did use twenty-four of Mack's slides, all but the last of which contained a chart with four counts mapped out, the final slide detailing the final charge.

At lunch, Mack waited in the attorney room as Dave and Mack's mom went to get sandwiches and salads. Mack took one bite of her kale salad and pushed it away, the pain in her ribs too intense to eat.

"You should try to have a bit more," her mom said, handing over her cup of tomato soup. "How about some of this, at least?"

Mack shook her head.

"You're gross and sweaty," Jess said. "Why are you nervous? I'm the one doing the talking."

"You're doing great. I just don't feel good."

Her mom put the back of her hand to Mack's forehead.

"You have a fever," she said. "When we leave here, you're going straight to the doctor."

Mack groaned. "Fine," Mack said. She leaned back, trying to relieve the pressure on her side.

Jess didn't eat much, either. She pushed her lettuce around with her fork until they headed back into the courtroom.

Mack took some more pain pills with the last sip of a bottle of water. Since sitting and standing were a challenge, she leaned against the low wall separating the spectators from the well of the courtroom until the jury came in and everyone retook their seats. Jess picked up where she had left off, explaining that "beyond a reasonable doubt" means only that the jurors needed to be firmly convinced of the defendant's guilt.

Jess returned to the table for a drink of water, and Schyanne's school picture filled the screen again. This time, however, it wasn't alone. All eleven school pictures were arrayed on a single slide.

"Ladies and gentlemen," she said, "this case is simple. These eleven girls went through hell at the defendant's hands."

The jury was rapt, their eyes on the photos.

"Now, they're in your hands. It is up to you to give them justice. Steve Andersen called himself 'the one mighty and strong,' but now he is in your hands as well. It is up to you to show him that he was merely the one who tried to steady the Ark. It is up to you to hold him responsible for his terrible crimes."

The screen went black momentarily, and then the word "guilty" faded in from the blackness.

"It is up to you to find the defendant *guilty* of all ninety-three counts. Thank you."

CHAPTER FORTY-SEVEN

Mack resisted the urge to applaud. She was on the edge of tears, and it was only partially due to the pain.

That was great, she wrote on her legal pad, sliding it to Jess as she sat down. Jess nodded slightly, but focused on Miller as he stood, taking a cup of water and a legal pad with him to the podium and angling it toward the jury. He approached them.

"Steve Andersen is innocent," he said. "He's not just 'not guilty,' he's innocent, and his life is in your hands."

Jess could have objected to that, since it was technically telling the jury to consider the penalty that Andersen was facing, which isn't allowed. She wisely resisted, knowing that objecting during closings was an amateur move, and let him continue uninterrupted.

His argument was, in many ways, great. It was easy to see why he was so successful as a defense attorney and why he had been so successful as a prosecutor. He was professorial without talking down to the jury or becoming repetitive. He very efficiently went through what he viewed as the holes in the

State's case, most of which they had expected: the bank account that had been emptied, Mellie's Facebook post, the perceived failure of the police to conclusively link the laptop to his client.

He spent a lot of time on the DNA results, which Mack had expected him to ignore. In her opinion, they were her strongest evidence, and the only thing for which there was no rational alternative explanation. Of course, she underestimated Miller's ability to make ridiculous arguments with a straight face. Although he had mentioned secondary transfer only briefly with the DNA expert, now he argued it extensively.

"Steve Andersen hugged his kids," he said, "and he participated in household chores like doing the laundry. Sometimes one of the kids would shower in the master bathroom if the kids' bathroom was occupied. His DNA could have gotten on Schyanne in any one of those ways and a hundred more." Mack noticed that he didn't address the issue of how the DNA got *in* Schyanne, but the jury appeared entranced. Juror Three, the older LDS woman who had nodded and smiled at Mack since day one, started nodding and smiling at Miller. She was taking copious notes during his discussion of the DNA.

Mack's skin felt hot and she was having trouble sitting still. She so badly wanted to rebut all the inaccuracies Miller was spoon-feeding the jury. It was incredibly frustrating to know that there was no longer anything she could do to change the outcome of the case. It was all up to Jess, who was preternaturally still. When Miller changed topics, she would write keywords on her legal pad, but she made no attempt to write his closing down verbatim like Mack would have.

"The prosecutors have made this case about Steve's religion," Miller said, walking back to the podium and taking a sip of water. "Really, though, this case has nothing to do with Steve's religion. Steve was, and is, an upstanding member of the Latter-day Saints. Bishop of his ward. Member of the Quorum of the Seventy." Juror Three stopped nodding. "This image of him as some sort of religious charlatan comes from Shannon—his wife who emptied his bank account at the first sign of trouble!"

Bank, Jess wrote, and underlined it.

"Don't get me wrong, ladies and gentlemen," Miller said, "Schyanne and Shaelynn and Sherrie are victims, but they're not victims of Steve Andersen. They're victims of their mother, who manipulated them into making horrible and unfounded accusations against their father."

He explained that the eight girls who came forward after the story hit the media were either victims of their parents' greed or, as in the case of Mellie, driven by greed themselves. "Even Professor Kimball said that it made more sense for a man in Steve's position to be subjected to religious libel—for the State to spread vicious *lies* about him, just because he belongs to a faith that's different—than for him to claim to be anything other than what he was and is—a righteous man trying to make his way, to guide his family, in these treacherous modern times."

Religious libel, Jess wrote.

Miller was talking about reasonable doubt when it was time for the afternoon break. Mack's pain pills must have kicked in because she was able to stand and walk to the attorney room with only moderate difficulty. James joined them this time, and they all sat quietly until it was time to go back into the courtroom. Mack's mom felt her forehead and shook her head. She immediately pulled out her phone, and Mack had the sneaking suspicion that she was texting Anna.

When they resumed, Miller had an easel with a large pad of paper on it positioned in front of the jury box. He wrote *BANK ACCOUNT* in black capitals in the upper right hand corner of the top sheet. *COMPUTER* went in the upper left corner. He filled the edges with more: *DNA, HE WILL PAY, PROFESSOR KIMBALL, SHANNON.* The jury watched him intently. Juror Three appeared to be copying his notes onto a blank sheet of paper.

"I've discussed each of these factors today," he said, turning back toward the jury. "Each of them, on their own, would be reasonable doubt." He turned back to the easel and drew lines from each phrase toward the center of the sheet, where he wrote *NOT GUILTY* in the same block letters. "When these factors combine, however," he said, pointing at the center of the paper, "there's only one conclusion you can draw. Steve Andersen is not guilty. Steve Andersen is *innocent*, and we ask you to find accordingly. Thank you."

Mack glanced at Steve Jr., who was staring at the back of his father's head. She wondered what it would be like to be in his shoes, and was suddenly grateful to be in her position, busted ribs and all.

Jess slowly stood and walked to the easel. She studied the sheet of paper, arms folded, then removed it, folded it neatly, and put it on the defense table. Legal pad in hand, she walked to the witness stand and leaned against it before speaking.

"You know," she said, "when I'm not at work I like to do jigsaw puzzles."

"Objection!" Miller said. "Facts not in evidence."

Jess snorted.

"Overruled," said Judge Donoghue.

"Recently," Jess said, smiling and making eye contact with each of the jurors in turn, "I was doing a puzzle, and I always do puzzles the same way. I put the box away and I start with the edges and work my way in."

Juror Three smiled. She looked like a puzzler.

"This puzzle I was working on," Jess said, "had a green stripey bottom border, and a blue and white top border, and over here"—she gestured vaguely to her right—"was something kind of brown, and over here"—she gestured vaguely to her left—"was something kind of red. And as I kept working on this puzzle, I put together this patch that looked kind of like whiskers, and this patch that looked kind of like grass, and this patch that looked kind of like a tail."

Mack smiled as much as her split lip would allow. She loved this metaphor, which was a common tool for prosecutors. Jess did it particularly well.

"Before long, ladies and gentlemen, I was firmly convinced as to what that puzzle showed. It showed a kitten playing with a ball of string in the grass with a blue sky overhead. I didn't need to fill in every last piece to be sure—beyond a reasonable doubt—of what that puzzle showed."

She crossed to the other side of the jury box. Sixteen pairs of eyes followed her.

"Defense counsel's job, which he has done well, is to point out to you the holes in the State's puzzle. But you all, every one of you sitting in that jury box, should be firmly convinced as to the picture on the puzzle that Ms. Wilson and I have assembled for you over the past several months. That puzzle shows the defendant systematically abusing eleven victims over a period of almost twenty years."

She went on to address each of Miller's points in turn. She reiterated her arguments from the first close about the DNA and the computer, about Mellie and Brig. Finally, she got to the heart of the defense's case.

"Is Shannon Andersen in the running for World's Best Mom?" she asked, shaking her head. "Of course not. But you saw her on the stand. She loves her husband. She's not trying to frame him for the most horrible acts that one person can commit against another."

Mack's eyes widened involuntarily. That was very close to the line separating allowable argument from vouching for a witness. She shot a glance at Miller, but he didn't object.

"The rest of the defense argument—that eight women and girls, or their parents, decided, independently, based on a press release about the defendant's arrest, to come forward and claim that he had abused them or their daughters in order to recover from his substantial wealth—is so ludicrous it's almost not worth responding to."

Feisty Jess was Mack's favorite Jess.

"But in an abundance of caution," she said, "let's think about what that would mean." She leaned forward, resting her elbows on the jury box and tenting her fingers against her face. "For that to be true, these eight girls would have had to independently guess about the specific sex acts that they would allege—and they would all have had to have independently guessed the exact same thing. These eight girls would have had to independently guess about the religious arguments Steve didn't use—and they would all have to have guessed the same arguments, based on an obscure revelation from 1832. Here's the kicker, though. It would have to mean that the DNA found *inside* the defendant's fourteen-year-old daughter was the freak coincidental result of them using the same towel."

She stepped back from the jury and made eye contact with each of them in turn as she removed the computer remote from her jacket pocket. The screen filled again with the school photos of the eleven victims.

"Ladies and gentlemen," she said, returning to her normal, measured tones, "the defense argument is laughable. What happened to these girls, however"—she gestured at the screen behind her—"is anything but laughable. What happened to these girls is tragic."

She took a long drink of water from the cup on the edge of the table.

"You should all be firmly convinced of what the defendant did to these girls. The tragic things he did in the pursuit of his own selfish desires. Now it's your turn. Go find him guilty on all ninety-three counts. Thank you."

Mack sighed. It was all over but the shouting, and the selection of the four alternate jurors who would sit out of the deliberation. The clerk took out an antique bingo set and spun the cage.

"Juror Two," she said. Juror Two, a young African-American man, looked relieved. Mack was disappointed—she had gotten good vibes from him for much of the trial.

"Juror Sixteen," the clerk said. Juror Sixteen looked disappointed, but Mack was thrilled. Spencer had told them to strike her, saying she seemed a bit too flexible in her religious beliefs, but they ran out of strikes before they got to her.

"Juror Seven," she said. Juror Seven had been an enigma throughout the trial, so Mack didn't know how to feel about his being selected as an alternate.

"Juror Thirteen," she said. Juror Thirteen was the presumed foreman—an older man who was not Mormon but had lived in Utah for many years. Mack's only concern in losing him was who would take his place as foreman. That decision could wind up making all the difference.

The courtroom stood one final time as the jury was ushered out. Jess wrote down her and Mack's contact details for the clerk so she could call when the jury had a verdict, Judge Donoghue directed everyone to remain within a thirty-minute radius of the courtroom during court hours until the verdict came in, and Mack, Jess, and Dave returned to the office to wait.

CHAPTER FORTY-EIGHT

Actually, Mack and her mother returned to the office to get Mack's purse, and then drove straight to the hospital. Anna called ahead and made an appointment with the physician who had treated Mack, and mother and daughter were ushered into an exam room without delay. The doctor removed the dressings on Mack's cheek and neck and looked at the healing cuts, checked her pupils and reflexes, and poked at her ribs, ignoring her hiss of protest.

"Given the fever," she said, pulling off her gloves, "it seems like infection. I don't see anything obvious, but your system has taken some punishment. Antibiotics and—more important—*rest* will help."

Mack slowly slid off the table and accepted the prescriptions without comment. Since the jury would start their deliberations on Monday, she had three full days to sleep on Anna's couch. Mack had given up the guest room to her mom, over her protests, since Mack was unable to get comfortable enough to really sleep anyway. Anna was waiting with a home-cooked meal when they got back from the hospital, and she had even gone to the grocery store. Her kitchen was stocked with ginger ale, orange juice, and an assortment of convalescent junk food.

For those three days, Mack lived like a kid home sick from school. Between naps, she and her mom watched old movies and played Monopoly. Her mom kept her quiet and made sure she took her pills at the right time. The doctor repeated her advice against spending time reading or on her phone, and Mack had forgotten to bring any files home with her. Jess came over on Saturday afternoon with a jigsaw puzzle.

"I heard about your closing," Anna said, hunched over a corner of the puzzle Mack thought might be the Eiffel Tower. "Never thought you would be a puzzler in real life, though."

Jess connected two long edge strips before answering, "I have many diverse interests," she said. By the time she left that evening, they had assembled one thousand pieces of what turned out to be the major European landmark buildings, and the other three finished it on Sunday.

On Monday morning, Mack's mom flew back to Cleveland and the jury began to deliberate in earnest. Anna's house was more than thirty minutes from the courtroom, so Mack went into the office to wait for a verdict. Jess had calculated that the sheer mechanics of voting ninety-three times and filling out ninety-three verdict forms would take several hours, so Mack took her time getting ready.

Anna drove Mack to a checkup with the neurologist, who cleared Mack to drive, a mere six days after Allen's attack. The cuts on her cheek and neck were healing nicely, and the black eyes and bruised ribs were fading to a sickly yellow-green. She still had another three weeks with the cast on her arm, and she was counting down the minutes until she was free. Mack had never realized how much she needed both arms until she only had use of one.

Mack was thrilled to get back behind the wheel, but she was unpleasantly surprised by how difficult it was to drive her standard transmission car with only one good arm. It was also the first time Mack had been alone since the attack, and she had not anticipated her reaction. She usually listened to music in the morning, and never paid much attention to the cars around her. That morning, however, she checked the mirrors at every red light, studying the surrounding cars and their drivers. She wondered if any of them were following her. Her knuckles remained white against the steering wheel for the whole drive. By the time she got to the parking lot, she was shaky and exhausted and had sweated through the Oxford shirt under her Monday suit.

Debbie Wood, the detective investigating the attack, was scheduled to meet her at noon, and Mack was sure that was contributing to her anxiety. They had not spoken directly. Mack had left the arrangements to Anna. When the receptionist showed Debbie to Mack's office, saving Mack the extra walk up and down the hall, she could tell Debbie did not know what to expect. Mack was leaning back in her chair, right hand over her closed eyes, trying to fight a headache.

"Mack?" Debbie asked.

Mack sat up and tried to smile. "Hi, Debbie."

She sat in the chair across from Mack and closed the door. "Not that people don't know," she said, "but let's keep the details private."

Mack nodded. Debbie removed a digital recorder from her pocket, but Mack held up a hand before she could hit record.

"Can we just chat for a minute, please?" she asked. "I know that the interview will need to be recorded, but, Jesus, Debbie, we've known each other five years. Can we acknowledge how weird this is?"

Debbie laughed. "I'm glad you said something," she said. "This is *very* weird."

"Not that you're not a great detective, but—"

The detective waved off the comment. "I get it," she interrupted. "If I were in your shoes, I'd be pissed off, too."

"I don't even understand why it's a sex-crimes case. There was no sex crime."

"Mack," she said gently, "you know he was the foothills home invader. You know what his plans were. He said as much in his interview."

The two women made eye contact and Debbie allowed her words to settle. Uncomfortable, Mack looked away.

"Speaking of which," Debbie said, taking a pen and notebook out of her purse, "I need to get a look at your car, at some point."

"My car?" Mack asked.

"There's a GPS tracker on it. He told us that's how he found you at the bagel shop that morning, and how he knew you were home that night last week."

"Of course it is," she said. "I should have thought of that."

"It's different when you're not reading reports," Debbie said.

"Yeah," Mack said, "I guess it is." She blinked as she looked at the folders on her bookshelf and cleared her throat. "Okay. You can turn on the recorder."

Debbie fiddled with it for a minute before setting it on the desk between them. Mack stared at the blinking red light.

"This is Detective Deborah Wood, Tucson Police Department badge number 122414. I'm present at the Tucson District Attorney's office with Mackenzie Wilson for an interview."

Her abrupt change from Mack's relaxed and concerned colleague Debbie to stiff and formal Detective Wood took Mack by surprise, as did the feeling of being interviewed. She kept her eyes on that blinking red light as they discussed the horrors of her assault. She felt like she was watching herself be interviewed from across the room and was disturbed by the lack of emotion she felt as she told her story. It was highly unusual to wait a week after an assault to interview a victim, and she hoped Allen's attorney would not be able to capitalize on the professional courtesy Debbie had extended to her, or on the clinical nature of the interview. She wondered what Linda Andrews had wanted when she'd called the week before and made a mental note to call her.

Debbie noticed her mind wandering. "I think that does it," she said, an hour after turning on the recorder. "Do you have any questions for me?"

"No, thank you, Detective," Mack said.

Debbie turned off the recorder. "How are you?" she asked,

relaxing her posture and instantly transforming back into the Debbie Mack knew and had worked with for years. "Really."

Mack bobbed her head noncommittally. "My answer changes from minute to minute," Mack said. "Now that some of the injuries are healing, I'm trying to deal more with the other stuff."

"Do you know MaryLiz Davidson?"

"The name is familiar," Mack said, "but I don't know why."

"She's a psychologist," Debbie said, "who works with the department sometimes. Did you know I saw a kid die a few years ago?"

Mack shook her head.

"That's why I switched from kid crimes to adult crimes," she said. "I got called out to this scene. A kid—a baby, really—got smacked around by Mom's boyfriend. When I got there, paramedics were treating him. They thought he was going to be fine, but he suddenly went into cardiac arrest and died right there in front of me."

"That's terrible."

Debbie nodded. "Yeah," she said, "it really was. He was about the same age as my Carson, and I knew it was time to switch gears."

"That makes sense."

They settled into a comfortable silence until Debbie sighed and shook her head.

"Anyway, even after I switched, sometimes this kid's face would pop into my brain. I would swerve my car while driving, or I'd suddenly run and throw up. It was really disruptive. The department hooked me up with Davidson, and, I have to admit, she helped." She dug through her purse and pulled out a business card case. She sifted through the cards before putting one on Mack's desk.

"Give her a call, maybe," she said, opening the office door.

"Thanks," Mack said.

Debbie smiled and disappeared down the hallway.

Mack stared at the card, unmoving, until 5:00 p.m. came and went with no word from the jury.

CHAPTER FORTY-NINE

Tuesday and Wednesday, Mack went in bright and early, just in case the jury wanted one more chance to sleep on their decision and planned to return their verdict early in the day. It just meant she spent longer unproductive days at work. She tried to organize her office and catch up on the cases she had neglected during trial, but she grew tired and sore too easily to make much progress. Jess really *was* catching up on her cases, as well as getting ready for another trial set to start the following week, so Mack saw little of her. Anna was busy with patients, getting home both nights after Mack had gone to bed.

On Wednesday, Peter Campbell made one of his infrequent and unwelcome appearances in the sex-crimes corridor, and Mack was called to James' office to meet with them both. Campbell stood as she entered the office, which Mack had never seen him do before. She eased herself into an empty chair, carefully guarding her ribs, and waited to be told why she had been summoned.

"Mr. Campbell has been inquiring as to your recovery," James said. "I thought it might be easiest to just bring you in and have you answer."

"I'm recovering," Mack said.

"Good, good," Campbell said. "Glad to hear it."

The office sank back into strained silence. James, hands folded on his desk, looked at Campbell. Mack looked at her shoes.

"I heard the incident adversely impacted the Andersen trial," Campbell said.

"We were dark for a day, and Jess Lafayette gave closing arguments," Mack said. "That was the only impact. It was not adverse."

Mack was nauseous with disgust. Seven months earlier, Campbell had tried to convince her that Andersen was innocent, and now he was using feigned concern over her health to cover his real concern—that she had screwed up a major media trial and brought dishonor on the office. Mack hoisted herself out of the chair and left the room without explanation.

"She's still dealing with a lot of pain," James explained, trying to cover her insubordination.

A bouquet of orange roses had arrived on Mack's desk. She looked at the envelope, right hand absently rubbing the edge of her cast, as she considered whether to read it. She was still frozen in the doorway when Jess found her, staring at the small white envelope nestled in orange blossoms.

"I don't think the card means you any harm," she said. When Mack said nothing, Jess grabbed the envelope and opened it. "Mackenzie," she read, "your mom called. I'm glad you're okay. I miss you. These used to be your favorites—I hope they still are. Love you, Dad." Jess handed Mack the card, and she put it back in the holder in the vase.

Mack cleared her throat. "What's up?" she asked, walking around her desk and sitting down. She rubbed her eyes with the heels of both hands.

Jess looked at her for a moment, seeming to weigh her next words. "Jury has a question," she said eventually. "We got the email while you were in with James and Pirate Pete. Judge wants us to call." She closed Mack's office door and sat down. Mack pulled up the email and they were soon connected with Miller, Grant, and Judge Donoghue.

"I'll read the question," the judge said, "and then the parties can comment." He cleared his throat and they could hear paper rustling. "What happens," he read, "if we cannot agree?"

Jess and Mack groaned.

Mack heard muffled conversation on the other end of the call before Miller spoke clearly. "I think you can just respond with the standard impasse instruction," he said. This instruction, known as the dynamite instruction, told the jury that they should deliberate fully, but if they could not reach a verdict they could inform the judge and the lawyers. It was only given if the jury indicated that they were having trouble reaching a verdict. If the jury couldn't agree, they would have to retry the case. The last three months would have been wasted.

Judge Donoghue cleared his throat. "State?" he asked.

"We agree," Jess said. "The standard instruction will be fine. If that doesn't work, we can cross that bridge."

Judge Donoghue agreed.

"What's the holdup, do you think?" Mack asked, once they had disconnected.

"If it is Juror Three," Jess said, standing to return to her office, "I will personally strangle Spencer for convincing us to leave her."

Thursday morning, Mack was running late. She took her first unassisted shower, finally confident in her ability to maintain her balance on the slippery tile. She dried her hair as best she could with only one good arm and even put on a bit of makeup. She was scared to look unkempt in front of the cameras, which would surely be on hand to capture a mistrial. Since it was almost nine before she got into the car, she got the call halfway to the office.

"Verdict's in," the clerk said. "We'll be starting in forty minutes."

Mack pushed the Saab to go faster and called Jess and Dave as she drove. Jess promised to call Schyanne's foster mom and the other victims and their guardians. Mack called Anna, too, but she didn't pick up.

"We've got a verdict," she said after the beep.

When Mack, Jess, and Dave rushed into the courtroom, it was packed. In the first two rows on the prosecution side were victims, victims' guardians, prosecutors, and cops sitting shoulder to shoulder. No one spoke. On the defense side, the only face Mack recognized was Steve Jr. The media and spectators took up the rest of the seats on both sides of the courtroom. It was easy to tell the difference—the reporters were all busy on laptops or phones, typing or quietly dictating stories, while the trial watchers were chatting pleasantly, as if waiting for the previews to start at a movie. Shannon was conspicuously absent.

They had barely gotten seated, legal pads on the table in front of them, when Judge Donoghue took the bench. The courtroom rose and then took their seats as one. The room was absolutely silent.

"Issues?" the judge asked.

Mack and Miller shook their heads, and everyone rose again as the jury filed in for the final time. Mack refused to look at them, superstitious about seeing someone smiling at the defendant. She kept her head down and began numbering her legal pad. It took two pages, three columns per page, to list all ninety-three counts.

"I understand you've reached a verdict?" Judge Donoghue asked when the jury was settled.

"We have," Juror Three said, rising to hand the binder full of verdicts to the clerk.

Jess and Mack exchanged a worried glance. Number Three, the older LDS woman who seemed undecided throughout the trial, was the only juror Mack had really hoped would not be the foreperson.

The clerk handed the binder to Judge Donoghue and he paged through it, ensuring each page was complete. Everyone except Mack watched him, anxiously trying to read the verdicts on his face. After ten minutes, he nodded and handed the binder back to the clerk.

"The clerk shall read the verdicts," he said.

She cleared her throat.

Mack's vision was gray at the edges, her heart was racing, and she could hear her pulse. She focused on the number one written on the legal pad and tried not to tap her pen on the table. She was starting to sweat. Count One required life in prison, so if Steve was found guilty on that single count, the rest of the verdicts didn't matter so much.

"We the jury," the clerk read, "duly impaneled on the above-listed cause number, do hereby find the defendant, Steven Andersen, as to Count One: Sex Conduct with a Minor, guilty."

Jess and Mack exhaled at the same time. There was an audible murmur from the gallery, and Judge Donoghue glared until the room returned to silence.

"We further find," the clerk said, "that it is proven that the defendant was over eighteen years of age. We further find that it is proven that the victim was under the age of twelve."

Mack marked a small "G" next to the number one, followed by two check marks. Regardless of the verdict on any of the ninety-two other counts, Andersen would never see daylight again. Mack set her pen down, done for the day, but then dutifully picked it up again as the clerk continued.

"We the jury," she read, "duly impaneled on the above-listed cause number, do hereby find the defendant, Steven Andersen, as to Count Two: Sex Conduct with a Minor, guilty."

Mack bit her lip to keep from smiling. She knew that the protocol was to look impassive for the jury, but she desperately wanted to turn around, to make eye contact with Emma, to give a thumbs-up to Mellie and the other victims, to tell them that they had won.

It took over an hour to read all of the verdicts, and Mack was exhausted by the end. The jury had convicted on eighty-nine of the ninety-three counts. After count five, she had stopped writing down the results and turned to watch Andersen respond as each additional nail was hammered into his coffin. He was expressionless, but any remaining color drained from his cheeks and his shoulders fell until he was hunched in his seat. He aged years in that hour.

All four of the not-guilty verdicts were on Mellie's counts. Mack was angry that the jurors were swayed by Miller's argument, that they thought Mellie came forward to get money from Andersen, rather than to get justice for his crimes. She worried that Mellie, already struggling, would be devastated, but the younger woman seemed upbeat when the jury was dismissed and the attorneys were finally able to turn around and talk.

"Screw them," Mellie said, giving Jess a hug. "I got what I wanted."

Sherrie lightly touched Mack's arm and nodded toward a quiet corner of the courtroom.

"Thank you," she said, when they were out of earshot of the rest of the crowd.

"You're welcome," Mack said. "Thank *you* for your bravery."

They looked at Steve Jr., still sitting on the other side of the courtroom, staring at the back of his father's head. His face was red and wet from crying.

"I can't believe Junior supported him," Sherrie said, disgusted.

"It's hard when your hero turns out to be the monster," Mack said.

Sherrie watched her brother for another minute and then touched Mack's arm a second time.

"I'm going to go," she said. "I have class this afternoon. Thanks again."

Mack smiled and watched her leave without acknowledging her brother. Andersen huddled with his attorneys until the deputy tapped him on the shoulder and had him stand up. The deputy secured handcuffs around Andersen's wrists and walked him out of the courtroom.

Miller stood and walked over to Mack. "If I ever know a victim, I hope they draw you as their prosecutor," he said, offering his hand. Mack noticed that the Breitling was back.

Mack shook it and smiled. "Thank you, Professor Miller."

"I think you could probably call me Robert," he said.

"Old habits die hard."

"Look," he said, "if you ever think about switching sides, let me know."

"Thanks," she said, blushing, "but it's not for me. I'm on the side of truth and light. Why in the world would I leave?"

He gestured at Mack's face. The bruises had faded, somewhat, leaving an overall yellow cast to her skin. The cut across her cheek would probably scar, but she thought it gave her face character. She thought she had earned it. She shook her head. Her phone buzzed and she excused herself.

She found a text from Anna. *Congrats!* The phone buzzed again. *Didn't want to bother you, but very proud. Celebratory dinner tonight?*

You were here? Mack typed.

Anna replied with a smiley face.

The clerk approached from the back hallway. "Counsel," she said, "the jurors want to talk to you, if you're willing."

Jess and Mack looked at each other, and reluctantly nodded.

"Sure," Jess said, and the four attorneys followed her back to the jury room.

"I hate talking to jurors," Jess whispered, nervously tugging on her skirt as they walked.

"I know," Mack said. "It has never once made me feel better about that whole 'jury of your peers' thing."

Eleven jurors were sitting around a conference table and turned to face the newcomers. Mack wondered idly why the woman who left hadn't wanted to stay. In a hurry to get home? Afraid she'd made the wrong call on Mellie's counts? Another question Mack would never see answered.

"Hi," Mack said, as she and Jess leaned against one wall and Miller and Grant made themselves comfortable against another. "Thank you all for your service. The clerk said you wanted to talk to us—just know that there are some questions we can't answer."

"We've just got to ask," Juror Three said, "what happened to you?"

The lawyers all looked at her blankly.

"You!" she said, pointing at Mack. "What happened to your face?"

"Oh," Mack said, blushing, "it wasn't a big deal. It looks much worse than it was."

"But what *happened*?" she asked.

"Umm," Mack said, and Jess thankfully interrupted.

"I beat her up," she said, raising her hands and miming a punch. "I wanted to do closings."

Mack laughed, grateful for her intervention. "That's exactly right."

"It's all we could talk about when we saw you," Juror Three said. "We were all so worried! Was it a car accident?"

Mack opened her mouth to respond, but thought better of it and looked at Jess, instead.

"Do any of you have any comments about how the lawyers did?" she asked. "Or questions? We're always looking for constructive criticism."

"Thank you," Mack mouthed, catching Jess' eye.

"I thought you did a very nice job in your argument, dear," an older African-American woman said to Jess. "And so did you," she said to Miller.

"Anything else?" Grant asked.

"Were you two always planning to have her do the closing?" Juror Three asked Mack. "Or did you have to because of your injuries?"

Jess sighed and stepped casually to her left, partially blocking Mack from view. "Ms. Wilson and I have done a number of trials together," she said, "and we try to split the trial pretty evenly."

"What's he looking at?" someone asked.

"Excuse me?" Grant asked.

"Is he going to prison?"

"We can't tell you that," Miller said. "Sorry."

They waited a minute to see if anyone had anything to say that was actually about the trial, but no one did. Finally, they excused themselves and returned to the courtroom.

"That was disheartening," Miller said.

"No more so than usual," Mack said. "You'd think they'd have real questions, after sitting through such a long trial."

"No," Jess said, "that *was* worse than usual. I'm so disappointed. Three months and all they can think about is your busted face. No offense."

Mack smiled. "None taken, for once."

The courtroom was empty. They picked up their bags and left, bracing themselves for a media onslaught that did not come. Mack shook her head—once the verdicts were in, Jeannie and her ilk apparently lost interest.

CHAPTER FIFTY

Anna took Mack back to Café Poca Cosa for dinner, where Anna slipped the maître d' a twenty to put them in a secluded booth in a back corner.

"You should have told me you were there today!" Mack said, once they had ordered guacamole and the daily special—carnitas tacos and spinach enchiladas.

Anna smiled and looked away. "I didn't want to distract you, but I wanted to see what happened."

Mack took a long drink of her first beer since the attack and sighed. She was exhausted after the stress of the day.

"I was really worried," Mack said. "I wasn't sure the jury would buy the religious stuff."

"You had an uphill battle against Miller, but you two did a phenomenal job."

"Thanks," Mack said. "I couldn't have done it without you."

"Sure you could." Despite her words, Anna looked pleased.

Mack shook her head, suddenly choked up. "No, really. There were so many places where Miller could have swayed just one juror. Just one hold out, and we would have failed all those girls."

"You wouldn't have failed," Anna said. "Your job is to present the evidence. The jury does what it does—that's out of your control."

"You really believe that?" Mack asked.

Anna's response was cut off as their salads arrived, and they ate in silence until the waiter returned to take their plates.

"I wanted to talk to you about my living situation," Mack said, focused on her fingers peeling the label off her beer bottle.

"You're welcome to stay as long as you want," Anna said cautiously.

"Thanks," Mack said. "But—well—we've been getting along really well, don't you think?"

Mack could feel Anna watching her, but she kept her eyes firmly on the bottle.

"I do," Anna said, and paused. "But, Mack, I don't think we should…"

"I know," Mack said, frustrated. "I just miss us, sometimes." The label finally off the bottle, she began to shred it. Anna placed her hands over Mack's, stilling them.

"I do, too," she said. "But after what just happened to you, I don't think you should be dating *anyone*. And we didn't work as a couple."

"I know," Mack said. "You're right. We're good as friends. You're one of my *best* friends. It's just—" Mack wasn't sure how that sentence was supposed to end.

Thankfully, their entrées distracted them from the suddenly awkward silence. Neither of them had much to say for the rest of the evening. Mack's post-verdict adrenaline was wearing off, and she felt tipsy from her single beer. She watched the streetlights and drifted off as Anna drove home. They each retreated to their rooms.

The next day, Mack left before Anna woke up for her run. She wasn't ready to face her after the previous evening's difficult conversation.

Mack and Jess bought Spencer a giant box of cookies from his favorite bakery as a thank-you present. Jess apologized for ever doubting his endorsement of Juror Three.

"Oh, she still might be crazy," Mack said, thinking back to their encounter in the jury room, "but it's a good crazy."

"That's the best kind of crazy!" Spencer said through a mouthful of chocolate chips.

Peter Campbell had Mack, Jess, and Dave attend a meeting in the executive suite that afternoon, where he gave them each a "distinguished service" certificate printed on regular copy paper. When Mack got back to her office, she closed the door, ignored the six new floral arrangements that had been delivered, ripped up the "certificate," and threw it away. Instead, she hung up Schyanne's school photo. There were a dozen or so on the wall across from her desk—victims' school photos from big trials—that reminded her why she kept putting herself through the sleepless nights and stressful days.

Debbie Wood called later that afternoon. "Congratulations," she said.

"Oh," Mack said, "thank you. You heard on the news?"

"The news?" she asked, sounding confused. "I'm calling about Allen."

Mack paused.

"What about him?"

"You haven't heard?" she asked. "He was killed in the jail."

Mack dropped into her desk chair. "Excuse me?" she asked, sure she must have heard incorrectly.

"His cellmate snapped last night," Debbie said. "Stabbed him through the eye with a golf pencil. By the time the detention officers got there, he was dead."

Mack gave herself a moment to absorb the news. "So," she said, her voice thick. She cleared her throat. "So it's done?"

"It's done."

They sat quietly and Mack listened to Debbie's steady breathing. Her head was pounding.

"Did he suffer?" Mack asked.

Debbie paused before responding. "I don't know," she said, "but I can try to find out, if you want."

Mack dismissed the offer but thanked her for the call and the information. She stared at the picture of Schyanne until it blurred and she realized that she was crying.

When she recovered, Mack picked up the phone and dug through the sticky notes on her desk until she found Linda Andrews' number. She also found the card for the psychologist Debbie had given her, resolving to call her, too. Linda picked up on the first ring.

"Linda, this is Mackenzie Wilson."

She sighed. "I'm glad you called." Mack heard shuffling and then a door closed. "I haven't stopped thinking about you since I heard what happened. Did you get the flowers I sent?"

Mack ignored the question. "What's up, Linda? You asked me to call."

"That morning at the bagel shop," she said, and paused.

"Yes?"

"That wasn't an accident," she said. "I think you have a right to know."

Mack didn't say anything.

"He told me he was in love with you," she said. She sounded almost hysterical. "He tracked you down to the bagel shop and thought, if he could just talk to you, you'd see he was a great guy and drop the charges."

Mack thought about what she was saying and suddenly realized what it meant. "That's what the *ex parte* hearing was?"

"Yes," she said. "I wanted to tell you. He hadn't made any threats at that point, but I was worried for you. Judge Spears said it was privileged communication, though, so I couldn't—"

Mack hung up on her without another word and went down the hall to James' office. She found him assigning files.

"Mack," he said, gesturing at a stack of five new files, "look what I got you!"

Mack made no move to take them. Instead, she told him about Allen's death and what Linda had said on the phone.

He whistled. "Well," he said, "I think that's ultimately got to be a relief, right? Are you okay?"

"I think so," she said. "I'm not sure. I may want to file a bar complaint against Linda. Maybe Judge Spears, too. If they'd told me what Allen had said, after the *ex parte* hearing..." Mack shrugged and cleared her throat. "They should have told me."

He considered that, capping the marker he was using and leaning back in his chair.

"Let me talk to Campbell before you do anything rash," he said.

Mack stared at her reflection in the window. She could only see the outline of her face and hair—the yellowing bruises did not show.

"Ready to get back to it?" he asked, gesturing again at the pile on his desk.

Mack shook her head. "I think I'm going to take some time off," she said. "Some sick leave. Get my head together. Maybe go home for a while. Spend some time with my folks. I've got some vacation time I need to use, too."

James looked up and rubbed his chin.

"That's probably not a bad idea," he said, finally. "There'll be plenty more files when you get back."

Mack scratched her arm under the edge of her cast.

"I suspect you were underwhelmed by your 'certificate,'" James said, "but you and Jess really did do great work on the Andersen case."

"Thanks," she said. "I hope we did enough. I hope Schyanne will be able to live something like a normal life. I hope she got out in time."

He nodded. "She has a hard road ahead of her," he said, "but she seems like a strong kid."

"I think so, too," Mack said. "She reminds me a lot of me."

Jess came into the office and collapsed into an empty chair, stretching denim-clad legs out in front of her. "Why are you still here, Wilson?" she asked.

"We were just catching up," James said. He winked at Mack.

"You ready to go?" Jess asked. "I can hear Happy Hour specials calling my name."

"That sounds good," Mack said. "I could do with a beer or three."

"You want to call Anna?" Jess asked. "Have her meet us there?"

"Really?" Mack asked.

"Of course," Jess said.

"Why? You don't like her."

Jess patted Mack's arm. "It's not that I don't like her, dude. I just worry about you, and I don't want you to get hurt. Weirdly, your recent misadventures have done nothing to assuage those fears. But I know she's your *friend* or whatever…"

"Nah," Mack said. "Maybe next time she can come. But tonight, let's celebrate just us. We earned it."

Jess got back to her feet, and, arm in arm, she and Mack headed out into the night.

Acknowledgments

This book would not exist without the passionate, dedicated, and brilliant women and men that I have worked with at the Arizona Attorney General's Office and Maricopa County Attorney's Office, many of whom offered their expertise and allowed me to pick their brains about specific legal and psychological issues. I am forever indebted to Elizabeth Reamer, Kyra Goddard, Jennifer Carper, Katie Staab, Erin Pedicone, Jordyn Raimondo, and Anna Park, all of whom read drafts, offered suggestions, and were endlessly kind as I struggled to get this story onto the page. Additionally, Cecelia Munoz, Jim Seeger, Steven Bridger, Treena Kay, and Steve and Carma Umpleby contributed many of the technical details in this book. Rachel Mitchell and Jeanine Sorrentino were always generous with their time and knowledge. Drs. Shelley Kaufman, Wendy Dutton, Kathy Coffman, Tina Garby, Holly Salisbury, and Nicole Pondell, this book relies heavily on the years of wisdom—of all sorts—that you, all encyclopedias in your fields, offered me. I rely heavily on it too, every day.

Thank you to the women who went before me and served as inspiration, particularly Linda Fairstein and Marcia Clark.

Thank you to the team at Bella Books for taking a chance on a new author.

I am grateful to my family, particularly my parents. Thank you Victoria Jones, Mom, for inspiring in me a deep love of reading and for all of your support during the writing process. I know I was miserable to live with during that time and you were patient and supportive as I found my way. Thank you Josh Pachter, Dad, for being my first editor and the one who loves me the most. You both make me a better writer and a better person.

Finally, thank you to Eli Ditlevson for believing in me, supporting me, and loving me.

Bella Books, Inc.

Women. Books. Even Better Together.

P.O. Box 10543
Tallahassee, FL 32302

Phone: 800-729-4992
www.bellabooks.com

CPSIA information can be obtained
at www.ICGtesting.com
Printed in the USA
JSHW022339010322
23465JS00001B/I